THE GENEVA CRISIS

Matti Golan is also the author of
**THE SECRET CONVERSATIONS OF
HENRY KISSINGER**

The GENEVA CRISIS

A NOVEL BY
Matti Golan

A & W Publishers
New York

Published by
A & W Publishers, Inc.
95 Madison Avenue
New York, New York 10016

Designed by Helen Roberts

Library of Congress Number: 80-66677
ISBN: 0-89479-073-0

Printed in the United States of America

To my wife Nitza, who helped to make it all possible.

My deep gratitude to
Angela Miller, Judith Sachs, and Maureen Heffernan
for their faith, support, and devotion.

THE GENEVA CRISIS

PROLOGUE

YOM KIPPUR, October 6, 1973

Amos Rimon raised his binoculars and squinted into the pale gray dawn light. The peaks of the Golan Heights were dim in the distance. He scanned the Syrian settlements below him. Darbel, Ein-a-Sha'lara, Orna. He stopped when his field of vision hit the village of Rima, approximately 1,350 yards from where he stood on top of Mt. Hermon. Something about this village was different. People going to their work in the fields, yes, that was normal, driving their wagons led by a horse or a mule. But he could make out other vehicles—trucks. He focused the binoculars for a sharper sighting. Probably nothing. Seven years since the last war, and the Arabs hadn't forgotten their lesson.

The other soldier on the northern wall of the stronghold's front-line position stirred.

"What's up?" Yoram Negbi called in a sleepy voice as he rubbed his arms against the chill.

(1)

Amos put down the binoculars and shook his head at his friend. "Perfectly quiet. As it should be on the Holiest of Holies. Even the Syrians respect Yom Kippur." Yoram gave a sarcastic laugh. He and Amos were among only fifty-seven soldiers and officers stationed in the "Katef Hachermon" stronghold. The other 250 had been given two days' leave so that they could spend the holiday with their families.

Yoram gathered up his rifle and ammunition and joined Amos. He raised his eyes. The gigantic radar plates continued to revolve in steady circles, their hidden eyes taking in the entire area from the top of Mt. Hermon to Damascus. The plates transmitted any and all activity to sophisticated equipment, buried deep underground, in a concrete fortress four levels deep. There was no better protected place in the Middle East—not even an atom bomb could penetrate the thick walls.

"Look now," Amos directed, pointing out to Rima. "People going to work. Over there." He indicated the Israeli side. "They're going to *shul*. The same people, same concerns, same sorrows. Even the same land. What makes them enemies is some imaginary border. Crazy."

Yoram yawned. "Don't be so naive. On both sides there are those who want this situation, profit by it." He picked up his equipment and walked around the position, surveying the landscape. Amos pulled his jacket collar up on his neck. This was the first Yom Kippur of his life he hadn't gone to synagogue with his father; instead of a prayer book, he held an American M-16 rifle. Yoram somehow didn't seem concerned about this, he thought. Perhaps his upbringing, his father being one of the most admired generals in the Israeli Defense Forces.

"Psst. Come over here," Yoram called.

"What is it?" Amos looked down and saw clouds of dust coming up from the direction of Rima. He peered through the binoculars again. "They must be having a market day or something," he said. "I see at least thirty trucks."

"So? The night is over. Don't worry, the Arabs have never attacked during the day."

Amos started to speak, but the sound of footsteps interrupted his train of thought. Their relief had appeared from behind the boulder which concealed the south side of the position.

"You're ten minutes late," said Amos good-naturedly. "Couldn't get up, eh?"

The two men shivered in the morning air although they were bundled up in heavy military gear. "You gotta be crazy to get out of bed in this cold," muttered one of them.

Yoram and Amos jumped out of the position. "We'll think of you when we get into bed," said Yoram. "Smart-ass," the other soldier responded.

The two men walked along the sheltered ditches until they reached the steel door. Amos pressed a hidden switch. "Password," called a voice from beyond the door.

"Landmarks."

The heavy door began to move, propelled by an electric motor. Amos and Yoram walked in and started the machinery to lock the door again. "How are things?" their captain asked, walking up to them. Gideon Lieberman was responsible for the position in the absence of its commander, who had gone home on leave.

"Quiet," Amos responded, shrugging off his rifle strap and jacket in one movement.

Gideon turned to Yoram. "You're guarding the door from two o'clock."

"How come?" Yoram scowled. "I just finished night shift."

"Sorry. We're short of personnel. That's the breaks, my friend. You can get a few hours' sleep, but we're on alert."

Amos swore. That meant sleeping with stinking clothes, hugging the cold steel rifle. But after a freezing, sleepless night, who cared? He plodded back to his bunk, lay down, and was asleep in minutes.

He was wakened by a strange noise and looked instinctively at his watch. 3:10 P.M. Yoram's bed was empty. He would already be on guard at the door.

What was that noise? The continuation of a dream.

. . . But there were shouts, hurried footsteps, shots. A paralyzing fear hit him. He heard the whir of helicopter engines.

Amos jumped out of bed, grabbing his gun to his chest, and ran toward the stronghold's main entrance. The front door was open.

There were six Syrian helicopters poised about seven hundred yards from the entrance. Scores of armed Syrian soldiers were running toward him. He threw himself down behind a rock and began shooting.

"Get inside! Fast!" Gideon ran past and motioned toward the back of the stronghold. "We don't have a chance out here! Get to the shelter."

Amos continued shooting while he withdrew, his body bent low to the ground. The Syrians could effect a total siege—they had the advantage of numbers and equipment, not to mention the surprise.

There were about forty men in the shelter and more were pouring in as Amos approached, breathless, sweating, frightened. The Hermon had fallen. They were lost. The realization hit him in one sudden, sickening wave. Someone had made the terrible error that everyone said could not be made. But at least they were safe in the fortress. The food stores could feed four hundred for sixty days, and there were only a few dozen of them here. The walls were concrete: nothing could penetrate.

Amos leaned against a wall, trying to quiet his panicky breathing. A red-headed corporal with glasses laughed nervously. "Unbelievable. This is just like '67, only they're doing it to us this time."

Amos felt a cold chill down his spine. What had just happened? He wheeled around like an animal sniffing danger, unable to locate it. His temples throbbed.

And then he knew. The echoes of shots.

He could hear them. Faint sounds, but then he shouldn't be hearing anything. Not through the walls and the steel door of the shelter.

Gideon listened briefly and then jumped to his feet. "My God!" His face was pale as he glanced around the bunker. He stopped, frozen with fear, when he spotted

Yoram. He lunged forward, pushing aside the men in his way. "What the hell are you doing in here?" he yelled, grabbing Yoram by the collar.

The young man didn't respond. His face was white, his lips trembled. His body seemed lifeless. Gideon pulled him closer. "Talk, man! Did you close the door?"

Yoram's eyes were blank and he began to shake uncontrollably. Gideon thrust him to one side in disgust. "Come on," he ordered Amos, and together they ran out of the shelter, stopping when they reached the corner that led to the long corridor before the main door.

Amos went down and peered into the dark hallway. He felt a terrible knot at the pit of his gut. A long narrow ray of light could be seen on the wall opposite the door.

"It's open," Amos whispered to Gideon. "And they're here."

They ran toward the door, shooting blindly in front of them. Suddenly Amos cried out and clutched his right shoulder. He felt a fire rage through him and rammed into the wall headfirst, thrown by the force of the bullet.

When he regained consciousness, Amos felt nauseated and weak. He was lying face down on the rocky turf, his hands tied behind him. A puddle of blood spread slowly on the ground.

He turned his head and his eyes met those of one of the two soldiers who had replaced him after the night shift. The man's mouth was slightly open, his gaze was unfocused. His stomach had been ripped apart with a bayonet.

Amos looked away and began coughing, tears filling his eyes. Coughing and crying hysterically. The soldier's legs had been amputated. The genitals were lying beside his body.

Amos felt a kick in his ribs and cried out. "You're making too much noise!" objected the Syrian soldier who stood over him. He was very young, with delicate features. He kicked Amos again and walked away. When the soldier's footsteps sounded faintly in the distance, he looked up.

Two men were standing about ten feet away. One was a Syrian officer, but the man with him was not wearing a uniform. He was very tall with a muscular body. His scarred face was accented with a thick black moustache. He wore khaki pants and a light shirt under his army jacket.

The two men were smiling with satisfaction. The Syrian officer waved his hand at the two Israeli soldiers. "Look at them now," he gloated. "No longer heroes."

"I always claimed that was a myth," said the other in a deep voice. "You just have to know how to hit them."

The Syrian officer waved and his adjutant ran over. "Take care of them," the commander ordered, nodding at the Israelis. "We're not holding any prisoners."

"Just a minute," said the man in khaki. "Who was their leader?"

Amos watched the adjutant point at Gideon Lieberman, who was bound hand and foot on the other side of the corridor. He was sitting up, the upper half of his body bent forward. His face was bruised and covered with blood.

"I'll handle him, if you don't mind," the civilian said.

The Syrian officer waved him on. "He's all yours, Awad."

The man walked toward Gideon with a firm step. And then Amos's field of vision was blocked as the adjutant came and stood over him. He saw the spear aimed at his own gut, and the rifle to which the spear was attached. Then he heard Gideon Lieberman's scream—wild, painful, inhuman—and after that there was only a quiet and peaceful darkness.

CHAPTER 1

IT WAS ONE of those October days that exist only in Jerusalem. Not yet winter, but a day that announced a definite change of mood and season—the sun's rays stroking the city's unclouded slopes; the air clear, with no sign of rain or haze.

On this day, Jerusalem's gold hit the tops of the mountains, the roofs, the curves of each mosque and the archway of each church. This day was one of peace, of purity and sanctity.

The summit of Mt. Herzl offered a perfect view of the city, but the thousands crowded on the peak were not aware of their surroundings. Their attention was riveted to the freshly dug grave before them, the grave that would be the final resting place of the young bodies wrapped in canvas lying at their edge. This military cemetery on the mountain had seen many such ceremonies over the past two decades, but each speech, each tear, only served as a (7) reminder that the war had not ended and more bodies would come to lie here before it was over.

Martin Silver, the American Secretary of Defense, stood in the first row with the President of Israel, the Prime Minister, and members of families whose father, son, or brother had fallen in battle. Silver was a tall man with a slightly stooped back, which made him look as though he had given up, after fifty-two years, in the attempt to hold his lanky frame erect. His features were blunt, not handsome but deliberate. He had a square protruding chin which gave him a powerful, determined look.

A platoon of soldiers wearing red berets stood fifty yards from him. Each soldier held a gleaming American rifle in his right hand. Every uniform was pressed; every man bore himself with stiff, military poise. Most of them were no older than his own son, Silver thought, picturing Richard in his mind. He shuddered at the notion that quickly flashed before him: different circumstances might have placed his firstborn in that platoon of soldiers. Or even among those whose shattered limbs and bodies had been hidden in these white sacks, unidentifiable and unviewable.

Silver shook the thought from his head. He should never have come to this damned country. Every sight fought to undermine the equilibrium that he'd won. In this place, one could not feel or think clearly. Everywhere, one was reminded of the biblical past and ancient ways. Everything was colored by events that had happened thousands of years ago, events that were echoed in the language and customs of the present day. The stones, the greenery, the rooftops brought back to Silver, with a force that surprised him, a rush of memories of his own past and the religion in which he'd been brought up.

He raised his hand to wipe the sweat from his brow and unintentionally jostled the elbow of the man to his right. Moshe Lieberman raised his eyes. He was shorter than Silver, and his broad frame accentuated their difference in height. Lieberman's face was harsh and angular. The blue eyes set over the high cheekbones and bony, prominent nose were filled with intensity—they were dark, deep, impenetrable.

"Excuse me," Silver muttered.

"I'm glad you are here," Lieberman said. "Please come later to my home." Silver nodded, and Lieberman returned his gaze to the gravesite. He looked down at the gaping earth coldly, his face betraying no emotion. *Martin Silver*, he thought again. And his thoughts stopped there, unable to proceed in the logical sequence. He caught the man's slightly stooped frame out of the corner of his eye. *What the hell*, he thought suddenly, *Mordechai Silverstone*. The use of the familiar name cleared the path for a flood of reminiscence: childhood, adolescence, the street in the big city, the friendship, the dependence. A world that was gone, irrelevant. Not appropriate, particularly given the present time and set of circumstances. Not right for either of them.

Lieberman's right arm embraced his wife's shoulder. She hid her face in his chest to muffle her sobs, and he looked out over her head, taking in the scene around him. This was not his first visit to Mt. Herzl. But this time was different from all the previous times, and would be different from any that followed. He had cared for each person he had accompanied to one of the thousands of graves on the mountainside. But this time it was Gideon, his only son. And that made all the difference.

A platoon of paratroopers in dress uniform stood waiting to fire salutes. All the country's leaders stood at attention: the President, the Prime Minister, the cabinet ministers, the Knesset members. Lieberman knew more information about each of these men than their own wives or children would ever discover. He knew so much because he, as head of the Mossad, was the only one with access to the huge files in the safe at Mossad headquarters. Yet for all his knowledge of the backgrounds, the secrets, the political intricacies, he had known nothing of the weaknesses and strengths of these men who had been responsible for Gideon's death.

These leaders, these men of "democracy" and "peace," had led Israel to the brink of military defeat. And they had led his son to his death. Lying here, not even as a whole man, but only as the bits and pieces of what was once Gideon Lieberman.

And the irony was that Lieberman had warned them.

Four days prior to the Arab attack, he knew what was about to happen, down to the last detail. But they preferred to hear those who said that no one would dare to provoke Israel on its holiest of holy days. Never on Yom Kippur.

The military cantor concluded the prayer. The Chief of Staff took his place on the podium. In a low, dramatic voice, he began to describe the courage of the fallen.

Lieberman looked at the faces around him. Only one man here had the ear of the country's leaders: Yedidia Rimon, the ideologue of the Labor Party, the prophet of peace. He stood only an arm's length from Lieberman, next to Martin Silver. The light wind ruffled his white hair and transformed it into a frothy mane encircling his tanned round face. His clear hazel eyes were firmly fixed at a distant point somewhere on the slope. The man who called for sacrifices for the sake of peace with the Arabs. The man, Lieberman believed, who was most responsible for the weakening of Israel's tough spiritual sinew.

Lieberman gazed at the beautiful young woman who held Rimon's hand. She was dressed in military uniform. There was no question that she was his daughter, he thought, comparing their round faces and fair coloring. She was delicate and petite—almost fragile. All those things that make a man feel protective. But there was something else about this woman. Lieberman sensed that a determined and strong person inhabited her angelic body. Perhaps it was the provocative nature of her bearing. Perhaps it was that not an eyelash, not a muscle moved in that beautiful face. Perhaps it was the way father and daughter stood together. It was she who held her father's hand—forcefully, ably, as if forbidding him to show any sign of weakness. And perhaps it was the way she stared at the white sacks on the ground.

"Mr. Lieberman?"

Startled, he turned toward the voice. A young soldier stood before him, wearing lieutenant's epaulets on his shoulder.

"*Shmee* Yoram Negbi."

Martin Silver overheard the exchange and looked over. *Shmee.* He recalled the word; it meant "name." After all these years, he still remembered. It annoyed him that the Hebrew had stuck with him.

"What is it?" Martin heard Lieberman ask the soldier.

"I was on the Hermon with your son."

Lieberman's face froze. This young officer breathed, spoke, moved. Why should this be so, when Gideon lay there, his body crushed and rotting? Who gave this damn kid the right to continue living while Gideon was denied it?

"He was one of the best."

Lieberman wheeled angrily away from Yoram Negbi, leaving the soldier momentarily stunned. He turned to walk away, embarrassed, and tripped on a stone in the process. He reached instinctively for the arm of the man nearest him.

Silver steadied him, and the young man regained his balance quickly. "*Slicha,*" he whispered, and Silver involuntarily translated the word into "sorry," the English equivalent. Another link.

"In their death they gave us life," concluded the Chief of Staff. He returned to his place near the Prime Minister.

"Present arms!"

The platoon of paratroopers raised their rifles. A group of bearded soldiers from the military chaplaincy approached three stretchers and lifted them high, moving them closer to the brink of the gaping grave.

"Fire!"

Jerusalem's hills reverberated with the sound. Everything was over so quickly that by the time Lieberman looked down at the stretchers, they were empty. The white sacks were already in the communal grave; the soldiers were already filling it with earth.

Only then did Lieberman begin to comprehend. The dirt was hitting his child, his son. He had never come home at night without looking in on Gideon. And now they were throwing stones and earth on him. . . .

Two pairs of hands caught him at the grave's edge. He twisted away, shouting at them, flailing with both fists.

Someone had to stop this, to protect his baby from the earth and stones. It took three men to subdue him and, finally, he ceased struggling. Every muscle and nerve gave way then, leaving him helpless. All his emotions were turbulently, violently released. Moshe Lieberman, head of the Mossad, the mere mention of whose name was enough to silence people, was lying on the ground, crying.

Silver stood over him, unable to move or offer a word of solace. His body felt frozen. He could not bear to see this man collapsed and broken. He felt deep sadness. But he said to himself, *You damn fool, I was right after all.*

CHAPTER 2

THE MEETING BETWEEN Israel's Prime Minister and Martin Silver took place in the Prime Minister's sparsely furnished office a few hours after the burial ceremony. He didn't know what to make of this man. Was he the Jewish American Secretary of Defense, or was he the American Secretary of Defense who happened to be Jewish?

On the surface, the conversation was friendly. Silver expressed the sympathy of the American President and government for Israel's casualties. What disturbed the Prime Minister was Silver's tone of voice: neutral, mechanical. Silver seemed to make a point of stressing that the sympathy was on behalf of an institution. The President. The government. Lip service.

After the initial exchanges, the Prime Minister noted, "We suffered heavy losses in equipment as a result of the war. Our financial situation is more precarious than before. I hope the American government is aware of these facts and will be prepared to offer us a helping hand." (13)

Silver's expression remained unchanged. "The war caused heavy losses to all its participants."

"The other side started the war," said the Prime Minister, making an effort to hide his disappointment and impatience.

"What constitutes a beginning of war?" queried Silver. "Firing the first bullet? Or the causes that lead to the firing of the first bullet?" He went on, not letting the Prime Minister answer. "The important thing now is to prevent developments that could lead to a new confrontation in the region."

The room was silent. The Prime Minister stared into Silver's expressionless eyes. Should he try? He couldn't resist the temptation.

"I am convinced that you, Mr. Silver, understand Israel's particular situation. Perhaps more than others."

"Why more than others?"

The question sounded very much like a challenge. A warning. *Should he say it?* pondered the prime minister. What kind of reaction would he get from the words, *Because you are Jewish?*

"Because you are familiar with the region's problems."

Silver blinked. "The region is not what it was prior to the war. We must examine the new circumstances and adapt our policy to them." He stood up and extended his hand. "Taking into account the interests of the *entire* region and the United States," he said.

The Prime Minister had no further doubts about Silver. He also knew the answer to the question that always troubled him in such cases: Was it good or bad for Israel when a Jew of another nation held a position of influence? In Silver's case, it was plainly evident that if his Jewishness did Israel no harm, it certainly did it no good.

The American Embassy's chauffeur opened the door of the black limousine for Silver. Several minutes later, the car was on the Jerusalem-Tel Aviv road with a police escort of two motorcycles clearing the way.

Ten minutes after they had left Jerusalem, Silver noticed cannibalized armored trucks lying on the sides of the road. Some of them were covered with flowers.

"What's that?" he asked the driver.

"Sir, those are the remains of the convoys that broke through the siege of Jerusalem."

"Siege?"

"Jerusalem was surrounded by Arabs. The only way to supply the residents with food and arms was by convoys of armored trucks. We suffered heavy casualties at the time. The trucks are here so that people will not forget."

"When did this happen?"

"During the War of Independence."

War. Everywhere war. In the streets, in the houses, on the roads. A nation that lives by the sword. People who live with memories of past wars and thoughts of future wars.

The car halted near a small apartment building on a narrow street in Tel Aviv. Silver entered and went up to the second floor. He knocked on the door and a few seconds later Lieberman opened it. He extended his hand. "Mordechai," he said softly.

Silver's body stiffened. "Martin," he corrected as he walked inside.

The living room was small, smaller than his kitchen at home. The furniture was simple and functional.

Rivka, Lieberman's short, gray-haired wife, sat on the sofa. She rose, extended her hand, and said, "I've heard so much about you. I'm pleased to meet you."

Silver sat on an armchair which creaked slightly as he put his weight on it. Lieberman sat in another chair, opposite him. There was an embarrassing silence.

"Would you care for a drink?" asked Rivka Lieberman. "Tea, coffee?"

"Coffee with milk, please. No sugar."

"Moshe?"

"Nothing."

Silver looked toward a photograph on a low end table. The young man in the picture looked confident, secure. He wore a carefree grin.

"Your son?"

"Yes."

"I'm sorry. Very sorry."

"Thank you."

He looked at Lieberman, waiting for some initiative on his part. But the dark blue eyes stared apathetically out the window.

"Here," said Rivka. "I hope it's strong enough."

"I'm sure it is," said Silver carefully, relieved that the silence had been broken.

"When are you returning to the United States?"

"Tonight."

"So soon?"

Lieberman shifted his head and gave his wife a long look. She coughed and said, "I'll leave you alone." She approached Silver and extended her hand. "Have a safe trip."

They were alone again. Lieberman returned his gaze to the window. But suddenly he said, "You *are* Mordechai. You cannot change that."

Silver was caught off-guard. "I was Mordechai for seventeen years. I've been Martin for thirty-five years. I made the choice."

"A change of name does not change your identity or your family."

I'll be damned if I'll let myself be dragged into this, thought Silver. "But you are wrong," he said. "I did become an American."

"You are a Jew." Lieberman's voice was calm, almost indifferent.

"Only by birth."

"By birth. By blood. Yours and others'. You are a Jew, nothing less."

Silver's face turned red. "I am what I choose to be."

Lieberman's eyes shifted to Gideon's photograph and his gaze rested there awhile before he turned back to Silver. Now his voice was sincere, apologetic, hurt. "But you're wrong. You are what society decides you are. Do you still not understand this?"

Still.

Warsaw, February 23, 1938. They were both seventeen.

Silver clearly remembered that Friday night. The table was covered with a sparkling white tablecloth. The white Sabbath candles stood in tall polished candlesticks. They had consumed the Sabbath meal—*challah,* gefilte fish, soup, and meat—and the other eight people in the household had gone to sleep right after dinner in preparation for the early-morning Sabbath service.

Only Moshe and Mordechai remained at the table, seated at opposite sides, their tired faces illuminated by the candlelight. *Where was it? In Moshe's home? In mine?* It was difficult to recall, because they were always together. They went to *cheder* together. They went to school together. They spent Friday evenings and the Sabbath together. One week at Moshe's home, one week at Mordechai's. Both houses were home to both boys.

It was difficult to recall because the two places were so similar, especially on Fridays nights. The same white tablecloth, the same candles, the same *challah*—and always the same enchanted solitude after the others had gone to bed.

It was already past midnight. The candles flickered, then went out.

"Do you really want to be a rabbi?" asked Moshe for the fourth time in a voice that was hoarse with fatigue.

"I think so."

"You want to be like Rebbe Mendel? To shout at children? To rap their knuckles? To study Torah all day long?"

"I want to be like the Baal Shem Tov."

"But there was only one Baal Shem Tov," protested Moshe.

"So there will be one Rebbe Mordechai."

The two boys were smiling when they heard the sound of breaking glass. Suddenly, blood was gushing from Mordechai's head. And then the gates of Hell opened: stones, broken glass, screams of the wounded, and the familiar cry, "Death to the Jews!"

Moshe threw himself over Mordechai and they both fell to the floor. He tore off his white shirt, rolled it up,

and placed it over his friend's forehead. His parents and
three brothers and three sisters had appeared in the doorway, and he screamed at them to get out of the window's
range. The white shirt on Mordechai's head had turned
scarlet. Was he dead? Moshe shook him. Mordechai opened
his eyes for a second, then closed them again.

"A hospital! He needs a hospital!"

Moshe lifted his friend's long, lean body, his left hand
steadying himself against the wall. He carried him to the
door, but Mordechai's mother blocked his path. "Where
are you going?" Her face was white, her eyes full of horror.

He continued walking, ignoring her broken voice.

The street was full of people. He had never seen so
many people. They shouted wildly and threw stones at
Jewish storefronts. Others were dragging Jews from their
homes and beating them.

Moshe moved slowly, close to the buildings, hoping to
get by unnoticed. The hospital was two blocks away. He
reached the corner and suddenly saw a face ravaged with
hatred; the eyes bulged and the mouth gaped at him. "Jew-
boy!" was all he heard. He saw a raised club . . . and
nothing more.

When he awoke in the hospital he felt sharp pain
throughout his body. His right leg was in a cast; his head
was bandaged. As soon as he opened his eyes, he saw his
mother. "Moshele, Moshele, how do you feel?"

"Where's Mordechai?"

His mother motioned to the next bed. Moshe recognized his friend's face. His head was also bandaged. Moshe
felt relieved. They were together again.

"How is he?"

"He will be all right. How do you feel?"

Moshe closed his eyes. If Mordechai would be all
right, so would he. It had always been so; it always would.

They left the hospital together three weeks later. On
Friday night, Mordechai did not come for the Sabbath
dinner. He came later, with his parents.

They had a cup of tea and a slice of challah. Then
Mordechai's father said, "We came to say good-bye."
Moshe looked at Mordechai, who lowered his eyes.

"We are going to America."

Moshe's father looked puzzled. "To America? What will you do in America?"

"It's our last chance to get out. Come with us."

Moshe's father laughed. "Last chance? Why?"

"There will be more riots. It will get worse."

"There have always been riots. Jews have always suffered."

Half an hour later, they got up to leave, but Mordechai stayed behind. The two boys were alone again.

"Come with us," said Mordechai. "My parents are willing to take you. You will be like a brother to me, like a son to them."

"Why?"

"The Jews have no future in Poland."

"That is true. But they also have no future in America. I told you about the group of boys who are going to Palestine. They're going to build a new state there. A Jewish state. I want to join them!"

Moshe's enthusiasm grew as he spoke. But he looked into blank, unsympathetic eyes.

"Palestine? How many times do I have to tell you? It's a desert. And full of Arabs. That's a crazy idea!"

"It's our only chance! The Jews have no future among the gentiles."

"Not all gentiles are the same. In America it's different."

"Different! It was different in Poland too! It's different everywhere until it becomes the same!"

Mordechai looked directly at Moshe. "I'm going to America," he said stolidly. Then suddenly, he began to weep. Moshe placed his hand on Mordechai's shoulder, swallowing hard, feeling separated already from his friend.

Two days later, Mordechai and his family left Poland for America. Five weeks later, Moshe Lieberman set out for Palestine. His parents refused to go with him and they, together with his six brothers and sisters, were sent to die in a place called Treblinka.

Thirty-seven years, and they were still debating the same question. They were no longer two Jewish youths at the mercy of the Warsaw mob. Now they had titles: the

American Secretary of Defense and the Chief of the Israeli Intelligence Service. But the argument was the same. Lieberman rubbed his brow thoughtfully.

"At any rate, I'm thankful you didn't become a rabbi," he said.

Silver smiled. "I would have made a lousy one. All that studying, all that ritual and mysticism. I guess I really never had it in me. Anyway, in the United States they don't even know who the Baal Shem Tov was."

"Do you have children?"

"Two. The boy, Richard, is twenty-three now. Barbara is fifteen."

They were silent. Both men realized that they shared an identical thought. Mordechai had gone to the United States and—even if wrongly so—had two children. Moshe had gone to Israel and—even if rightly so—had *had* one son. Now dead.

Lieberman stood up and Silver did likewise. They shook hands and walked to the door together. "I can't forget," Silver said in a low voice. "The night of the pogrom is something that will be with me forever."

Lieberman's face hardened. "You owe me nothing."

Silver slumped back into the seat of his limousine and felt his tension begin to ease. He bit his lip and looked out the window at the passing landscape. He yearned with all his heart for the past when he had known exactly where he stood and why. It was more difficult now, and friendship was no longer a criterion for his decision-making. On the plane back to Washington, he breathed a sigh of relief. Never in his life would he have to visit Israel, or his past, again.

Or so he hoped.

CHAPTER 3

THE RIMON LIVING ROOM teemed with people after the funeral. Not just the close friends who would have been expected to come, but the politicos, the Zionist activists for whom Yedidia's words were gospel.

Deborah sat in a corner of the living room, watching the people milling around her father. Their voices penetrated her consciousness from afar, as if through a fog.

"If not for the Americans, we would have easily destroyed the Egyptians."

"We needed only another twenty-four hours."

"Now the Egyptians claim victory and the world applauds them."

A brief silence ensued, and then Deborah heard her father's quiet voice. She opened her eyes.

"Perhaps it's better this way. Perhaps they need the illusion of victory to make peace."

Deborah saw the people around her father nod in agreement, even in admiration. Here was a man who had just lost his son saying it might be better that the enemy had not been defeated. Even at this difficult time, he placed the national interest above the personal one.

Deborah felt a strong urge to shout at her father that he still didn't understand anything. This war also could have been prevented, Amos would have said, had his father and his colleagues understood the root of the problem.

But she didn't say a thing. Not because of the occasion, or the people, but because she knew it was pointless. She and her father thought in different terms, on different levels.

Deborah rose and left the room. She wasn't surprised that her movements went unnoticed.

She had wanted to go to her room to gain the solitude she needed to rethink the reality of life without the brother she had raised as a son. But on her way, she stopped at the closed door to Amos's room. She hesitated for a moment, opened the door, and walked in.

The room was sparsely furnished.

That's the way Amos liked it. That's the way Amos was.

She sat on the only armchair in the room, trying to feel Amos's presence, but there was nothing. Perhaps because he had spent so little time at home since joining the army. Three months had passed since his most recent stay in the room, on the last leave he had received before being transferred to the Hermon.

She turned her gaze to the far corner of the room where, on the desk, she saw a photograph of a smiling young woman. Their mother. Deborah had always thought that the face showed remarkable hopefulness.

She had died when Deborah was four years old, and the passage of time had erased any of the memories Deborah had of her very early years. But she never forgot her father's story of his first encounter with Sarah Braun.

Deborah smiled as she recalled it. Her father had been so proud when he had told her, "You know, I actually carried your mother on my back to Israel." That had been in 1947, when the Hagana had organized illegal immigrant

ships to smuggle Jews into Palestine past the British naval
patrols. They would row out in small rubber dinghies,
under cover of darkness, to transfer immigrants from the
boats to the beach, and from there to a secure haven. Sarah
was one of those immigrants, and Yedidia, then a young
Hagana officer, carried her on his back to the beach. Six
months later, he carried her in his arms as his bride into his
small apartment on the outskirts of Tel Aviv.

Yedidia Rimon had saved Sara from the British patrols, but no one could save her from cancer.

After her death, he made an unsuccessful effort to be
both mother and father to his two young children. But he
was already involved in public affairs that demanded
most of his time. Deborah and Amos grew accustomed to
spending long periods of time on their own. In the course
of time, Deborah became the axis around which the small
family revolved, either because she was two years older
than Amos or because she had the more independent
character.

Deborah heard sounds of people coming and going.
More came in than left, she thought bitterly. And the
monotonous sound of voices, a sound she had lived with
all her life.

In her younger years, there had been nothing she
admired more than her father's quiet, cultured voice speaking of ideals, ideas, the past, and plans for the future.
Over the years, she grew to doubt this admiration. Later,
she exchanged it for bitter disappointment.

She and Amos spoke of this at length. They both
sensed something tasteless and futile in the endless verbi-
age. It didn't lead anywhere. Her father talked and talked
and the wars continued to be fought and the blood continued to spill forth in the towns of Israel and the towns
across the border.

Why? The question tortured her; the answer was even
more difficult. Deborah concluded that her father had
built himself a world of his own with its roots in the
forties. He was unable to disengage himself from that
world and to adjust to the new reality. He still thought in
terms of Egypt, Jordan, and Syria, whereas the real problem, in Deborah's view, was the Palestinians.

They had had many arguments on the subject. When Deborah accused him of not making enough concessions to the Palestinians, he replied angrily that many in Israel accused him of the reverse. Deborah knew this was true. Her father was considered an extreme "dove" because he favored certain territorial concessions on the West Bank. What he failed to realize—and she told him so—was that the Arabs perceived him as no less "hawkish" than the most extreme "hawks." She demanded of him, almost begged him, to go one step further by agreeing to the establishment of a Jewish-Palestinian state. At this point, the conversation would turn into a loud preaching session. One day, however, father and daughter simply ceased discussing it.

Someone knocked at the door and pushed it open without waiting for a response. Deborah turned around to see a slim, tanned young man wearing lieutenant's stripes.

"Do you mind?" she said curtly. "Well?"

"I'm Yoram Negbi," he said weakly. "I was with your brother on the Hermon." She motioned for him to sit in one of the chairs.

He remained erect and still, watching for her reaction. "Were you close to Amos?" she asked.

"We were good friends, yes. Us and Gideon."

"Gideon Lieberman? I remember him. He was here several times."

"So was I. I never met you, though."

"Right." There was silence again. Deborah was annoyed that this man was soliciting her for some reason when she had her own problems to deal with.

"I recall Amos telling me that Gideon's father was someone in the Secret Service," she added to keep the conversation alive.

"The head of the Mossad."

"Oh, yes."

She had been as cordial as could be expected, but this was ridiculous. "Look," she said as she got up, "I'm awfully tired and I hope you won't mind if I just show you back to the living room." She wasn't trying to be rude; she just preferred being straightforward.

"But," he said, "I wanted to talk to you about the plans that Amos and I had."

"What do you mean?"

"Can you give me a few more minutes? Please, sit down."

She sat on the edge of her chair.

"The army, service—it was terrible. The plans for afterward were the only good thing about it. But it was all in vain, you see, if we don't act on them. Amos would have insisted. He thought they would be the only way to bring about peace.

"This house is full of talk about peace," she said testily after a long pause. "Welcome to the club."

She noticed a new quality in his blue eyes, a mixture of pain and insult. "I don't just talk," he said. "I haven't sat quietly since the war. You're not the first person I've approached about this. And you know what? People listen now. They are beginning to realize that we can't put on uniforms every few years, take up arms, and defeat the Arabs in six days. That illusion is finished, dead."

"I wish you'd come to the point," she said impatiently. "What people? How many?"

"I've spoken to approximately thirty, all young army veterans or students. Eighteen of them expressed willingness to cooperate. A few weeks ago, we held our first meeting and chose a name for ourselves: Ishmaelites: The Front for a Jewish-Palestinian State. We set up two cells: one will concentrate on activity among Jews; the other, on cooperation with Palestinians. But for the time being, we decided to focus on widening our base and increasing our membership. There will probably be thirty at our next meeting." He quickly added, "It's not much, I know, but it's a *beginning*."

"It's not the first beginning. It's happened before." His eyes narrowed.

He looked angry, and Deborah noted that this way he seemed older and more mature.

"Well," he asked, "what are we supposed to do? Forget the whole thing just because a few attempts failed?" He took a deep breath and leaned forward. "We can't afford

another war. And if it does come, you and I and hundreds
of others like us won't be able to blame the leaders. If we
sit back now and let things develop on their own, *we* will
be the guilty ones."

He sighed as though a heavy burden had been lifted
from his shoulders. Deborah was intrigued. Perhaps this
was what she had been waiting for, what she and Amos
had discussed since the time they realized that their father
and his friends, for all their fine notions, had not touched
even the tip of the problem.

"When is your next meeting?" she asked quietly.

And as soon as she did so, she saw across from her
the most beautiful smile she had ever seen—happy, innocent, with an additional quality she could only describe
as devoted. She had shown just that much interest, and it
had convinced him. It was as though Yoram was now
prepared to give himself over to her with unquestioning
faith, just because she had faith in his idea. In that instant,
she actually found him attractive.

"In four days," he said. "I'll pick you up."

He was about to leave when, for some reason, she
suddenly remembered.

"The Hermon . . . you were the only survivor, weren't
you?"

He froze. "Yes." And before the next question could be
asked, he quickly left the room.

CHAPTER 4

THE PRIME MINISTER thrust the letter back across his desk at Moshe Lieberman. "I do not accept your resignation," he said.

"You must accept it. It is final."

"Why?"

"I no longer have faith in the government, or in you."

The Prime Minister rose and walked to the window. "You're not in such bad company," he said with a bitter smile. "I'm not so sure that *I* have faith in myself and the government."

Lieberman raised his eyes. The Prime Minister continued to stare out at the sky. "We have all lost a great deal of faith and trust," he said softly. "Especially in ourselves. This is not unnatural. All these years we reassured ourselves that we were invulnerable. It suddenly became painfully clear that this was not the case." (27)

"We would have remained untouchable, if only you had listened."

The Prime Minister turned to look at Lieberman. "We were unwilling to pay attention because we were arrogant, feeling pretty smug, I admit. But the war is not yet over. On the contrary, now it will be more difficult. There is serious cause to suspect that the PLO will increase its activities." He walked over to Lieberman. "I need you."

Lieberman lowered his eyes. This state of uncertainty was new to him. He was accustomed to making swift decisions. But this time he was confused. He was contemptuous of his political superiors and no longer trusted them. But precisely for this reason, was he not obliged to keep doing his job? Could he leave the most essential security matters in the hands of those who had proven to be irresponsible?

"I will think about it."

The Prime Minister picked up the letter of resignation and slowly tore it in half, then in half again. "We Jews," he said ironically, "are lucky. There is nothing to think about. Nothing to consider. We have no choice." He threw the bits of paper into the wastebasket and turned to Lieberman. "We took a beating. So what? What do we do, close up shop? Tell ourselves that we tried and it didn't work? Is that what you suggest?"

"I said I would think," protested Lieberman.

The Prime Minister's face hardened. "What about? If you are correct in saying that we are weak—and I'm not saying you're wrong—then we need people like you." He softened his voice. "There are too many unfinished matters. The Munich murderers. Ma'alot. Na'hariah." And almost in a whisper he added, "Maruan Awad."

Lieberman's body stiffened. He looked at the Prime Minister. That name had not been mentioned accidentally. The old political fox knew that the leader of the Holy Front for the Liberation of Palestine had become an obsession of Lieberman's. And the Prime Minister was the only person who knew what Lieberman had accidentally discovered.

A few days after the end of the war, the Mossad caught a group of PLO terrorists who had infiltrated Israel from Lebanon. Lieberman took part in the interrogation.

The commander of the terrorist unit, a blustering coward under pressure, went out of his way to satisfy his interrogators in order to save his life. When he was asked to name his leaders, he mentioned, among others, Maruan Awad's name. He had met him, he said, prior to the operation, to receive instructions. In the course of the meeting, either to inspire him or to boast, Awad told him that during the war, he had joined the Syrian force that captured the Hermon.

As soon as he heard the word "Hermon," Lieberman's face stiffened and he grasped the Palestinian terrorist by the arm. "What exactly did he say?" he demanded.

The commander of the unit seemed happy to satisfy Lieberman's curiosity.

"Well, he asked me, 'Did you hear what happened to the Jews we caught on the Hermon?' I said I had. He went on, 'And did you hear what happened to their commander?' I said yes, and he bragged, 'I did that with my own hands!'"

Leiberman's face paled. He tightened his grip on the Palestinian. "More! More! What else did he say?"

The Palestinian choked and drew back. "I don't know . . . I don't remember." The two other interrogators grabbed Lieberman and pulled him away. One of them muttered, "I think he's telling the truth. Are you all right? What's the matter with you?"

Lieberman looked at his subordinate as though he had just awakened from a deep sleep. "Never mind," he said finally. "Nothing."

Since then, he had been unable to think of Gideon without recalling the image of Maruan Awad, whose photograph he always kept in his jacket pocket. Almost with as much care as he had kept Gideon's childhood photograph.

The Prime Minister cleared his throat and Lieberman shook the memory off. He rose and walked to the door. "I

know you paid a heavy price," the Prime Minister called
after him. "Think about what I said. I need you."

Lieberman walked slowly down the corridor, lost in
thought. He left the building and got into the back seat of
his car. "To the office," he told the driver. He leaned his
head back and shut his eyes. *No*, he told himself, *the
Prime Minister has no idea. He knows the details, but he
knows nothing else.*

The Prime Minister knew nothing of Lieberman's
horrible uncertainty after he learned of the fall of the
Hermon. When Lieberman first heard about it on the second
day of the war, he had an instinctive sense that Gideon was
dead. For days he attempted to confirm his fear, but without success. Then, on the twentieth day of the war, one
day before the fighting ended, Lieberman asked to be
attached to the force sent to take the Hermon back from
the Syrians. His request was rejected. But he was in the
first helicopter which reached the mountaintop after its
recapture.

The corporal who led the party from the copter was
sick immediately. He had killed in battle himself, but he
could not stomach the task of collecting the pieces of
hands, feet, faces, genitals, and other human organs which
were strewn all over the mountain. Not a single corpse
was found intact. Consequently, it was still unclear who
had fallen in battle and who had been taken prisoner. The
distraught parents were told they would have to wait
days, possibly weeks, before eyes could be put back into
faces, before hands were joined to shoulders and sexual
organs sewn in place. But Lieberman did not wait. He
carefully examined each piece of the revolting debris. His
search was painstakingly slow because he was careful not
to show any disrespect.

The commander of the assault force tried to get him to
leave. He explained that it would be better to leave the
task to the experts whose laboratories were equipped to
deal with the job. Lieberman could not hear the man's
words and turned back to his search in a daze. The head of
Northern Command approached him then. "If he's dead,"
the man told Lieberman, "you won't lose anything by

finding out in a few days' time." When he got no reply, he shrugged and said, "My son was also here." He pulled a piece of paper from his pocket and handed it to Lieberman. "If you find anything, I'd be grateful if you'd let me know." With that, he went back to conducting the battle. The piece of paper contained a six-digit figure: the dog tag number of the general's son.

Lieberman spent eighteen hours on Mt. Hermon without food or rest. In the course of the nineteenth hour, he found what he had dreaded finding: three beauty marks, which would have meant nothing to a laboratory staff. They were on the arm, near the place where it had been severed from the shoulder. Three brown marks in a triangle, precisely the way they looked when Moshe Lieberman first picked up his hour-old son and held him in his arms. "It's a sign of the evenness of his character!" he had boasted at the time. "Look how perfect this triangle is!" Consequently, he had not the slightest doubt as to whose arm this was.

He left the rest to the laboratory staff. He told them he would come himself to identify the body when they were finished. They begged him not to do so. "Sir, we've succeeded in locating all the limbs, but. . . ."

He insisted, and there was no way of preventing him. It was the first time in his life he had ever broken down. He did not cry or shout. He just broke down totally. Everything collapsed within him, he could not hold himself upright. Two forms swam before his eyes: Gideon, with his smooth handsome face and his shock of blond curls; and a rounded hunk of amorphous flesh. The two forms mingled, one trying to obliterate the other.

Then came the information about Awad; it injected new meaning into his life. How ironic, he thought. Before the war Gideon had been everything to him, he had been the goal and purpose of his existence. Now it was his murderer, Maruan Awad.

The car halted near an old three-story house with peeling walls. A sign hung at the entrance: "Meat Products Marketing Board." Lieberman climbed the stairs to his office on the second floor and sat down behind his massive desk. He took a big cardboard file from the pile awaiting his attention and opened it. Intelligence reports from Bagdad. His eyes skimmed the printed letters, but his mind absorbed nothing.

Is Israel worth it? he found himself asking. *Is it worth such sacrifices? God! Liberate me from these thoughts! It's a sin, an anathema! I, Moshe Lieberman, who sent other men's sons on missions from which they did not return, I, of all men, cannot have these thoughts.*

He rose quickly and almost ran to the bathroom next door to his office. He placed his head under the tap and opened it all the way, letting the cold water flow over his hair, his face, his neck. Finally he closed the tap and returned to his office. He walked over to the window and looked out. There were a few military trucks driving north. A police car. Pedestrians. Civilian vehicles.

A noisy, vibrant city. And the place where he now stood had been desert sands only thirty years earlier.

Run away? Never. How could a Jew even conceive of life in this generation without participation in the special experience of building the Jewish state? And it had to be preserved so that "Martin Silver" and his like would always have a refuge.

CHAPTER 5

"MEET NABIL BUTRUS," said Yoram.

Deborah extended her hand to the young Palestinian. She guessed that he was in his late twenties. He was tall, slender, and unattractive. But there was something pleasant in his manner.

"I'm very glad to meet you," said Nabil. "Yoram has told me a lot about you."

Deborah smiled. "Thank you. I am glad to be here." Which, she thought, was a gross understatement. It hadn't been easy to reach this place or to achieve this moment.

More than three years had passed since she had participated in the first meeting of the Ishmaelites, three years packed with conflict and soul-searching. Every issue, every particle of an idea, had been subjected to marathon discussions that lasted weeks and months. What kind of Palestinian state, where, when, how?

Deborah's position in support of a joint Jewish-Palestinian state was the least popular. When originally
presented, it had been greeted with open hostility. Deborah
reasoned that there was no need for a new movement to
meet the Palestinians halfway. The other political parties
were already doing just that. Her opponents claimed that
the Palestinians would be the majority in a joint state,
which would then lose its Jewish character. It had seemed
like an endless argument, and Deborah had begun to lose
patience and to contemplate resignation. And then the
Geneva Conference was convened. That changed everything.

The United States had finally managed to convince
Syria and Jordan to participate together with Egypt and
Israel in a conference, to be held in Geneva, that would
strive toward an overall settlement of the Middle East
conflict. The Palestinians were not invited.

Deborah had no difficulty in persuading her colleagues
that the entire affair smacked of betrayal of the Palestinian
cause by the Arab states. The danger was that Geneva would
result in a solution that ignored the Palestinian problem.
Deborah was convinced with all her heart that such a
solution would not only fail to solve the problem, but
would exacerbate it. The price would be ultimately paid
by both the Jews and the Palestinians.

The Ishmaelite movement, which comprised seventy
members three years after its establishment, accepted
Deborah's proposal to attempt direct contact with the
Palestine Liberation Organization. Furthermore, the movement authorized Deborah and Yoram to be its representatives in any such contacts. And so they reached Nabil,
who had been described as "having connections with the
PLO."

Deborah looked around. The house, furnished oriental-
style with low tables and stools, was built on one of
Hebron's eastern slopes. The view from the window was
pastoral. The small houses on the hillsides were built of
clay and looked as though they had sprouted from the
earth. Herds of sheep nibbled at the green grass. A light

spring wind ruffled the rows of olive trees which stretched as far as the eye could see.

"It's beautiful," said Deborah quietly.

"It's even more beautiful at sunrise," said Nabil. "When I'm not too lazy, I get up very early in the morning to see one of the most breathtaking sights in the world."

"It's a crime to have wars in this beautiful country of ours," she said.

"Yes, it is," replied Nabil. "Perhaps we shall succeed in bringing them to an end. It's obvious they won't do so in Geneva."

"I'm afraid they'll do *something* in Geneva," said Deborah. "That's why we must meet with authorized representatives of the PLO."

"Excuse me for being so direct. But what do you think you can contribute? You seem to have had very little impact in Israel." And after a short pause, Nabil added, "If any at all."

"That's the reason we're here," Deborah said. "We believe that together we can have greater impact. Maybe even a decisive one."

Nabil reflected over her words, and Deborah heard goats bleating from the distant valley. Finally he said, "Maybe. It's worth a try. When can you be in Paris?"

"Paris?" asked Yoram. "Why Paris? Why not here?"

"Too dangerous. Can you come to Paris?"

"Yes," Deborah quickly answered. "Any time you say."

"Next Wednesday," said Nabil. "The Imperial Hotel. Are you familiar with it?"

"We'll find it," said Deborah.

After seeing them out the back door, Nabil returned to the house and entered an adjoining room through a side entrance. An old man sat at a small card table, puffing at a nargila.

"Did you hear?"

"Yes," replied the old man.

"It doesn't look serious," Nabil said. "What can they do to help us?"

The old man's face remained expressionless. "They can let us undermine the Israelis from within." And he continued puffing.

Outside Nabil's house, Deborah said, "Well, we did it."
"Yes," said Yoram in an edgy voice.
Deborah knew what he was thinking. A meeting with members of the PLO was not only unconventional, but illegal. He was thinking of his father, General Yitzhak Negbi, and of his reaction if he found out.
She put her arm through his and they walked toward Hebron's central square, which was filled with tourists hunting for souvenirs and bargains from the Holy Land. On the western side of the square, tourists, mostly pilgrims, pressed into the narrow, low entrance to the Church of the Nativity.
The sun was hot and Deborah began to perspire. She gently pressed Yoram's arm. He looked at her. She smiled.
"Sure," he said eagerly. "Why not?"
Yoram wasn't surprised. Since they had become lovers two years earlier, he had learned that Deborah liked to top off any excitement with sex. Sorrow, disappointment, enthusiasm, hope—she turned every strong emotion into a sexual high.
At first, he deluded himself that she loved him. Later, he came to terms with the fact that for her, he was only a convenience. She was a woman, and he was the man with whom she spent more of her time than with any other.
They took a room in a small, neglected hotel overlooking the square. Deborah undressed nonchalantly, as though preparing for a bath. They didn't touch each other until they got into bed. He stroked her breasts and she closed her eyes. She felt his hand on her stomach and then on her groin. She responded by taking his penis, which was hard and ready, in her hand.
She enjoyed him immensely but she never came. Not once.
"Was it good?" he would always ask after his orgasm.
"Yes."

But her tone was dull. Her head rested on Yoram's chest, her naked leg encircled his.

In the Israel of the early sixties, neither money nor education nor titles could have given young Yoram more prestige than his father's rank. He was the kid who came to school with emblems of paratroop units, of the artillery, and of the infantry sewn on his jacket. The whole school came out to gaze at the brown military car which drove up to collect him and at the tall man sitting inside with the red beret on his head. Whenever there was a battle or some other military operation, everyone listened to what Yoram had to say, assuming correctly that his insights came directly from the source: the General. A visit to Yoram's home was a much-coveted prize; those granted the honor were proud of it. And it was a unique privilege to be Yoram's friend, because it granted one the privilege of being near his father.

Yitzhak Negbi was a living legend in Israel. His deeds of valor were the inspiration for books and movies. Since most of the yarns about him were a mixture of truth and fantasy, he himself often found it hard to make the distinction.

He was typical of those husbands and fathers serving in the combat units. He came home only on occasional weekends, and always unexpectedly. It depended on where he was stationed and on whether or not he had a mistress at the time—usually one of the office clerks serving in his battalion, later on in his brigade, and then in his command. These were bright young girls with a proper respect for men of rank who had a glorious past and an assured future.

Few people had any doubt about Yitzhak Negbi's future. At the age of twenty-nine, he was a colonel; at thirty-three, a lieutenant colonel; at thirty-eight, a general. Everyone knew it was only a matter of time before he became chief of staff.

From an early age, Yoram heard his mother tell of the great and important things his father was doing as defender of the state. Yoram, however, only understood that he missed his father, and he would sometimes cry at night, wondering why the General did not spend more time at home like other fathers.

Later on he did understand, and so did his friends— that was his compensation. Nevertheless, throughout all those years, he retained a hidden measure of bitterness about the time when he needed a father, not a war hero.

At fifteen, Yoram, like his fellow students, began his cadet training. The first day, the instructor took Yoram's section to a field where they were led to a one-story house. The boys were ordered to clamber up on the roof, and a blanket was stretched out down below. The instructor ordered them to jump. Without a second thought, they all stepped back to let Yoram go first. He looked down and felt his stomach turn over. It seemed so high. He could get hurt. Even so, he closed his eyes and jumped. Nothing happened to him.

The next time, they were to slide down a rope from one side of the Yarkon River to the other. When Yoram's turn came, he discovered that the fear he had felt on the roof had returned full force. It was harder this time to convince himself and the others that he considered the task routine. When he was first required to train with a rifle and bayonet, he began to shake uncontrollably.

From this point onward, all his thoughts focused on a single purpose: to conceal his dreadful secret from his friends, his officers, and, above all else, from his father.

He became a proficient and highly sophisticated liar. He began to get violent stomach pains at the right moments and missed school on the right days. But the more evasively he behaved and the more he lied, the more he feared the day when the mask would be ripped off, revealing him to the world exactly as he was.

But it didn't happen. The only person who knew the truth was Yoram's mother. He fathomed this from the manner in which she spoke to him and from the topics she discussed. She never once said that she knew, but she began telling him stories about people who were never lauded for their physical courage who had nevertheless distinguished themselves in other areas. In her delicate fashion, she spoke to him of intellectual or moral courage. Who was braver, she sometimes asked rhetorically, the man who stormed forward under fire or the one who stood up against prejudice and corruption?

Yoram's father had his own answer to that one. There was no difference, he told his son. Whoever feared for his life or his body was equally fearful in spirit.

When the time came for Yoram to enlist, he went to the medical board with a fervent prayer that he would be found unfit, that they would discover some ailment which would disqualify him from serving in a combat unit.

He was found to be in perfect health, and he did what his father expected of him: he volunteered to join the paratroopers.

He hoped that the unique atmosphere prevailing in the elite unit would leave him with no room for cowardice. If his fears did not vanish there, perhaps, at least, he would grow accustomed to them and go on with his duties despite them.

What happened was precisely the opposite. His fears increased, particularly his fear of heights. He could not lie his way out of it, nor absent himself from action. And then, inevitably, came the day Yoram would never forget.

His father drove up to the camp in his big car, wearing his red beret and his glistening insignia; everyone jumped to attention and saluted as he strode past. He marched into the office of the camp commander, and the two men shook hands warmly. As befitted a military officer, he did not hug or kiss his son when he came into the room. Instead, he returned his salute. This was a great day in his life: he had come to receive an account of the paratrooper who was destined to follow in his footsteps.

Ten minutes later, he walked out of the office a changed man. His shoulders slumped and he gazed absentmindedly at those around him. His eyes were downcast, and he could not look at Yoram, who had accompanied him back to his car. Father and son exchanged not a single word, not a single glance.

Yoram was transferred to the infantry, to the Golani brigade stationed in the north. This too was a combat unit, but he was not required to jump from planes. Yoram completed a section leader's course, and in September 1973 he was posted to the Hermon. He was a sergeant when the Yom Kippur War broke out.

After the war, nothing was the same. The atmosphere of the country had changed, and so had values—and heroes. Military men were no longer omnipotent; they were vulnerable, they were ordinary human beings.

Returning home from service, Yoram saw his father in a completely different light. The handsome, invincible war hero, erect and powerful, now suddenly looked ludicrous, beaten, helpless. Now, for Yoram, there was no longer any shame in being a coward.

But he still could hardly believe that he had run away while his comrades fought to defend the fortress. For two days, he hid in one of the many caves on the mountainside. Occasionally, he heard the Arabic-speaking voices of the Syrian patrols. He didn't dare look out, but his hunger and thirst finally overcame his fear. On the third night, he began crawling along the mountain's northern slope. He lost consciousness when he reached the Israeli lines.

He awoke two days later, in the hospital, and discovered that he was the sole survivor. Two intelligence officers interrogated him regarding the events that preceded the capture of the mount. "How did it happen? How did the Syrians succeed in penetrating the fortress that was considered impenetrable?" Yoram replied that the attack had come as a stunning surprise. Other than that, he said, he couldn't recall a thing. The interrogators persisted. "Why was the electronic door open? Who opened it? Why?" Yoram tiredly closed his eyes. "I can't remember. I can't remember. . . ."

He covered Deborah's mouth with his and felt his cock harden. He was completely involved in the feeling of her hot breath on his face and the union of their bodies when something outside exploded with such force that

Deborah and Yoram could feel the blast. They wrenched apart and ran to the window.

Outside, hundreds of people were running in search of cover. A tour bus in the parking lot at the edge of the square was on its side and was totally demolished. Ambulance, police, and army sirens shared the air with the screaming of wounded men, women, and children. The torn and broken bodies lay strewn about the street.

"PLO," Deborah said quietly.

Not a muscle twitched in Moshe Lieberman's face as his eyes scanned the photographs on his desk. He gazed, mesmerized, at the silent, twisted corpses.

Lieberman had already grown accustomed to the sight of corpses. But children's corpses—they were different. And children were always the target of terrorist acts by the Holy Front for the Liberation of Palestine.

There was a knock at the door. Without raising his eyes, Lieberman answered softly. His secretary, Zipporah, a stocky, severe-looking woman, entered the room and placed a typed page on Lieberman's desk. "It's Maruan Awad again. Porat wants to speak with you."

"Show him in."

Lieberman lit a cigarette and picked up the paper. He quickly skimmed the notice by the Holy Front for the Liberation of Palestine which proudly announced the successful act of sabotage in Hebron. The announcement set the number of dead at twenty-nine. No mention was made of the fact that half the casualties were children.

There was a knock at the door, and David Porat walked in. Lieberman greeted his young, boyishly handsome aide with a thin but affectionate smile. Porat sat down opposite Lieberman, who put down the paper and held up one of the photographs.

"If we didn't kill this child, we are accomplices to the murder," he said.

"It is impossible to prevent every act of terror."

Lieberman banged his hand on the desk. "'Impossible' never was a word in our dictionary! We did not use it in the early years of our statehood. Only recently have we become experts at finding explanations and excuses."

There was silence between the two men. At last Lieberman broke it. "Four years—years!—we have been pursuing Awad. All that time, and nothing. We are accumulating failures and he is accumulating acts of terror."

"We've done all we could."

"Not for this child." He pointed to the photograph in his hand.

Porat cleared his throat. "Maybe I'd better come back later."

"Sit, sit. What is it?"

"Remember the Ishmaelites?"

Lieberman nodded.

Porat drew a piece of paper from his briefcase and perused it. "Two of the Ishmaelites were seen yesterday at the home of Nabil Butrus. Probably something to do with the Geneva Conference. It seems that they are planning some meeting with the PLO's people in Paris."

"Are you sure?"

"We received this from a good source. How should we handle it? Should we stop the meeting?"

Lieberman pondered a minute, then shook his head. "Let the matter develop. Let's see where it goes. Notify the office in Paris to keep their eyes open."

"I feel that we should prevent it."

Lieberman looked at Porat with growing interest. If Porat disputed his orders, he must have good reasons.

"The two Israelis at Butrus's home—a young man and a young woman. The man is the son of General Yitzhak Negbi. The woman is the daughter of Yedidia Rimon."

The picture immediately flashed through Lieberman's mind. The cemetery. The young beauty who held Yedidia Rimon's hand. The young man who said that he had been on the Hermon with Gideon. What were they doing in the home of a PLO member?

"They are very active in the Ishmaelites," said Porat. "Actually, the young woman heads the movement."

Lieberman was stunned. The daughter of a Zionist

leader and the son of a general, traitors? "There must be a mistake," he said.

"No mistake," said Porat decisively. "They are going to Paris. My recommendation is to prevent the meeting with the PLO. The situation is too sensitive now, Moshe. There might be a scandal when it becomes known. And think of Rimon. It will be a blow, for him and for the public."

Lieberman's smile was tense. *Always the politician, Porat. Always searching for the public and political implications.*

"No," he said. "We will treat these two just like any others. I want to see where the collaboration goes. Notify Paris."

CHAPTER 6

THE IMPERIAL HOTEL was located on a side street on the Left Bank of the Seine. It was an old establishment, and the owners, Moroccans, made little effort to maintain a decent standard. The walls were peeling, the doors creaked, some of the chairs were broken, the drapes were stained.

For the purposes of the young people gathered in the small meeting room, the hotel was adequate. The only thing that mattered to them was the Jewish-Palestinian revolution.

Nabil introduced Deborah and Yoram to two Palestinians, who came to Paris, they said, especially for this meeting. Halid Ismail came from Holland, where he headed the PLO office. He was twenty-seven years old, short, and thin. The other man, Omar El-Kudsi, was introduced as a member of the political department of the PLO. Deborah guessed that he was in his mid-thirties, but it was impossible to be certain because of the thick, black beard that covered much of his face.

Deborah soon found that the Palestinians knew exactly what they expected from the Ishmaelites. Omar El-Kudsi, in a quiet and businesslike voice, outlined the objectives: a series of well-prepared demonstrations in Israel, intended to create the impression that Jews as well as Palestinians opposed the Geneva Conference and supported a Jewish-Palestinian state; participation of the Ishmaelites and other Jewish supporters in demonstrations on the West Bank; and infiltration of the Jewish press. Each proposal was discussed at length. By the end of the day, most of the points had been covered.

Deborah was in high spirits. Not only was the first cooperation with the PLO established, but in one day they had managed to work out together the beginning of a practical plan for political action.

She went to her room, took off her clothes, and stepped into the shower. She turned the hot water tap, but nothing came out. She hesitated, then turned the other tap. The first shock of the icy water took her breath away, but once she got used to it, she felt refreshed and recharged.

She came out of the bathroom drying herself and saw Yoram, sitting in an armchair, smiling hesitantly at her naked body.

"How did you get in?"

"The door was open. You should be more careful."

Yoram kept staring, overwhelmed by her beauty. The cold water had reddened her smooth skin. She seemed much younger, almost like a child. Her eyes shone, her cheeks were flushed.

She threw the towel on the bed and reached for her panties. Yoram got up. She looked at him, deliberating. Then she smiled and let the panties fall on the floor.

She reached out for him and his excitement turned to uninhibited desire. Her lips pressed his, her tongue searching his mouth, and she shifted her hips to be close to his erect penis. He stroked her breasts. The nipples were hard with desire. Her hand was on his belt when someone knocked loudly at the door.

"Don't open it," Yoram whispered pleadingly, feeling he would burst with his need for her.

They stood frozen, waiting for the sound of retreating footsteps. Another knock.

"They know I'm here," she whispered. And then she called, "Just a minute."

She arranged her clothing, brushed a hand through her hair, and walked to the door. Nabil was standing to one side of the doorjamb, leaning heavily on his good leg. He looked at her, then at Yoram, and said, "I'll be back later."

"No, no. It's all right. Come in," said Deborah. When she glanced at Yoram, she was half-sorry that she hadn't let Nabil go. Yoram's face was suddenly a mask of defeat—the whipped dog again.

Nabil seemed amused, perhaps because of the situation he had evidently interrupted. "Until we establish our ideal state, how would you like to go out and have some fun? I know a terrific little cabaret near here. You'll enjoy it." He looked questioningly at Deborah, then at Yoram.

"Maybe later," Yoram answered quickly.

"Why not now?" Deborah's voice was animated, happy. "I think we've earned some entertainment."

On their way out of the room, Deborah put her hand on Yoram's arm. "We have the whole night before us," she whispered, trying honestly to assuage his hurt feelings. But her urgency for him had passed.

The cabaret was just a big room, sparsely decorated. A waiter led them through a cloud of cigarette smoke to a low table near the far wall. They sat down on the squat wicker chairs.

When Deborah's eyes had become accustomed to the dark, she realized that another man was sitting at their table. She saw Nabil, obviously surprised to see him, shake his head and murmur something. A waitress in a floral skirt and apron approached the table. She asked for their order in French.

"What will you have?" Nabil asked.

"A beer," Yoram told him.

"Deborah?"

"I don't know. No alcohol."

"Don't be silly. You've worked hard today. A drink will help you to sleep. Just one," Nabil urged.

She shrugged. "All right, whatever you say . . . you can order for me. But nothing too strong—I'm a terrible drunk."

"*Un gin-tonic pour mon amie; un whisky pour moi, s'il vous plaît,*" Nabil told the waitress.

Deborah watched the stage. The singer had just finished a number, acknowledged the applause, and started a new song. The lights were dimmed and only one spot illuminated her face. The woman had an earthy sort of beauty; she was not pretty, but she had deep, marvelous looks. Her voice was low and warm. The soothing, almost monotonous tune, together with the singer's rich voice enveloped Deborah in a pleasant haze.

She clapped loudly when the singer took her bows. The stage lights were switched off abruptly and overhead fixtures came on in all corners of the room. The waitress returned and placed the drinks on the table.

The stuffy air and cigarette smoke had dried Deborah's throat, and she took a long sip of her drink. When she replaced the glass on the table, she felt dizzy and closed her eyes. The feeling passed and she was suddenly relaxed and mellow.

Nabil laughed. "You better watch it. That stuff is potent."

"I always forget about the alcohol." Deborah smiled.

"She's not used to hard liquor," Yoram said. "I once saw her get bombed on half a shot of whisky."

"What's she like when she's drunk?" asked Nabil.

"Sad," Yoram answered.

Nabil covered Deborah's glass with his hand. "No more then. We want you happy."

She laughed. "Don't worry. I feel good tonight—wonderful, in fact." She picked up the glass and took another sip, looking across the table as she did so. She couldn't help wondering who the stranger seated with them was, and why Nabil had not introduced them. She noticed his thick black moustache; it seemed to complete his face rather

than adorn it, as did the facial hair of so many men she had
known. This man did not wear a moustache to create an
impression or to hide anything.

He was not handsome; compared with Yoram's classic
features, his looks seemed roughhewn. His nose was flat
and wide. His eyes were too far apart and his ears stuck
out slightly. But those eyes—very black, very big, and
deep. The man radiated strength without doing or saying
anything. His shoulders were broad and his hands were
large and strong. Although he was seated, she could tell
that he was tall.

Why am I so curious about him? Deborah asked herself. It was his presence, she concluded. He had a kind of
magnetic, hypnotic quality that almost frightened her,
and Nabil's humble and respectful attitude toward him
confirmed her feeling.

Deborah stretched out her hand. "Deborah Rimon,"
she said.

The stranger looked at her through the glass of whisky
in his hand, as though contemplating what to do with the
outstretched hand. He finally smiled and placed the glass
on the table. "Ahmed Said," he said. He had a thick,
soothing, bass voice.

"Did you enjoy the singing?" Deborah asked.

"Yes."

"Have you heard her before?" she went on after an
awkward silence.

"No."

The man was really infuriating. After all, she was
only attempting to be polite.

"Are you a Palestinian?"

Finally, she thought triumphantly, she must have
touched some nerve, because he looked surprised and
threw a furtive glance at Nabil.

"I'm an Arab," he said.

She burst out laughing. "That's no answer. I'm a Jew.
But I'm an Israeli. You *are* a Palestinian, aren't you?"

He smiled. "How do you see yourself? As a Jew or as
an Israeli?"

"An Israeli of Jewish origin."

"Well, I'm an Arab of Islamic origin."

He drank up the remaining whisky in his glass. His eyes were somewhat blurred. It was clear that this was not his first drink that evening, and he ordered another one.

Nabil was impatient and seemed nervous about the turn of the conversation. "The show's over. We can go."

"Go?" asked Deborah. "Why? We just got here."

"There's no rush," said Said. Nevertheless, he did not contradict the other man.

Deborah introduced Yoram. Said nodded, and immediately turned back to Deborah. "I understand that you met today to discuss the Palestinian problem."

"You make it sound so theoretical. There is no Palestinian problem. There's an Israeli-Palestinian problem. God, how I hate that word. There are nations—people who are killing each other. It has to be stopped, as fast as possible. Don't you think so?"

"That's easy," said Said slowly, an ironic look in his eyes. "Give back what you took."

"It's not a question of give and take," said Deborah, in growing anger at Said's condescending attitude, which he didn't bother to hide. "We're there, and you're there. The logical solution is to live together as equals. In other words, a Jewish-Palestinian state."

Nabil cleared his throat. "Really, Deborah, the forum is over for the day. This is time for recreation. Give it a rest until tomorrow, why don't you?" He glanced at Said, as if concerned that he might have aroused his anger.

But the man was clearly not interested in him. He glared at Deborah. "Just like that, eh? You come, steal our homes and our lands, then turn to us and say, 'You see how good we are? We're prepared to be partners. These are the terms of our partnership: We'll continue to hold on to what we took from you, and you can share with us whatever is left.' Your generosity disgusts me! You are no different from all those bastards about to gather in Geneva in several weeks. All those Arabs and Jews dividing up the spoils. What sellouts you all are!"

There was silence. The only sound was the clink of

the ice cubes in Said's glass when he raised it to his lips.
Deborah swallowed hard. *Patience,* she told herself. One
couldn't blame these people for being angry.

"So you *are* a Palestinian."

He gazed at her thoughtfully. "I'm hot," he said. "Let's
go for a walk."

He stood up. Nabil quickly followed suit, touched
Said's arm, and whispered something in his ear. Deborah
watched as Said pushed Nabil away and muttered a few
words in Arabic. She guessed from the tone of his voice
that Said was not interested in his company.

He turned back to Deborah. "I want to walk with you
alone," he said. The three remained frozen in their places,
startled by his forwardness. Deborah was put off by this
direct approach, but still, she could not deny that his
manner intrigued her. Men did not usually treat her so
offhandedly. This stranger was a challenge.

"Wait for me at the hotel," she told Yoram.

"I don't think you should go with him," Yoram responded quickly in Hebrew. "You don't even know him."
His hand on her arm felt damp, clammy.

"That's why I'm going," she replied firmly. "To get to
know him."

It was already past midnight, and a light rain had
begun falling on the city. The fresh moist air chilled
Deborah's warm cheeks and diminished the effect of the
gin. Said stood at the door of the cabaret, hesitating
briefly. Then he fastened his coat and strode off without
saying a word, as if he expected Deborah to follow him or,
Deborah thought, as though indifferent about what she
might or might not do.

They walked silently for ten minutes. The lights of
the *quartier* flashed in the dark sky and shone hazily
through the rain on the small old buildings. They walked
down the long hill of the rue Mouffetard, passing the
vegetable markets and small restaurants shut up for the
night. As they walked around the Pantheon a few students, rowdy and drunk, reeled along behind them,
singing a popular song and attempting to harmonize with
one another. They turned onto the rue Descartes. The rain
had flooded the gutters, which were oddly illuminated in

the lamplight. Finally, they left the more populated neighborhood and started down the somber rue Soufflot leading to the Luxembourg Gardens. The rain had grown heavier and there was no one else on the street. When they were through the gates, Said led the way to a bench and sat down. Deborah joined him, keeping a small space between them on the seat. She was soaked to the bone but was determined not to voice a word of complaint.

"Why are you staying in Palestine?" he asked, as though continuing their conversation from the cabaret. "You have nothing but trouble. You can go anywhere— Europe, America, Australia. The world will be only too happy to give you a piece of land anywhere you want in order to solve this problem. What's keeping you? Why do you remain there?"

"I was born in Israel. It's my home," she said simply but firmly, and quickly added, "It's your home too. That's why I am suggesting a joint home. What do you suggest? Terror? Murder?"

He laughed loudly, but there was no humor in the sound. "You're making a big mistake. I'm not suggesting anything. I'm not a PLO man or a member of any other organization. I'm an independent observer. I have no personal involvement."

"Oh, I see," she said, surprised at her disappointment.

She raised her hand to brush the wet hair from her face. She felt his steady breathing nearby. Why didn't she get up and leave?

"You're worse than your government leaders," he said quietly. "At least with them, we know where we stand. You pretend to be charitable and succeed in confusing our people."

"Some of your own leaders support the idea of a Jewish-Palestinian state."

"They're damned fools. They don't understand the injustice of such a solution. They don't want to understand. They are totally corrupt and tired of fighting. They'd rather sit around at the Geneva Conference and divide up a map than help the Palestinian cause. They want power, they want to govern." He took a breath. "Are you cold?"

"They may want power," Deborah countered, "but

that desire, in and of itself, is not invalid if through it the fighting can be stopped." She decided to ignore his question about the cold.

"You're naive. You're . . ."

"Don't call me naive!"

He looked up sharply, and, for the first time, she noticed real interest, perhaps even a glimmer of respect, in his eyes.

"You don't know what that means!" she went on angrily. "I hear that word constantly in Israel. If you have claims and arguments, let's hear them, but don't tell me that I am naive. I'm sick and tired of all the grown-up, smart, sophisticated, and not-naive people. What they have achieved are four wars and incessant fighting in between. It's time for the rest of us to try to do something."

"What can I say then?"

"You can say I am right."

If he thought she was joking, he realized his mistake when he examined her face closely. Her expression showed just how serious she was. He continued to gaze at her. "I could say many things, but that is one thing I shall never say to you." He lowered his eyes. The full lips were slightly open. Her breasts were prominent and clearly outlined through the completely soaked thin blouse.

Beautiful Jewish bitch, he thought. He got up. "It's late."

She began trembling. *Because of the cold*, she told herself. But she knew it was also the way he had looked at her.

They walked out of the gardens and he hailed a taxi at the corner. He opened the door and climbed in after her, giving the driver the name of her hotel. She was surprised that he knew it, but she didn't say a thing. They remained silent throughout the trip.

When they reached the hotel, he paid the fare and they stood outside for a brief moment together, letting the rain drench them all over again. *He wants to come to my room*, she thought. She entered the hotel and nodded to the night desk clerk, aware of Said's footsteps behind her and of the way her heart was pounding. He followed her into the elevator, and she pressed the third floor button. When the door opened, she stepped out and walked in the direction of her room, convinced that Said was following her. She opened the door and turned around. The long corridor was empty.

Her heart beat wildly. In disappointment, in shame, in regret. After several deep breaths to calm herself, she regained control of her senses, and felt relieved. *Better this way*, she told herself. She was still troubled by the thought that this man—any man—could confuse her so completely and could make her lose her self-control. She promised herself that it wouldn't happen again.

She opened the door to her room and was startled to see a light on. Yoram was sitting there in an armchair.

He jumped to his feet and rushed to her. "God, you're completely soaked. What happened?"

"Rain. What did you think?"

She went into the shower and closed the door behind her. She quickly undressed and turned on the hot water. It felt so good. The heat stroked her skin and penetrated her pores. She stood still and let the water stream over her.

A few minutes later, she got out, dried herself, and put on a bathrobe. Yoram was exactly where she had left him.

He came to her and cupped her face in his hands. "I was worried about you," he said softly. She could not help but think—though she realized she was being unfair—that he was worried about himself, and what might happen if she did not return.

"There was no need," she said.

He touched his lips to hers, but she did not—could not—respond. "The entire night is before us," he whispered. "You said so. Remember?"

For heaven's sake, she thought. *It wasn't a note with a date of payment.* "I'm tired, I want to sleep," she said brusquely. Her voice was cold and impatient, and Yoram flinched.

"Are you sure everything's all right?"

She touched his cheek with her head, hearing how

harsh her own voice had sounded. Why did this man make her want to crush him? He seemed so weak, so easy to conquer. Whereas Said. . . . She stopped her thought.

"I'm just tired. Really. I'll see you in the morning."

He turned around, opened the door, and turned back again. "I love you," he said, and it sounded like, "I hope you still love me."

"Good night," she said, unable to tolerate his presence any longer. The door closed and she let out a deep sigh.

CHAPTER 7

SHE TURNED OUT the light and closed her eyes, exhausted and confused. The conversation with Said had unsettled her conviction about everything that had taken place earlier. Could it be that he was right, while all the other participants in the meeting were wrong? It didn't matter who was right or wrong, she decided, but who had the power to convince more people that his aims and methods were right. She could be right, but as long as most people thought like Said, the Ishmaelites would fail.

What exactly had the man said?

It was difficult to recall. She made another effort to think of him in terms of views and theories, but failed. The only terms in which she could think of him were as a person. As a man.

She saw his deep black eyes, perhaps the only part of his body that did not lie. Even when the lips smiled—usually bitterly or ironically—the eyes were sad and full of pain. It couldn't be, she thought, just the burden of his political problems. It was too real and deep. It had to be a very private, very personal pain. Was it related to his family, perhaps? She had no idea. She only knew that she wanted to know.

And because she was not in the habit of deceiving herself, she admitted that had the eyes been set in a different face, she might not have bothered. Maybe it wasn't noble or fair, but her interest in the man was not divorced from the broad shoulders, the solid chest, the prominent chin, and the thick moustache.

To think of him as a person. As a man.

Her eyes closed involuntarily, and she finally fell into a restless sleep, only to be awakened by the sound of screeching brakes from the street below. She went to the window. Two drivers stood in the middle of the road, yelling at each other, but the rain proved a sufficient deterrent to the argument. Eventually they ran to their cars and drove away.

She glanced at her watch. Two-thirty. She had just managed to get to sleep, and it would be daylight in a few hours. She returned to bed and closed her eyes.

She heard muffled voices in the corridor. Whispers. Her body aching with exhaustion, she got out of bed and was about to go out and complain, but her hand froze in mid-air. She could have sworn that one of the two voices belonged to Said.

Slowly, cautiously, she turned the doorknob. Through the narrow crack she saw Said standing nearby. Nabil stood opposite him, engaged in an intense monologue, but all she could here were the words, "Geneva Conference." Several seconds later, they parted with a handshake. Nabil disappeared immediately into his room, which was close to hers. Said began walking toward the stairs.

Had she thought first, she probably wouldn't have done it. But something drove her to action. She left her room and ran along the stained carpet. Said turned around with a panther's speed, the look on his face tense and grave. Only when he saw who it was did his features relax, and then only partially.

He measured her with his eyes, slowly taking in her body from head to toe. She was wearing only a nightgown.

"You look as though you need a bit of brandy," he said quietly. "Am I wrong?"

"I couldn't fall asleep. And when I finally did, you woke me up." She didn't really want brandy—she knew that. And probably he knew it as well. She saw in his eyes the same blend of curiosity and irony she had learned to recognize.

"Come," he said.

He led her up one flight to his room, and went to the bathroom for glasses. Deborah looked around. The same hotel furniture as in her room. But she noticed that the closet was empty. His clothing was piled up in a big suitcase, which was filled to capacity. *As though ready to leave any minute*, she thought.

Said returned to the room with a half-empty bottle of cognac and two glasses. He poured for Deborah and himself.

She took a quick sip and inhaled sharply. It tasted like medicine. But afterward, when the taste had passed, she sensed a pleasant warmth in her chest and her stomach. She looked at him. He had finished his drink and held his glass between his hands.

"You *are* involved," she said quietly.

He dismissed her remark with a wave of his hand. "With Nabil? Nonsense. I'm a businessman. I asked Nabil to look into a deal on the West Bank. That's all."

"At two-thirty in the morning?"

"I couldn't fall asleep." His voice had a tone of contempt again. As if he was annoyed by her piddling questions.

She smiled. "I don't believe you."

"As you wish."

They continued to sit silently, gazing into their glasses. Finally, he raised his eyes. "I believe we've exhausted all the topics of conversation. I'm sure we can both fall asleep now."

She remained in her seat. She told herself that if she was only patient, she would eventually discover who he was and what he did. Silence troubled him, and he would talk. She had only to be patient.

"Well?" he said.

"Well what?"

"What do you want?" He measured her again with his eyes, stopping at her breasts. "If you weren't what you are, I'd think you wanted to sleep with me."

"You're right not to think so. But what do you mean, if I wasn't what I am?"

"A Jewess. An Israeli. Sure, to talk of brotherhood and cooperation is one thing. To sleep with an Arab is something altogether different."

There was no bitterness in his voice, only a challenge.

She burst out laughing. "My God, what an original approach. I'm almost prepared to believe that that's a line. You thought that as soon as you spoke it, I'd spread my legs for the sake of Arab-Jewish brotherhood."

She stopped laughing, and there was disappointment in her voice. "Don't you understand? Had I done that, I would have proved just what you assumed. That I wanted to sleep with you because you are an Arab—and that in itself would make you different for me, a novelty."

The man was clearly more sensitive about their ethnic differences than she. It was maddening. She only wanted to know what he really thought about her—Deborah. Was the look in his eyes respect for her ability to argue a point? Was it appreciation of her whole self? Or was it lust, plain and simple?

"No, Said," she continued. "In this room, you're not an Arab and I'm not a Jew. You're a man and I'm a woman and that's the only reason for our being here."

She breathed heavily, her face tense and determined. He placed his glass on the table, his eyes piercing her like X rays.

"Well then. . . ," he began hoarsely. But he stopped speaking and stood up, came to her, and, his legs parted, began to unfasten his shirt buttons. She stared at him, paralyzed. What had she done? Was this really what she wanted? What she had, in fact, asked for?

He took off his shirt and threw it on the bed. Then he unbuckled his belt. Deborah continued to watch, mesmerized, as he unzipped his trousers, as they fell to the floor.

He stood before her naked. He was dark and hairy. She looked down, but could not keep her gaze off him. Slowly, then, she raised her eyes. His penis was erect.

This was far more than a sexual challenge. He was testing her. His manner of standing—legs apart and hands on hips—and the half provocative, half-amused look in his eyes fascinated her. It was as if he were saying, *What will happen now, Jewess? After all the talk of peace, coexistence, brotherhood, can you also give your body to a Palestinian man? Come on, talk's cheap. Let's see if you can get beyond it.*

She stood up and quickly removed her nightgown. She walked toward him, her eyes glued to his, returning his challenge. Her look implied, *Of course I can. And you?*

She felt the touch of his skin and the heat of his breath on her neck. She waited for his embrace, his kisses. But instead he grabbed her hands, lifted her, and threw her on his bed, pinning her down with his body. She felt a sharp pain as he entered her. The pain increased with the swift pace of his movements. She fought, shouted, pounded with her fists on his chest. Suddenly, he was still. Then he rolled off her.

Silently, she got up and dressed. He remained on the bed motionless, staring at her. She hissed at him in a low voice, "You prick."

She left without looking back. When she reached her room, she threw herself on the bed. Her body ached. But her bruises were not physical. What an ignorant, naive child she was! She had let herself in for this. Intrigued by his arrogance, his sense of strength. And he was just another Jew-hating Arab after all.

She closed her eyes, hoping to fall asleep or to try to forget. She dozed briefly, then was engulfed by dreams that left her restless and anxious. A knock on the door awakened her. What time was it? She opened her eyes a

crack and dragged herself to the door, expecting to see Nabil
or Yoram. But it was Ahmed Said. "You!" she spat at him.
"Get out!"

She tried to force him into the corridor, but his body
was firmly wedged in the doorway. He entered the room
and shut the door behind him. He took her face in his
hands and tried to bring her mouth to his. She turned her
face away.

"Now that the war is behind us," he said with the
trace of a smile on his lips, "can we make peace?"

His touch was light, fleeting. She felt only his finger-
tips on her neck, her back, her buttocks, her stomach, her
groin. And despite herself, she was aroused. Waves of
pleasure made her shudder. He slid his hand under her
nightgown and drew it up over her head. He quickly
stripped off his own clothes. Still uncertain of him, she
took a step backward, but he caught her with one arm.
"Don't move," he said quietly.

His hands slid down from armpits to her waist and
then to her legs as he slowly kneeled before her. He stroked
the insides of her thighs, coaxing them to part with a
touch unlike anything she had ever felt. She looked down
and saw his black hair between her legs and felt his
tongue inside her, searching, probing, exploring every crev-
ice. She placed her hands on his head, directing his
tongue, searching for more, as her body swayed in rhythm
with his kisses. Her eyes were closed, her lips parted.
With the last vestiges of consciousness, she reproached
herself: *This is inconceivable, forbidden, you can't lose
control of yourself so totally, you can't give yourself so
openly to this person.* But then even those thoughts fled as
a long, sharp cry of release escaped her lips.

Slowly, he stood up. His arms embraced her trembling body, and she clung to him. He stroked her hair, gently
kissed her neck and her forehead. She pulled his mouth to
her, tasting her own juices, inhaling his tongue into her
mouth, sucking and licking, while her right hand held his
cock. She caressed him, stroking and rubbing, until she
felt his powerful shudder, and she placed her hand on the

tip of his penis, smiling with satisfaction as her hand absorbed the sudden, powerful, warm flow.

And then they got into bed, silent and stunned, lying in each other's arms. Deborah was still trembling. She looked at Said. His eyes were closed, but she could feel that he was not asleep. His cock, resting on her leg, was becoming hard again. She reached for Said's arm and gently turned him over on his back. She straddled him, her hands on his shoulders, her face close to his. He opened his eyes and their lips met. She stretched back, grasping his penis, and slowly directed it inside her as she watched his face, taut with pleasure. When she could feel him at the very peak of her vagina, she began moving up and down, languorously and rhythmically. Said shook his head from side to side, licking his lips, trying to raise himself and reach her mouth. But she moved her face away, watching his eyes, full of a sense of victory that she could reciprocate the pleasure that he had given her. Reciprocate the loss of control that he had caused her.

Now he, too, lost control. His body shook with pleasure. He moaned and pressed his hips upward, trying to bring their two bodies even closer together. Finally, he let out a cry that blended with hers. And again there was silence.

Deborah tightened her legs around him, wanting to absorb as much as she could for as long as she could. She lowered her head to his chest and breathed quietly with him, listening to the steady beat of his heart.

And then she saw Yoram standing in the center of the room, his eyes uncomprehending. She had never seen him so pale. When his eyes met hers—no less stunned than his—he muttered, "I'm sorry. The door was open."

Deborah moved off Said's body and covered them both with a sheet.

"I . . ." She had no idea what to say, but she wouldn't apologize. "What's the time?"

"Eight. I came to take you to breakfast. The meeting begins in half an hour."

"I'll be right there."

Yoram left. Deborah turned to Said. "You sleep with him," he said. It wasn't a question. She didn't respond.

He stroked her hair and bent over to kiss her cheek. He then quickly got out of bed and began dressing.

She watched his every movement. She could do it again, she thought in astonishment. She could do it again and again and again. Her body was alive, pulsating with something totally new for her.

As he started for the door, she sat up and reached out a hand to him. "I don't know how to say this. I'm not a very . . . articulate person when it comes to my emotions. But . . . will I see you again?"

He didn't answer right away and she sensed that it was a struggle for him. When he finally spoke, it was as if he had reached a compromise with himself.

"Keep in touch with Nabil."

He stood there a moment looking at her and then briskly turned and left the room.

When she had finished dressing, she walked to the elevator and rode to the small meeting room on the second floor. The five men were already there. She sat down next to Halid Ismail, the head of the PLO office in Holland, who was going over the resolutions—dates for demonstrations, places, methods of communication, a list of potentially sympathetic journalists and public figures—all of it aimed at establishing public opinion against the Geneva Conference.

Deborah only half-listened to Halid's monotonous voice, and she was glad when it was over.

They all shook hands warmly, and Deborah felt that the three days had brought them close together beyond the boundaries of political cooperation.

On the plane back to Israel, the stewardess offered Deborah the London *Times.* Although her mind was elsewhere, she took the paper and flipped through it casually.

On the third page, her eye caught a headline: the third article in a series on the Palestinian terrorist organizations, illustrated with three photographs of the organizations' leaders. Deborah's eyes stopped at the middle picture. The man's face was clean-shaven. But there was no doubt that it was Ahmed Said. And in smaller type it said, "Head of the Holy Front for the Liberation of Palestine."

Her heart beat wildly. She closed her eyes. He was not just a Palestinian. He was not even just a member of the PLO. He was leader of the most radical, murderous organization. She felt an emptiness in her stomach. She closed her eyes and saw corpses of men, women, and children. She banished the scene from her mind. In place of the corpses she saw his body: large, dark, muscular. She felt his strong hands on her neck, her breasts, her stomach. And again the corpses, and his body, and corpses, and his body. . . .

"Are you asleep?"

She opened her eyes. "No, just dozing."

Yoram hesitantly placed his hand over hers. She knew that this was his way of saying he was prepared to forget what he had seen, if she was prepared to forget what had happened.

She pulled her hand away. Then she looked again at the photograph and at the name under it. It was not "Ahmed Said."

It was "Maruan Awad."

CHAPTER 8

LIEBERMAN WAS MORE than angry. He was filled with revulsion. Another defeat. Another failure.

Once again, he read the surveillance report on Deborah Rimon. Maruan Awad had stayed at the same hotel for an entire day. Another case when Awad's whereabouts were known and Lieberman found out too late. Another opportunity blown.

Aside from this detail, there were very few interesting facts in the report. The group in the hotel were like so many others that spent time in futile talk over a senseless matter. Lieberman attached no importance to the decision regarding continued cooperation and activities aimed at recruiting additional members. The entire affair smacked of amateurism.

Toward the end of the report, mention was made of the fact that Deborah had spent some time in Awad's room, and that he had spent time in hers. The writer expressed his view that the two had had sexual relations.

(64)

Lieberman threw the report down on the table. *This woman is not only a traitor*, he thought in disgust, *she is a whore as well.*

"Does Rimon know anything about his daughter?" he somewhat rhetorically asked Porat, who was seated opposite him.

"All indications are that he knows nothing. He doesn't see her very often these days."

The two men looked at each other, thinking the same thing. It was possible—and certainly decent—to warn Rimon, who might be able to prevent further involvement on his daughter's part. But was that wise? If an intimate relationship had indeed developed in Paris, then maybe it would continue. And Deborah could lead them to Awad.

Lieberman rose slowly and walked to the window. This line of thought was useless. He shouldn't delude himself and encourage another bitter disappointment. He gazed at the rows of cars streaming down the noisy Tel Aviv street. It was evening. People were on their way home, others on their way out for the evening. When was the last time he had gone home at a reasonable hour, had gone out and enjoyed himself, laughed and joked?

Gideon had been dead for some time now, and his death had been responsible for such a tremendous change. The same sort of change might come upon Yedidia Rimon— if he knew.

It was horrible to lose a child. To lose two, thought Lieberman, would be unbearable. Rimon might not be able to survive the consequences of his daughter's dangerous games. Lieberman had the power to stop her, but not the will. In this war, Maruan Awad was more important—far more important—than Yedidia Rimon's pride. He surely was immeasurably more important than Rimon's daughter.

Deborah paced back and forth across the floor of her room at the Imperial Hotel. She had looked in the restaurant, the coffee shop, the lobby, and the corridors, without finding any sign of Awad. Where was Nabil? Why didn't he bring her some word?

There was a knock, and she rushed to open the door. Yoram stood before her. "They're waiting for you downstairs," he said. "We'd like to begin the discussion."

"Start without me," she said impatiently.

"Deborah, I . . ." His eyes shifted over her head to the bed. "We haven't talked about this, but we must."

"Not now."

"I'm not saying this to protect myself, or because you've hurt me. It's more important than that. You don't realize what can . . ."

She cut him off sharply. "My personal affairs have nothing to do with you. You let me know when you think they're hampering my work, all right? Until then, I'm not interested."

He turned sheepishly. "We'll expect you downstairs then." She shut the door and, breathing heavily, returned to the chair. What was the matter with her? There was no need to behave like that—certainly not with Yoram. But she just couldn't help it.

Nabil did not come until midnight. "A car is waiting for you," he said.

She grabbed her suitcase and rushed downstairs. Yoram was standing at the bar in the lobby, a glass in his hand. He averted his eyes. She ran out and got into a gray Citroen that was parked in front of the hotel. The driver was very young, a dark, thin Palestinian. He said nothing, simply started the car and drove away.

"Where are we going?"

"You'll see when we get there," said the driver in a thick accent. "You may as well sleep. It's a long drive."

They traveled for hours, stopping only to buy gasoline. Each time they left a service station, a white Peugeot drove up, filled its tank, and continued after their Citroen.

Deborah could not sleep and was exhausted by the time they arrived in Rome. The car halted near No. 23, Via Della Lungara, and Deborah climbed out. It took her a moment to force her legs to move, but she kept close behind the driver as he walked quickly through the entrance and into a waiting elevator. The elevator door opened at the fourth floor, where two men with drawn guns stood guard. They spoke with the driver in Arabic, and then waved him on. Deborah and the driver walked down the corridor, turned a corner, and stopped in front of a wide door. The number 705 was engraved in bronze. The driver knocked and a man with a drawn gun opened the door and allowed them to enter. For a moment, they stood there in silence, but then the door of an adjoining room opened, and Maruan Awad walked out. He motioned with his head to the driver and the guard, and they left, locking the door behind them.

Deborah no longer felt any fatigue. Only a quiver which grew in intensity and stopped only when she was held tightly in his arms. She wanted him at once, quickly, totally. But each time she grabbed him, he pulled back. "Not so fast," he whispered.

He undressed her slowly, removing one piece of clothing after another, not caressing her, but intent on his task. His eyes moved over her breasts, her belly, her legs, and buttocks. When she was naked, he laid her on the bed but did not stretch out next to her. He sat beside her, his hands fluttering over her body, until his fingers disappeared between her legs. She began to arch and moan. She begged him to take her. And then she could bear it no longer and pulled him savagely over her, tightening her legs around his hips. She tore at his clothes as her mouth licked and sucked his lips, his chin, his tongue, his ears, and his neck. At last she wholly absorbed him, craving and demanding more, still hungry, until finally her eyes clouded over and she felt as though her soul was leaving her body.

Her head lay, helpless, on the pillow. The strands of hair around her face were wet with perspiration. She stroked Awad's head, which was resting on her stomach.

When she caught her breath, she asked, "Why didn't you tell me the truth?"

Although she couldn't see his face, she sensed a tiny smile at the corners of his mouth. "Which truth?"

"You didn't tell me that you were Maruan Awad. Why?"

He turned his head and his eyes gazed into hers.

"Because a name does not tell the truth. It actually distorts the truth."

"How?"

He gently kissed her navel. "Maruan Awad means leader of the Holy Front, which means terror, sabotage, murder. That is only part of the truth."

She stretched her arm and lightly touched his mouth and his eyes. "Tell me."

He could see her face between her lovely rounded breasts, the most beautiful he had ever touched. She was the first in his life to impress him both as a person and as a woman—she was both intelligent and sexual, fragile in appearance yet strong in character. He had never felt this way toward any woman, but it was still difficult for him to express his emotions.

He turned his head from hers and kissed her pubic hair. He stroked her legs and slowly closed his eyes. This way it was easier. As though he were talking to himself. . . .

The walls of the little hovel in the Jabaliya refugee camp near Gaza were built of dirt; undoubtedly they would not hold up long.

The most popular—in fact, the only—topic of conversation in the camp was the good old days in Jaffa, and the houses the people used to live in. If one were to believe all the stories and reminiscences, pre-1948 Jaffa was a city filled with palaces and ornamental gardens, and not a single one of its inhabitants had a bank account of less than six figures.

At first, Maruan swallowed these tales greedily. But by the age of fourteen, he was fortunate enough to grasp that these were daydreams of people left with little else. He would certainly not permit himself to be drawn into this snare. He would build his future in accordance with his own wishes; his first step would be to leave the ramshackle camp and cut himself off from his people's senseless hopes for days gone by.

Visitors to the hovel would find him sitting in one of the corners immersed in a book or a notebook, oblivious of the din raised by his brothers and sisters or the tumult from the unpaved road outside, which served the children of the camp as a football field.

Consequently, no one was surprised when the Egyptian authorities gave him the chance to continue his studies in Cairo, as part of the quota allocated to Palestinian students. Possibly, Awad himself was the only one who was surprised—but only by the fact that there was a quota. After all, every Palestinian willing and capable of studying ought to be admitted by any Arab university. But since he was included, he soon pushed his resentment aside. He was not interested in fighting the wars of the Palestinians. He would fight the wars of Maruan Awad.

On arriving in Cairo, he encountered great difficulties in finding a room. "Awad? Maruan Awad?" After a time, he learned to recognize the meaning of that particular glance: "A Palestinian, eh?" Only the worst, the dirtiest, and most remote rooms were available, those rooms desired by no one who was not totally impoverished or rejected.

Here he learned a lesson he would never forget. The Arab world admired and pitied the Palestinians, but only from a distance. It loved the Palestinian cause, but not the Palestinians.

After four years' study, he got his architect's diploma. His first step was to collect every available scrap of information about the various Arab states. He was looking for a state—any state—where the demand for professionals like himself exceeded the supply. After careful consideration, he chose Kuwait.

This would be his transit station, not by any means his final destination. Here there was a dearth of expensive nightclubs and theaters, and of all the other hallmarks of a metropolitan city. Not that he had savored such entertainment in Cairo. But precisely because they were beyond his reach, he dreamed of the time when he would be a regular visitor in these places he had seen only from the outside.

During his first year in Kuwait, he engaged far less in architecture than in public relations. He did all right with

the salary he received from the large, well-established
architectural firm for which he worked. But not for a
single moment did he intend to build his future within the
company. He chose it only because it gave him the chance
to make the acquaintance of the right people—the ones
with plenty of money.

He was young, attractive, educated, and ambitious,
and he took advantage of his appeal. He made himself a
favorite of high society and soon learned the secret of
success: the rich Kuwaitis were interested not in the best
architects but in the most well-known and sought-after
architects.

And so he became one. Clients began to request that
Maruan Awad, specifically, be given the job of designing
their palaces. When the demand for him was great enough,
he took his leave of his employers and set up a company of
his own.

It was then that he learned a further secret to success.
The only thing his clients wanted was his name on the
plans. They were completely indifferent about the actual
design. Awad hired an additional architect, while he himself continued to engage in public relations. Three years
after going out on his own, he employed fourteen architects.

At the age of thirty-six, Awad was immensely rich,
and he intended to make the most of it. The time had come
to make up for everything he had missed—and he had
missed almost everything he wanted.

He began to buy houses the way other men buy cars.
His greed was appeased only when he owned property in
Aswan, Cairo, Akaba, Damascus, and Riad. But he was
not satisfied. The list would not be complete until it included Gaza, even though there was nothing about his
former home which could persuade him even to visit there
several days a year.

But he had to do it. He had to own the elegant house
on the highest hill in Gaza. The bright lights of this very
house had preoccupied him each night during the dreary
years in the refugee camp. For him, that house was a
symbol of everything he wanted—and finally attained.

As Awad spoke of Gaza again, Deborah saw his eyes cloud over. She could see the torment of his past in those eyes, and they helped her to understand the brutality with which he had taken her that first night. Like a possession, a house, something to be grasped at the earliest opportunity. And used for his own purposes. It was only afterward that he had been able to see her as a woman.

"You are torturing me," he complained in a whisper, looking down at her.

She held his stiff penis in her hand, brought it to her mouth, and kissed the root at his groin. She felt his hair tickle her chin and cheek.

"Later," she said.

"Now!"

"Later! I want to hear the rest."

He put his head back on the pillow. He could not treat Deborah the way he treated most of his women; he would have to accept that. At first, something in him had rebelled against such a change. He wanted to use her as he had the others—purely for his own pleasure. But he needed more of her than the delights her body offered. Her strong character was part of her, and he saw no way—or need—to separate that part from the rest.

He placed his hand on her face, and she kissed his fingers. He continued, lapsing back into the hypnotic tone with which he had begun his story.

No man could have been more pleased than he was the day he brought his family to see the house he had bought. As they drove up the hill in his black Mercedes, he was proud to be able to show his relatives the tangible proof of his success. Up to now, they had seen only the big car, the elegant suits, and the banknotes he scattered lavishly. But there was something reserved about their response. The house on the hilltop would overcome this.

His middle brother and his sisters reacted exactly as he had anticipated. Each room provoked a new cry of admiration. Each piece of furniture was a jewel to be discreetly stroked. Each flight of stairs was a cause for excitement.

His youngest brother, Hassan, did not utter a word, however, and his face was expressionless. His parents, too, were polite, no more.

Awad said nothing until they were seated in the roomy guest chamber, while cups of steaming black coffee and plates of sweetmeats were placed on the tables. When they had all uttered the traditional sigh of pleasure on taking their first sip, Awad turned to his brother and asked cooly, "How do you like it, Hassan?"

"It is wonderfully beautiful," said Hassan abruptly.

"But something is troubling you?"

Hassan averted his eyes. "You have spent enormous sums on this house. It would be discourteous of me to say anything unfavorable."

Awad shrugged as he struggled to contain his anger. "Speak frankly, my brother. I respect your opinions."

"As you wish, Maruan," said Hassan, stroking the small porcelain cup with his slim fingers. "The house is beautiful, as I said. But it seems to me that you have forgotten we had a similar house not very far from here. In Jaffa."

Awad was unable to control his fury. "That belongs to the past. The time has come for us to learn to live in the present. In the future."

"That is your prerogative, Maruan. I bear no grudge against you. But you would do a greater service to us, to yourself, and to your people if you were to dedicate your energies and wealth to regaining the house in Jaffa. Gaza is not our home. We have no need of houses here."

"What are you talking about? How could we have that house again?"

"There are ways."

Awad grasped the drift of his brother's words. He leaned forward. "Are you involved with the terrorists?"

Hassan made no reply but fixed him with burning eyes. Awad turned to his father. "Do you know of this, my father?"

"The war has not ended," his father responded. His yellow-white moustache scarcely moved as he spoke. His face, with its dozens of wrinkles, did not betray any emotion.

"There will be another war," said Hassan. "In another year or two."

"How do you know?"

"There has to be!" replied Hassan decisively. "And then we shall return to our home in Jaffa."

"Or you will lose this house too," added their father softly.

Awad felt the two men across from him change before his eyes. They were strangers, belonging to a different world with a different goal: to attain the unattainable, to recapture the past. Not that Awad had any more affection for the Jews than they did. But he did not intend to permit this issue to determine his path in life.

That was in April 1966. On June 5, 1967, Awad was sitting in the exclusive poker room in the casino at Monte Carlo with three other men. They were seated at an ancient mahogany table covered with a soft green baize, while a gilt chandelier dangled overhead. Tens of thousands of dollars changed hands every few minutes. Whether winning or losing, none of the players displayed any particular agitation.

Awad was holding three aces, and the stakes were mounting rapidly. He had the feeling he often had in his business dealings, the sense that he knew something of great importance unknown to everyone else. And when they found out, it would be too late.

"*Hawaja* Awad! *Hawaja* Awad!"

Awad raised his eyes, surprised by the interruption. The others did likewise. Abdalla, his personal secretary, was trying to enter the room, while the armed guard kept him at a distance.

Flushed with anger, Awad stood up. Laying down his cards, he apologized to the other players and walked to the door.

"What's the matter?" he hissed furiously.

"War! War!"

"Where?"

"Israel is attacking Egypt and Syria."

Awad grabbed his secretary by the lapels. "For that you dare to disturb me? Get out of here immediately." He pushed Abdalla away and hurried back to the table.

When the game ended, Awad was $85,000 richer than the day before, but $40,000 poorer than the day before that. Still, who kept count?

He returned to his apartment on the seventeenth floor of the hotel, where he found Abdalla awaiting him. "You disgraced me!" he spat at the quaking man. "Tomorrow we are leaving."

"Where to?"

"Cairo. But on the way, I want to visit my family."

"You cannot do that, *hawaja*."

Awad's eyes glinted murderously. Abdalla hurriedly added, "The Israelis have taken Gaza."

"What did you say?"

"That's what I have been trying to tell you."

That night, Awad headed for Cairo. When he arrived, sleepless and impatient, he made inquiries and learned that his family was in Gaza when the Israelis occupied the town. Now they were no longer refugees. They were captives.

This thing was endless. No matter how hard he tried to evade the problem, it haunted him. The Israelis wouldn't allow him to ignore it. They were never content with what they had. They wanted to swallow up everything. Any Arab sitting about with folded arms was helping them to gain their objective.

With these thoughts running through his mind, Awad traveled to Algiers to meet Ahmed al-Khalid, head of the Fedayeen for Palestine, regarded as the most extreme of the organizations affiliated with the Palestine Liberation Organization.

Al-Khalid was bent on gaining control of the PLO. He told Awad that if he succeeded, he would restore the organization to what it had been in the past, when its members were not concerned with speeches and politics but with laying bombs; when they spent less time in intellectual salons and more time hijacking planes. Awad's money could be of great assistance to the cause.

Awad had doubts about al-Khalid's motives. He suspected that this man, like the other leaders of the PLO organizations, was plotting in anticipation of the day when a Palestinian state would be established alongside Israel.

Awad left Algiers with a promise to al-Khalid that he would think it over. He headed for Beirut, where he took an apartment in the Moslem sector. Word traveled quickly that Awad had come to recruit men who were prepared to continue the war against Israel. The telephone never stopped ringing. Of the scores of persons he interviewed, he selected two dozen. Instead of pouring money into property, gambling, and mistresses, he used his millions to finance the most efficient Arab murder apparatus the world had ever known.

It was not long before Awad became a target, not only for the Israelis but also for fellow-Palestinians. His sophisticated operations embarrassed them because he stressed the impotence of the clumsy Palestinian maneuvers. And so he became responsible for the brutality, the killing, the destruction.

His voice dropped almost to a whisper as he concluded. He sat up and roughly pushed Deborah aside. His thoughts propelled him away from her, and he went to the window, where he stood looking out. The memories had reminded him that the woman in bed with him was Israeli, Jewish.

She looked fondly at his firm back, his muscular legs. She slowly got off the bed and went to him. If only she somehow could show him that to her he was not a murderer but a lover—an exciting, mysterious, dramatic new presence in her life. If they could forget their origins when they were making love, perhaps they could do as much when they sat together at a conference table. She touched his arm, but he continued to stare beyond her, his eyes roving. Where? To Jaffa? To Gaza?

Without speaking, she knelt before him and gently took his penis in her hands. She ran her tongue along the length of it and eased it into her mouth. He looked down at her, unmoving.

He could not decide what gave him the greatest pleasure right then: the touch of her full, moist lips on his cock or the sight of an Israeli Jewess kneeling before him. Deborah had faded for the moment, and an image, an old fantasy, had taken her place.

He sensed how she was rapidly bringing him to climax and he tried to pull back. But she grasped him with both hands, preventing his escape, and this stimulated him even more. He shut his eyes and permitted himself to float away with her to heights he had never before experienced. It was true, she was more than a Jewish woman. She was his. The old fantasy dissolved. He muttered the words he had never said before, "I love you, I love you. . . . I love . . . you!"

His chest heaving, he felt her mouth release him. He glanced down and saw her blue eyes shining softly as she tasted him for the first time. Then she rose and wrapped her arms around him.

"Oh God, I love you. So much," she said intensely.

They walked to the bed holding each other and lay down as one person. In a few minutes, they were asleep.

CHAPTER 9

THE STREET BELOW was so silent that nothing seemed to stir, not even the Tiber, whose ripples clearly reflected the lofty apartment blocks, illuminated by millions of tiny specks of moonlight. Only the most acute ear could have picked out the sound of tires turning slowly down the nearby Via Del Riari. The green Fiat and the blue Alfa Romeo were both in neutral. Two hundred yards from the intersection between Via Della Lungara and Via Del Riari, the driver of the blue car carefully pressed down on the brake. Behind him, the driver of the green car noticed the other's lights, and he also braked. Both cars halted noiselessly at the curb on the left of the street facing the river.

At some command, three of the blue car's doors opened. From the left rear door, a tall man emerged, the pale moonlight glinting on his smooth blond hair. The man who got out of the rear door on the right was about the same height, but stockier and barrel-chested. It was (77) almost impossible to make out his swarthy features and black hair, which merged with the darkness. In the moonlight, his brown eyes appeared to be holes in his round face.

The man who emerged from the third door, beside the driver, was the smallest of the trio—not more than five foot six. He approached the man in the passenger's seat of the green car with a rapid, almost springlike gait.

Antonio Rigaldi put his hand on the window and peered at the man coming toward him. This was the one he had been told about, the one he was to call Cerberus. He could make out the man's gray hair, turning white at the temples, the deep furrows running down from the top of the nose, growing deeper and wider as they sloped in toward the corners of his mouth.

Rigaldi opened his window, and Cerberus leaned forward, permitting Rigaldi a glimpse of the most interesting feature in his face, the eyes. The somberness within their depths gave the whole face an expression which Rigaldi found hard to define. On the few occasions he had met the man in the past, his eyes had taken on differing and conflicting degrees of hardness. At times they seemed almost kind, but then they shifted with lightning speed. Rigaldi knew one thing: it was better not to have this man as his enemy. The eyes told him that.

"Make certain we're not disturbed." Rigaldi scarcely comprehended the words, whispered in English with a heavy Slavic accent.

"Try to hurry," he replied.

Only the driver remained in the Alfa Romeo. Rigaldi glanced at his watch. "I wish all this was behind us," he muttered nervously. His driver grinned but said nothing. Rigaldi watched as the three men approached the intersection. The blond man walked faster, the other two hanging back about fifteen yards.

Suddenly, Rigaldi sat bold-upright, an expression of amazement on his face. The stillness of the night was shattered by the blond man's high-pitched tenor. He was staggering as he made his way down the road singing. A few moments later, Rigaldi could still hear him but had lost sight of him after he turned off to the left. His two colleagues were leaning against the wall of the house on the left-hand corner, apparently deep in conversation.

The only person to see the blond man staggering along, singing at the top of his lungs, was a short man in an overcoat, who sprang from his post beside the entrance to No. 23. As the stumbling figure approached, the guard instinctively thrust his hand into his right-hand pocket, his fingers grasping the butt of his gun. He moved slowly out of the gateway, his eyes following the drunk's every movement. When he had ascertained that the man was harmless, he let go of the gun.

Suddenly, the blond man's right foot tripped over his left leg, and they fell together. The guard got out a weak cry before the blond man's right hand drove a knife blade deep into his stomach.

Not for a single moment did the blond man cease his toneless melody. But now, as he dragged the corpse into the courtyard, the words of the song sounded loud and clear: "O sole mio . . ."

The two men standing on the street corner listened for only half a line before starting toward the singer. They turned into the courtyard and helped their colleague, one grabbing the legs of the corpse, the other taking the torso. Together, they carried it around the back of the building. Cerberus opened the door of the incinerator, and his two companions flung the body inside.

The trio entered the building together. The blond man halted beside the elevator, while the other two started up the stairs. The blond man glanced at his watch; after four minutes had elapsed he pressed the elevator button.

In the car, Rigaldi looked at his own watch. Another six minutes—if all went well. The road surface reflected the lights of a car approaching from behind. He turned around. The car drove past slowly: police. Suddenly, the patrol car halted, reversed, and parked on the opposite side of the street, parallel with the blue car. The policeman in the passenger seat got out and sauntered over to the blue car, while his companion remained in the car, his left hand on the steering wheel and his right hand on his holster.

The approaching policeman whipped out his pistol and halted in the middle of the street, his legs wide apart. "Don't move! Stay where you are!" he called toward Rigaldi, who was getting out of the green car.

"What are you doing here?" he demanded suspiciously.

"I'll show you if you let me put my hand in my jacket pocket," said Rigaldi quietly.

The policeman blinked cautiously. "Don't try anything funny," he growled. "Easy, easy," he yelled, as Rigaldi moved his hand.

Very slowly, Rigaldi put his hand in his pocket and produced a leather pouch. The policeman took one pace forward and stretched out his left hand to seize the pouch. With a swift flip, he opened it up, but it was too dark for him to read the contents. "Alberto," he called, without turning his head, "bring the flashlight."

The other policeman quickly sprang out of the patrol car and came up to his companion, directing his light at the document. "Security service," he read out. The two policemen put their pistols back in their holsters. "Sorry," said the policeman, returning the document to Rigaldi. "Do you need any help?"

"No. Everything's okay," said Rigaldi.

The policemen turned on their heels. A moment later, their car had disappeared around the corner. Rigaldi returned to his car and slumped into his seat. With the back of his hand, he wiped the sweat off his brow. "Lucky they didn't come two minutes later," he muttered.

On the fourth floor of No. 23, a sound alerted the guard sitting on a chair facing the elevator. Looking up, he saw the light flashing rapidly upward on the elevator scale. Instinctively, he drew the small revolver that had been tucked into his belt and pointed it at the elevator door. A moment later, the door opened and a blond man emerged, gazing right and left, and then—startled— straight ahead at the gun barrel pointing at him. Cau· tiously, he began to turn to the right, but the guard grabbed him and began to run his hands over his jacket pockets.

"Where do you think you're go—"

His words were cut off and his face sagged as the five middle vertebrae of his backbone were smashed by the bullet which came from the stairway, where two men—one swarthy, the other gray-haired—were now standing. They hurried over to the blond man, who was supporting the body, to prevent any noise from its fall. Together, they dragged the lifeless body away and laid it on the floor behind the door to the stairway.

The three men now hurried over to the door which bore a bronze plate with the number 705. The blond man whipped out a key, and the lock turned on the first try. Gently, he pushed the door open, allowing the other two to slip inside. He remained in the doorway for a moment, checking the hall behind him.

Like two prowling cats, the two men kept perfectly still for a few seconds, while their eyes grew accustomed to the darkness. Then they glanced about, the pale moonlight giving them a glimpse of every piece of furniture and every fold of the drapes. Cerberus jerked his head toward a door to their right which was half-open. He led the way, followed by the blond man. Without touching the door, the two men entered the bedroom. They froze as the couple on the bed groaned and turned over.

After making sure that the couple was still fast asleep, Cerberus took a few steps forward to catch a clear glimpse of the face he had never seen but which had not left his thoughts for many years now. As he glanced down, one thought ran through his mind: "I have him!"

The blond man was the first to make a move, stepping up to the bed and reaching for the reclining figure. But suddenly, his hand stopped and his heart froze. The eyes of the man on the bed were wide open, alert, as though they had never been shut at all. Without a twitch of his facial muscles, he had changed position on the bed and was stretching out toward the bedside table. Only after the man's fingers fumbled slightly did the blond man pull himself together and act. The man on the bed shut his eyes again as a clenched fist landed on the back of his neck.

The girl groaned, but did not wake up. The blond man lifted his prey off the bed and propped the senseless body upright while his companion wrapped it in an overcoat he found in the closet. The swarthy man seized his victim's left hand and twisted it around his neck; then he moved the body out of the room. Cerberus followed the other two, glancing back just once to be certain they had left no trace of their visit.

And then there was a scream.

Cerberus blocked the path of the naked girl who was struggling past him toward Awad's motionless body. He caught her by the hand and, for a split second, the eyes of Moshe Lieberman and Deborah Rimon locked. There was madness in Lieberman's eyes, and his voice was full of hatred and contempt. "Whore!" he spat at her. He slapped her face with all the strength he could muster and left her lying on the floor, unconscious.

Lieberman was the first to emerge from the darkened doorway into the street. After glancing left and right, he beckoned to his companions, and the three men sprinted toward the open doors of the blue car parked opposite, ramming the senseless body of Awad inside.

Out of the corner of his eye, Lieberman picked out the green car parked without lights at the intersection behind them. "Go!" he muttered swiftly to the driver.

Eighteen minutes later, the blue car halted beside a large iron gate in the fence surrounding the airport. A mile away, the lights of the control tower were clearly visible. The men remained in their seats until they heard the sound of a motor and saw the green car approaching rapidly. Lieberman got out and walked over to the gate. Rigaldi was waiting for him, a half-smile on his face.

"Everything okay?" he asked.

"Okay."

From his pocket, Rigaldi produced a key, which he inserted into the heavy padlock. The lock wouldn't budge. "Rusted right through," Rigaldi complained. "It's not used much." Nervously, Rigaldi continued his attempts, until finally there was a click and the lock slid open. He thrust open the heavy iron gate with his leg, and it swung back with a slow, piercing creak. Rigaldi slipped the key back into his pocket and seized the outstretched hand of Lieberman. "Thanks," said the head of the Mossad. "I won't forget it."

Rigaldi smiled. "I would prefer that you *do* forget. Good luck."

Lieberman clambered back into the blue car, which moved off through the gateway, heading onto the airfield. Four minutes later, it halted beside the gangway leading up to the front doorway of a Boeing 707 El Al passenger plane whose upper wing bore the emblem of the state of Israel.

The plane's heavy door began to open, and two men in civilian clothes appeared on the ramp. The blond man and his swarthy companion lifted up the senseless form of Awad and rapidly mounted the gangway, with Lieberman hurrying behind them. One of the two men in the doorway raced down the gangway and jumped into the car, which he gunned toward an empty hangar. Twenty-five seconds later, the door of the plane closed once more. No one had seen their proceedings.

Four-and-a-half hours later, the first of the plane's passengers began to file into the tourist section. Five persons claiming to have purchased first-class tickets were told regretfully that the air-conditioning in the first-class section was out of order. The passengers complained but finally consented to take the seats they were offered in the tourist section.

There was no way in which these five, nor any of the plane's 234 other passengers, could have guessed that just a few feet away from them, in the comfortable, well-ventilated first-class section, lying on the floor, covered by a piece of brown material, Maruan Awad, the brain and the long arm of the Holy Front's terrorist operations, was slowly opening his eyes. Just as he was beginning to make out the blurred objects around him, a cloth saturated with chloroform came down on his face, rendering him unconscious once more.

CHAPTER 10

WHEN DEBORAH OPENED her eyes, she was aware only of an ache. She saw the two brown dressers, the white curtain, the orange rug. Nabil and Yoram were standing beside the bed. *Rome. Awad.*

She remembered, and raised herself on her elbows. She looked again at Yoram, and then at Nabil. The Palestinian's eyes were hard and cold.

"What happened?" he asked dryly.

"They kidnapped Maruan."

"We know that. Who did it? How did it happen?"

Her head reeled with pain, and she touched her cheek, which still smarted from Lieberman's blow. "Israeli agents. I don't know how they found us."

Nabil sat on the bed next to her and grabbed her arm. "How did it happen?" he shouted.

"You're hurting me!"

"Talk to me."

"Leave her alone," said Yoram. His voice was subdued, weak.

Nabil loosened his grip but continued to stare at Deborah. "Who are you?"

She felt increasingly angry. "What do you mean? You know who I am."

"Who are you *really*?"

"He thinks that you led the Israelis to Awad," explained Yoram, embarrassed.

Deborah couldn't control her bitter laughter. "You idiot. You stupid fool. Don't you understand? I love him. I love him more than anybody or anything."

She got out of bed, wrapping the sheet around her. Then she went to the window and stood looking out. "For you, he is merely a fighter, a commander," she said softly. "But he is everything to me." She paused. "Who knows what they'll do to him now."

Nabil's eyes were not quite so hard then. "I was upset."

"I know," she said. Then she added, "Nevertheless, I must have led the Israelis to him. Unintentionally."

She sat on the bed again. "I betrayed him." The words came out in a kind of toneless wail. She let her head fall on her chest and her blonde hair covered her face.

"You couldn't have known," said Yoram awkwardly, attempting to comfort her.

"I should have known. Or at least suspected."

Nabil sat beside her, his face pale. "It screws up everything. It screws up everything," he muttered.

"What are you talking about?" asked Deborah.

He looked at her carefully. An idea was beginning to shape in his mind. "It was supposed to be our biggest operation. Do you remember when we were first together at the hotel in Paris? He said over and over that he would remind the world, especially the Americans, of the Palestinians' existence. 'I'll hit them where it hurts,' he said." Nabil rubbed his brow, dejected. "Now it's finished."

Deborah stood up and looked down at him. There was a new strength in her voice. "Not necessarily," she said quietly. "What was the plan?"

"What difference does it make now?"

"Tell me!"

He raised his head and began to talk. When he concluded, half an hour later, she understood completely. Awad was going to undermine the Geneva Conference. He had worked on the plan for months.

"Is that why he was in Paris?" Deborah asked, remembering their first night together.

"And Rome," Nabil nodded. "There was a great deal to take care of."

Deborah's mind raced. In her gut she was against the whole thing, against all violence. But she could not deny that she had no experience with the tactics of which Awad approved. Maybe there were other ways . . . but maybe his was the *only* effective way. Then another thought hit her hard. *And if I don't do it—if I don't do something— won't I be exactly like my father?* The image of Yedidia Rimon floated before her eyes briefly, but it was quickly replaced by that of Awad, her lover, being hit and dragged off as she lay helpless beside him. She was overwhelmed with guilt and the horror of what she unwittingly had done. She might never see Awad again, certainly not if she didn't do this for him.

"When?" she asked.

"It was to have taken place in five days."

Deborah's glance swept over the two men, and her eyes were alive with excitement. "There will be no change in plans," she said.

Nabil made an effort to hide his satisfaction. This would be much better than the original plan. The Palestinian torch would be carried not by PLO people but by Israeli Jews.

The single ray of light which made its way into the narrow cell was enough to send waves of pain through Awad's skull.

This has to be done slowly, he thought. Sitting up on his bed, he placed the palms of both hands over his face, his eyes turned downward. Very slowly, he opened his eyes once more and gradually spread his fingers, allowing the light to filter through to his pupils. The throbbing pain subsided as he fixed his glance on the dark floor.

Now he could take his hands away and lift his eyes to the lighter-colored walls. The pain was gone, leaving only a dull heaviness. This would pass in time.

But there was something else which would not pass away so easily: the sense of nausea which filled his thoughts and penetrated the corners of his soul. How had he failed? How had he permitted them to take him? Had he not sworn that he would come to Israel only as a triumphant conqueror?

He looked carefully about him, but there wasn't much to see. Four high walls, white and stained. One square window, little more than a foot square. An iron bed. A wooden chair. A wash basin. A toilet bucket. That was all.

It was a prison cell, normal in every way—except for the complete stillness. He had never been a prisoner, but in the course of his life he had visited various prisons. Even the harshest and the most isolated jail always showed some kind of activity.

What was happening here? Where were the little sounds, the scratching, the conspiratorial whispers—all the signs indicating the presence of other living beings?

He had been placed in a new wing of an ordinary prison. There was nothing to distinguish it from the older wings; it, too, was an ugly block with only a few windows breaking its symmetrical lines.

The difference was within. Instead of the usual long narrow corridor with cells leading off it, the eleven cells in this wing were constructed as separate units. Each cell had its own entrance and its own window, but there was no way the occupants of the cells could see or hear one another. The prisoners had no way of knowing if there were any neighboring cells or if they were alone.

The wardens in the special wing were as isolated as their prisoners. They had no contact with the wardens in the other wings. They had their own dining room and washrooms, and an office administering exclusively to their affairs.

Their uniforms resembled those of the other wardens: their shirts read "Prison Service." But they were paid by the Mossad. Theirs was a double function: they guarded the special prisoners who came from the elite of the Palestinian terrorist organizations and they pumped them for information. They were promised that no one would ever ask them how they acquired the information—as long as they got it.

The occupants of these cells were never placed on trial; they were detained by administrative order. Only seven people in Israel knew the identities of the prisoners in the special wing. Aside from the wardens, they were also the only persons who knew of the existence of the wing. Since its construction, no prisoner had ever left it alive, although one of the cells would be vacated every now and then and remain empty until a new prisoner was brought in. Only three people in Israel knew what became of the prisoners who vanished.

Awad had no idea where he was, nor had he ever heard of the special unit. But after a swift reconstruction of the way he had been kidnapped, he came to the conclusion that he had lost in a game which did not allow for more than one setback. He reached this conclusion quite cooly. He felt no sorrow or regret. After all, he had chosen the game. He had played it well for a long time. Now it was over.

Suddenly, the electric light was switched on, and Awad shut his eyes. When he opened them, he saw a tanned, gray-haired man, broadly built and of average height. Awad managed a slight smile.

"Lieberman?"

Lieberman could not speak at first. He had not felt such excitement since his first encounter with a girl, when he was fifteen. But considering the manic twists and turns of a man's life, this was not, after all, such a bizarre analogy. With the exception of his wife and son, no person had ever taken up such a large period of his life or occupied more of his thoughts. Years of persistent pursuit, marked by repeated failure—until now.

"Why didn't you kill me?"

"We have other things in mind."

Awad bowed his head. "I see. A historical pageant. The Palestinian Eichmann."

"No. We hope you're going to be reasonable and work with us. Willingly."

Awad sensed a splitting pain pierce his head as he burst out laughing. "I thought we understood one another," he said. As suddenly as it began, his laughter subsided and was replaced by fury. "Who do you think you're dealing with? Some little terrorist from Kalkilyia?"

"I apologize." Lieberman conceded his mistake. He rose. "I should have known it would have to be the hard way."

Awad felt a tremor in his heart. For the first time in years—he couldn't remember how long—he actually felt fear.

"You know you aren't going to get anywhere that way," he said feebly, but he regretted his words instantly. They sounded more like a plea than a statement of fact. They were going to try. They had to. "In any case, I don't think you have a lot of time at your disposal. My people won't rest until they set me free, and you know it."

Lieberman was standing by the door with his back to Awad. He glanced over his shoulder. He pictured his desk with the blown-up photographs. His vision focused on one single picture: the disfigured face of a thirteen-year-old girl after the terrorist raid on the school in Ma'alot.

Slowly, almost as though he was talking to himself, Lieberman whispered, "That won't make any difference to you, Awad. Because by then you won't be the same man." The heavy steel door slammed shut with a sound like a mighty explosion.

CHAPTER 11

"WILL YOU BE needing the other garment bag as well, Mrs. Kraft?" the maid asked.

Susan thought a moment and put her clipboard down on the comforter. "No, that's all right, Delia. I think I have sufficient clothing packed to cover a Senate filibuster. Is Eli ready to leave?"

The maid smiled. "He was set for the trip about a week ago."

"Fine. Well, give me another minute to go over these details with Barbara and you can call the car." She smoothed her neat cap of auburn hair and pressed the buzzer by the side of the bed that would summon her secretary.

It had been years since she'd had a real vacation. How long? Let's see. There was the summer before Phil's cancer, when Eli was ten and she was pregnant with Jimmy. They had left Eli with her mother and taken off for Greece.

Basking in the hot white sun with a plate of figs and some strong retsina. She shook the memory away. Her husband's cancer had hit them suddenly, like a thunderclap, sending their lives into turmoil. It was only after he died that she had come into her own as a correspondent, that she had turned into "the" Susan Kraft, she admitted reluctantly. One of the highest-priced reporters in the country, with her own following, her own direct line to the White House. All this, and half a family too. She gave a short laugh. How ironic the whole thing was. Phil had never cared much about her career.

She looked up abruptly as her secretary came into the room. Barbara Andelman was her right hand; she could never leave her New York responsibilities and waltz off to Geneva without her.

"So," the woman began as if they had just been interrupted in the midst of a conversation. "You want me to keep tabs on Jerry and make sure he doesn't throw any zingers into your reports. Seems to me, the job is pretty cut and dried. Just be certain they photograph the American ambassador on his good side and that he doesn't get into any arguments with the Egyptian representative like he did at the UN last year."

Susan shook her head and gathered her notes. "I don't know why I even bother. You always read my mind. Have Pete do your hair like mine and you can take over the show."

"Not likely. Come on. The car's ready and your sons are about to fly to Switzerland without the airplane."

Susan flipped the lock on her attaché case, then picked up her mink from the chaise longue and threw it over her arm.

"Don't do anything I wouldn't like to," Barbara admonished as she swept her out the bedroom door and down the long hallway to the front door.

The two boys were already fidgeting. Jimmy attempting to pummel Eli, who was dodging back and forth between the rooms. "Hey, you two." Susan laughed. "This is countdown. Zero minus ten. Let's go."

"Oh, Mom, we've been ready for hours." Eli walked to

her and held his arm out impatiently for her coat. He wore
a brown corduroy suit and a baseball cap, and looked just
like her image of the all-American kid. "C'mon. We'll miss
the plane."

Barbara Andelman gave Susan a quick kiss and held
the door open for them. "Nope, Eli. For your mother, they'd
hold the plane."

Little Jimmy reached up and Susan lifted him into
her arms. "But I'm not carrying you around Geneva, understood?" He nodded. The maid took the children's luggage and followed Susan and Barbara down the steps to
the limousine. "Bon voyage," Barbara yelled as they
speeded down the driveway. "Remember, all work and no
play. . . ."

On the way to the airport, Susan felt a marvelous
lightness, the way she used to feel after finals at college
when the whole summer stretched before her. This assignment was a breeze, her producer had seen to that. Just
a few days of interviews with the representatives at the
Geneva Conference, a windup editorial, and the rest of the
time free to be with her children and to be alone with
herself. Yes, she decided, that was what she missed
most in her celebrity life: the luxury of evenings alone
without obligations, the pure comfort of not being on all
the time.

Jimmy slept in her arms until the limousine stopped
in front of the VIP lounge and Eli woke his brother with a
"Hey, look at the 747s coming in. That is a neat golf cart—
the one for the suitcases. Real efficient."

Susan had an aisle seat in first class and was gratified
that Delia took the boys off into a corner to keep them
busy until they got tired. The stewardess came by with
complimentary champagne and offered newspapers. Susan couldn't resist, or, more accurately, felt a pang of guilt
about her desire to resist. She flipped through the *Times*,
then the previous day's *France-Soir*. The French were not
exactly enthusiastic about President Kelly and predicted
he would lose the nomination as his party's candidate
for another term. She had interviewed the President on
numerous occasions and could not help thinking, all fem-
inist sentiments aside, that his wife would be a far more

effective leader than he had been. Of course, her late husband would have been horrified by the very thought of a woman in the White House.

And suddenly she remembered the phone call. It had come through in the middle of that busy afternoon when she was arranging her time in Geneva to interview George Williams, the American ambassador. The man had identified himself as Henry Clements, and Barbara had put the call through, thinking that it was someone from the American Embassy. When Susan asked what the man's business was, he laughed.

"Don't you remember? Chicago? The political science department? I'm in New York on business, thought perhaps we could get together for a drink."

She wasn't sure why she agreed. Certainly she didn't have the time. She hadn't been interested in Clements at school despite his persistence, and she certainly wasn't interested now. It had to be some corny yearning for her old college days. So she suggested they meet at her club the next evening, before the dinner party for Senator Grimes which she was obliged to attend.

They spent the hour reminiscing. Then, just as she was about to call her car, Clements leaned over and with a roguish smile asked, "By the way, whatever happened to that Israeli? Do you see him? What was his name?"

Susan grew pale. "I don't remember," she said, and quickly tried to change the subject. "Stamitz has joined your department, hasn't he? The Middle East consultant?"

Clements wouldn't let go. "Oh yes—Eli, Eli Goren. You were very close, weren't you? If I'm not mistaken, you were inseparable for a time."

The damn fool. When would he stop? She fixed him with a look, the look that had won her many an interview, that had speeded her rise to the top of her field. "I think you must be mistaken. He lived over on Green Street with some other foreign students."

Clements took a sip of his drink. "I guess you're right. Memory fails, hair thins. It's been a lot of years." He got up and gave her an odd little bow. "Time's been good to you, Susan. I'm real happy about your success. The right people so rarely get ahead. You're the exception."

Her heart beat wildly and she felt the blood rush to her face. Even now, miles away, eons away from that encounter, it still affected her.

The plane's tires screeched as they touched the concrete runway. Susan unbuckled the seat belt around her slender waist and looked across the aisle to see the maid getting the boys ready to deplane. Eli yawned and came over to his mother. "A perfect landing," he said. *Precocious child*, she thought. And again the thought of that conversation rose up before her.

By the time they reached the Bristol Hotel, it was near midnight, but she was too exhausted to think about falling asleep. Nor, apparently, could anyone else in Geneva. The lobby was swarming with people, those checking in and those desperate for rooms. It was clear that the peace conference had taken over the city. Although it had been going on for two and a half months now, space was at a premium.

Susan, Delia, and the boys were led through the crowd to a private elevator, which took them to their suite on the eleventh floor. The management was used to having celebrities as guests, but they had not lost the touch of making a subtle but noticeable fuss. Flowers in each room of the suite, a basket of fruit, the bedclothes turned down on each bed with a Godiva mint on each pillow. Susan felt comfortable immediately, already on vacation.

She took Jimmy into the smaller bedroom and undressed him, but he did not wake even when she kissed him on the forehead. Eli claimed that he wasn't tired, but at Delia's insistence he put on his pajamas and got into the bed across from his brother. When Susan came in to check ten minutes later, she heard his steady, regular breathing.

"You want me to help you unpack, Mrs. Kraft?" the maid asked, stifling a yawn.

"God, no, Delia. Just go to sleep. I'll see you in the morning."

"Thanks, Mrs. Kraft. Good night."

"Good night."

Susan lit a cigarette as she went to the window and pulled open the drapes. Geneva's lights shone out through the blackness. The lake was directly across from the hotel, and the water shimmered in the moonlight. One of her favorite lakes, enhanced by the tallest fountain in the world: the *jet d'eau*. The powerful wall of water shot to the sky as the multicolored spotlights played over it. Magnificent, she thought with a sigh. Somehow the grandeur and freedom of it mirrored her own feelings about this trip. There was, she recalled fondly, something magical about vacations. You could pretend to be anyone you wanted, you could melt into your surroundings and escape the persona that everyone at home knew and loved, or hated. You could just be yourself, the plain old ordinary Susan you had been for years before the calamity (read "fame and fortune") struck and turned your life to solid gold.

When she finally climbed into bed an hour later, she was sure she was too excited to close her eyes. But exhaustion won and sleep overcame her immediately.

As usual, Jimmy was the first one up. Eager to get a start on the day, not the least disoriented by the new room and strange bed, he ran across to his brother's bed to shout in his ear. Eli protested and turned over, but when he remembered that he was in Geneva and on vacation he opened his eyes again. When Delia came in to dress them, the brothers were already on their way out the door of the suite, eager to explore.

"Just a second there," the maid cautioned, hauling them in by one arm each. "I think it might be polite to wait for your mother this morning. How about it?"

"Okay," Jimmy grinned, running to Susan's room and barging in. He slammed the door and she jumped up in fright.

"I've told you not to do that!" she said angrily, catching her breath. He had interrupted a dream, and she realized her pulse was much faster than normal. Jimmy responded by climbing into bed with her, hugging and kissing his mother until he coaxed a smile from her.

"You're a devil." She shrugged.

"What's a devil?"

"It's you!"

She got out of bed and walked to the window. The sky was clear and the streets were bathed in sunlight. The fountain spurted majestically above the lake. "Fabulous day," she said.

Eli came in softly behind them. "Well, what are we waiting for? You . . . you aren't going to work today, are you, Mom?"

"I am not," she proclaimed fiercely. "This day is ours and nothing will interfere. They don't need me until the day after tomorrow," she added, knowing how much of a disappointment it was to the boys to learn secondhand that their mother had been called away on business. Better to prepare them, always, for the harsh blows she had to deal them.

"So, I'm open to suggestion. What do you want to do?" She grabbed them up in her arms and bundled them toward the bed, where they fell together in a heap, laughing and pummeling each other.

"Ice cream, ice cream," cried Jimmy gleefully.

"To take a boat ride," Eli chimed in.

"No, ice cream, ice cream."

"I want to get right up next to that fountain!" Eli insisted over his brother's smaller voice.

"Okay, guys," Susan said, hushing them. "Stop yelling. We'll do both." For the first time in longer than she liked to remember, her work would come second to her children for two days. Susan the mother was about to take precedence over Susan the million-dollar commentator.

They had a light breakfast in the hotel's coffee shop, where Susan anxiously peered from under her large dark glasses to be sure that she was not recognized. Fortunately, the place was so packed with delegates and tourists that no one paid them any heed except for the attentive waitress, who couldn't do enough to please them. When they walked out, Susan decided against taking a taxi. The day was so beautiful, she could not bear the notion of being shut up in a car. After a brief check of her street map, and a wave at Delia, the three of them set off for the lake.

Numerous convoys passed in the crowded streets. Each was led by two police motorcycles, three or four black limousines, and, finally, additional motorcycles. Even the faces in the limousines were similar. Frozen, serious.

Only the flags waving on the cars were different. The American stars and stripes, the Soviet scythe and hammer, the Arab crescent, the Israeli Star of David, and the UN's pale blue globe.

Susan and her children joined the numerous onlookers crowded near the entrance to the Palais des Nations. She lifted Jimmy so that he could watch the scene.

Traffic returned to normal once the last convoy had entered. Five minutes later, they were at the lake.

"There are the boats." Eli pointed as he pulled his mother toward the pier.

"First we'll have some ice cream," said Susan.

The look on Eli's face was imploring. He pointed to a large sign in front of the pier. "The boat leaves in ten minutes!"

Susan pulled her arm away. "There's always another!" she said impatiently, and walked toward a nearby cafe.

When she recalled the scene a few days later, she could have sworn that the look on Eli's face was one of fright, almost desperation. But maybe she only imagined this, because of everything that happened later. And what difference did it make? For the rest of her life, she would regret not taking the first boat.

But they didn't. Instead, they sat at one of the tables on the sidewalk and ordered two large portions of ice cream. Eli wasn't hungry.

CHAPTER 12

THE DEPUTY SECRETARY-GENERAL of the United Nations pounded three times with his gavel, and the sound reverberated off the impressive marble walls of the council chamber of the Palais des Nations.

To the right of the chairman sat the American ambassador.

The Soviet delegate took his seat and nodded to the men facing him at separate tables arranged in two rows. The representatives of Egypt, Syria, Jordan, Lebanon, a Palestinian delegation, and Israel were all present.

The conference had lingered on for two and a half months. When it had first been convened, it had electrified the entire world. There was an optimistic sense that this time, in this most peaceful of states, some lasting good could finally be done. The gallery had been filled for the first ten days with journalists and TV cameras from around the world.

Now the gallery was sparsely populated by just a handful of media people. Down below, in the chamber, boredom reigned, now that the serious problems had already been treated. As one of the journalists had written several days ago, the historical confrontation of men and ideas had degenerated into technicalities, numbers of guns, inches between borders—all the mechanics of peacemaking.

How ironic that this particular conference was taking place in the very building where, in September 1937, the League of Nations had first convened, presided over by the Aga Khan. How meaningless was the splendid bas-relief, depicting the creation of man, with its motto: "Man was created in the likeness of God." Even more meaningless were the two statements carved beneath it, expressing the view of Robert Cecil: "The nations must disarm" and "Be just and have no fear."

During its four decades of existence, the chamber had housed numerous conferences. A few were successful, the majority proved how wrong Robert Cecil had been. It was never enough to be just.

That was the reason why, on this occasion too, no one in the chamber mentioned justice of fraternity. The delegates argued over kilometers of security, guarantees, commercial treaties, cultural agreements; they talked of oil, arms, and money.

It wasn't exciting. It wasn't impressive. But it was effective. And now, after six weeks of discussions, the conference's objective seemed to be within reach, more than ever before.

"Distinguished delegates," said the chairman, "we have three more items left on the agenda. With regard to the warning stations along the borders, we have reached an agreement in principle, and now—"

"Mr. Chairman, Mr. Chairman!"

The chairman lifted his head, and removed his spectacles. He saw that the head of the Syrian delegation had his hand raised. "Yes, sir?"

"I regret, but we made it clear that our consent in principle is conditional upon an agreement concerning the number of stations and their location."

"Of course," said the chairman. "That is self-evident."

"I request that my remark be recorded."

"The remark will be recorded," said the chairman in a weary tone. It had been like this all along. Reservations, comments, clarifications. He would be overjoyed when this whole thing was over.

"On the Golan Heights," the chairman continued, "Israel proposes warning stations ten kilometers apart—in other words, a total of six stations. Syria holds that three are sufficient. I propose that, before going on to the next item, we solve this problem, which does not appear to be grave."

Even before lifting his eyes, the chairman knew that when he did so he would see the Syrian's hand.

"I deplore the comment made by the chairman," said the Syrian. "We consider this to be an extremely grave issue. In our view . . ."

The debate was launched. The chairman stifled a yawn as he leaned back in his seat. In the course of these last few weeks, he had become proficient at listening in a manner which did not occupy his complete attention. In this fashion, he was able to take in something of the beautiful vistas of Geneva which were visible through the expansive picture window, and to contemplate his next move in the fascinating chess game which he was conducting in the evenings with the Norwegian ambassador.

Susan let the sun's rays warm her face. She could never sit in an outdoor cafe and sip a coffee like this in New York even if she had the time, which she never did. The nature of New York was such that when you weren't busy, you got anxious and proceeded to create something to do rather than luxuriate in idleness.

Geneva, on the other hand, was completely the opposite. Being busy simply didn't match the scenery—the blue lake whose waters could never become turbulent, the small white houses with their neat red roofs, the country estates on the opposite side of the lake partially hidden by a mass of lush green foliage and banks of extraordinary flowers.

Susan examined the faces of the passersby. Did they share her feeling? No one seemed rushed; in fact, their pace was so slow one might almost believe they were making an effort not to hurry. The expressions were serene, almost blank. Most of the strollers were tanned, fashionable, and dressed in the height of the *grande mode*. They knew exactly how they were supposed to look and they worked hard at making their chic seem unstudied. *What a city,* Susan mused. *Even its inhabitants look like tourists.*

She could have sat there forever, enjoying the sun. But then she felt a tug at her sleeve. "Mom, snap out of it," Eli urged. "We'll miss this boat too!"

Reluctantly, she summoned the waiter for the check and lazily hauled herself out of the wicker chair. Eli, with Jimmy in tow, was already on the other side of the street near the entrance to the pier. A large placard on the dock read, "Tour Lake Geneva. Adults:—francs. Children:—francs," in three different languages. The prices had been obliterated. Currency values had been fluctuating so crazily in Europe lately that it apparently didn't make sense to advertise, in case the price changed the next day.

Susan purchased three tickets and stood looking at the magnificent spectacle of the fountain. Eli pulled her arm again.

"Let's get on!"

"We've got ten minutes till it starts, hon."

"Let's get on!"

She let the boys propel her forward. Two young men and a young woman who had been sitting together at the sidewalk cafe had followed them out onto the pier. The young woman was a thin, frail-looking blonde struggling under the weight of a heavy backpack. Her companions were dark. One walked with an almost military gait, despite his slight limp. Both men wore packs. Susan had a sudden flash of memory and smiled to herself, recalling how she had first traveled abroad after her junior year at Chicago. *They still look the same,* she thought ruefully. *Just as poor, but just as eager.*

The boat was ancient, but roomy and quite comfortable. The forward deck was open, dotted with about twenty benches which were starting to fill up. The middle deck, somewhat larger, was closed in and heated for those who couldn't take too much of the sea air, and had space for about eighty passengers.

Susan and the boys took seats in the sun on the outer deck. There were only about twenty passengers on board and Susan wondered about the financial viability of tour boats on Lake Geneva.

But her concern was premature. Two minutes later, she saw a tour bus screech to a halt on the pier and about fifty people pile out. They raced toward the boat, filling the vacant seats quickly, while their guide handed their tickets to the crew member on the gangplank. The previous peace and quiet was replaced by noisy laughter and talk. "Americans," whispered one of the first group of passengers, an Englishman.

Two men released the heavy ropes mooring the boat to the thick iron pilings on the pier. The captain gave a yank at a short cord in the steering cabin and the loud whistle made several people start. He then began flicking his finger at a faulty microphone on the instrument panel.

"Hello, hello, can you hear me? What's all this? Damn it! What . . . is it working?"

Everyone laughed as attention turned to him. The captain was wearing a white sailor's cap with gold trim. He was a genial-looking man in his late sixties. He stood behind the rudder wheel looking as though he had never done anything else in his life.

"Ladies and gentlemen," he announced, clearing his throat, "the captain and crew are happy to welcome you on board."

Eli laughed. "What's he talking about? He's the captain, and the crew is that kid standing next to him."

Susan patted his arm. "True, but a good public relations man always knows a way to convince the people they're getting more than they bargained for."

Suddenly Eli spun around and pointed. "Look!"

Susan followed the direction of his finger. Gradually, everyone on deck turned toward the fountain. The gush of water was sinking lower and lower; within two minutes, it had vanished completely.

"What's going on?" Susan wondered softly.

Eli looked serious. "Maybe they ran out of water?"

Jean Dromier knew, without any doubt, that it was the switch. The reason the fountain had ceased to function had to be the switch. For over three months, he had been warning everyone that this was about to happen, but did anyone take any notice? All of his careful memos and phone calls were regarded as so much aggravation. Well, now they knew!

It was high time the directors of Geneva's water corporation realized they had to take what he said about the fountain seriously. He, Jean Dromier, was the master of that *jet d'eau*. Maybe not as young as he used to be—well, sixty-three wasn't exactly old!—but he had been doing this job for the past forty years and there was no one who could ever equal him at it.

Every moring at seven, Dromier would arrive at the powerhouse and carefully scrutinize each of the two 2,400-volt fuses of the two motors which kept the fountain pumping. They were his children, and he understood their temperamental fits and starts. After that, he would scrupulously examine the transformer's 18,000-volt fuse. Then, satisfied with the major components, he would check out the motors' various sections. There were cogs, wheels, screws that could and often did come loose. Why, it was nearly three months now since he had reported that the switch of one of the motors was wearing out. By his assessment, the wheel-shaped device would not hold out more than a few weeks longer.

Without the switch, there was no fountain. What the directors failed to see was that the apparatus was a brilliantly designed machine with a rhythm and a heartbeat. One motor into action; then, once that was spinning nicely, the second. When the two sang together, the fountain jumped to life. But each motor depended for its life blood on its own automatic switch. Should one switch break down, both motors would stall. And this was precisely what had happened.

And so, now at the twelfth hour, now when the directors realized the gravity of the situation, they were running around like panic-stricken mice. Dromier had to laugh. He could have solved the whole matter weeks ago, but, no, they *would* wait until things had reached crisis proportions. After all, Geneva without its fountain was not the same city. The tourists expected it, just as they expected the view of the mountains. So suddenly everyone listened to Dromier. They needed his advice and counsel; he was no longer the nuisance. Everyone was begging. "Do whatever is necessary. Quickly."

That morning he had called the National Electrique, the only company with all the necessary parts. An hour later, they called back. Awfully sorry, but they did not have the switch in stock. No delivery for another three or four days, at the inside.

Dromier could not believe his ears. It was unheard of. They must make a supreme effort. The patient official assured him he would do everything in his power, but he could not promise results.

Dromier walked to the window and gazed out at the lake, which appeared still and empty. He was responsible for its glory and, even without the lofty column of water in action, he knew precisely where the base of the fountain was located. A boatload of tourists was slowly approaching the spot from which the *jet d'eau* had gushed, just a few minutes ago. Dromier shook his head. That it should come to this. . . .

CHAPTER 13

Only a short plane ride from Israel, but there it's a different world, Deborah reflected as her eyes took in the blue lake, the picturesque houses on its banks, and the yachts anchored at its pier. And the fountain. Tons of water gushed into the air and returned to the lake in tiny flakes that formed a wondrous rainbow of blue, yellow, and red. She smiled as she thought of the wasted energy. A typical reaction of a young woman from a country where energy was considered too valuable to squander on improving the scenery. She shifted her glance to the first row, and Yoram looked back at the same moment. She turned her head to the left. No one else could have noticed Nabil's imperceptible nod. Deborah felt something surge inside her, a kind of power she had felt only in bed with Awad. . . .

Deborah had a clear view of the Palais des Nations to her left. The honchos were all there, wheeling and dealing. The men who talked. Of peace. Of an international accord. **(105)**

Always talk. Endless talk. Never mind, all that would end momentarily.

Deborah looked down at her watch. 9:57. The boat was rapidly approaching the fountain. She could see the tension in the faces of Yoram and Nabil.

Three minutes to go. And then the water stopped. The fountain had simply melted into the lake.

Tak-tak-tak.

At first, Susan thought it was the engine. It was only when she heard the screams that she turned her eyes toward the captain and noticed the blonde young woman. She was holding an Uzi submachine gun and pointing it directly at the passengers.

Susan was uncertain whether it was the woman who had fired into the air or whether it was one of the two men who were likewise holding submachine guns. One of them was pointing his weapon at the elderly captain, who was clutching his chest and looking dazed with fear. The other terrorist had taken up a position on the far side of the boat.

"Nothing will happen to you if you obey instructions!" the girl shouted into the microphone.

The captain had stopped the boat, as he was ordered. The vessel now drifted silently in the middle of the lake no more than fifty yards from the source of the fountain.

"Everybody inside!" Deborah shouted. "Go inside bench by bench, just in the order in which you're seated. Come on, move!"

Susan picked up Jimmy, hugging him tightly. "You stay close to me, okay Eli?" she said to her older son. "That way we all get seats together inside."

"Sure. You know what's going on, Mom?"

"Not yet, hon. We'll have to see what they tell us. Let's go."

When all the passengers were herded into the closed central cabin, Yoram picked up his large backpack. Placing his submachine gun on the deck, he began to empty out the contents of his bag. It was filled with a number of small, carefully wrapped packets.

He lined the packets in a row and began to join them together with a thin wire which was enclosed in a black plastic covering. Nabil came over and, together, the two men trailed the explosives around the passengers' seats, every now and then laying one of the packets on the deck boards.

After completing their turn around the deck, the two men joined the end of the wire to a square box with an iron bar at the top. They took the box into the steering cabin and laid it on the deck, under the structure to which the rudder wheel was attached. "Outside," said Deborah nervously. "We don't want anybody setting it off accidentally."

"We're surrounded by explosives," Susan said under her breath.

"Boom-boom!" Jimmy shouted cheerfully.

Susan gazed outside. On the shore, about two hundred yards away, she could clearly see the growing crowd. It seemed that people had noticed that something was happening, although they did not know precisely what.

A police car drew up, its siren shrieking. The driver got out and made his way to the barrier separating the sidewalk from the lake. He turned and shouted to his companion, who emerged from the crowd a moment later, carrying a bullhorn. He lifted it to his mouth.

"You people in the boat, can you hear me?"

The hijackers glanced at one another.

"Is there anything wrong with your engine?" the policeman shouted again.

An additional police car drove up and the commander of the Geneva police got out. The onlookers stepped aside to let him through.

"What's going on?" he asked the two officers.

"We're not sure yet, Inspector Pascal," replied one. "There's no answer from the boat."

"Let's go find out then," Pascal said. The three men ran to the pier, where the police motorboat was moored.

Deborah saw them coming. She opened one of the bags and produced a powerful bullhorn.

"Don't move. Don't get any closer or else the boat will be blown up!"

Gasps of astonishment arose from the crowd, and the policemen stopped dead in their tracks. Peering through

his binoculars, Pascal could clearly see the man standing
on the open forward deck. He focused on the enclosed
cabin, but could distinguish nothing more than shadowy
figures. He started when the woman's voice again boomed
out from the boat.

"We want one man to come out here. Only one. No
weapons."

Pascal glanced slightly nervously about him, encoun-
tering the stares of the people standing nearby. Someone
handed him the bullhorn, and he lifted it to his mouth.

"This is Police Inspector Claude Pascal. I'm coming
right away."

He laid down his gun holster and climbed into the
small boat that awaited him, its motor already humming.
He slowly lowered himself into the seat beside the tiller,
revved the motor, and sped toward the pleasure boat. It
had begun to rain lightly. In two minutes, he had reached
his destination. A fair-haired man was standing above
him on the deck.

"Are you armed?"

"No."

"Climb up!" ordered Yoram, letting down a rope ladder.

Pascal grabbed on and started up. When he had nearly
reached the top rung, he slipped; he would certainly have
fallen into the water had Yoram not taken his arm and
yanked him aboard.

"Thank you," he said quietly to the terrorist.

"Come with me."

There were cries from the cabin. "Inspector, what's
happening? Why don't you get us out of here?"

"Shut up!" Yoram's shout silenced them. Pascal was
brought into the helmsman's cabin, where Deborah was
waiting for him. It struck him as he looked at her that she
didn't seem like a terrorist, but then what did he know?
He'd never seen one before.

"Do you speak English?"

"A little."

Deborah handed him two typewritten pages. "This is
our statement with our demands. Read it to the journalists,
okay?"

"Yes."

"We plan to be here for quite a while. We'll need fresh water, no food. Everyone here is on a hunger strike. You'll understand that when you've read our statement. You bring the water in five-gallon cans in a boat which will stop thirty yards from here. No closer. One of us will come in a dinghy to collect it. At that time we will deliver a list of the hostages' names. Remember that if anyone tries to approach the boat, we will be obliged to make use of that." Pascal glanced over to where she was pointing and saw the box with the handle. It was connected to the line of explosives that circled the deck.

"That's all," she finished.

As he walked toward the rail of the forward deck, Pascal heard Deborah's steps behind him. "You better go see what's happening at the rear of the boat," she told Nabil.

Nabil walked away and Pascal swung his leg over the rail, stepping onto the top rung of the rope ladder. Deborah seized his arm. "Don't say this in public, but you can tell those who need to know: I want Awad. The joint communiqúe and Awad. As for the rest of the prisoners, we can come to some arrangement."

"A joint communiqúe?"

"You'll understand later. Don't forget. Maruan Awad."

Deborah moved away. Pascal stared at her, feeling a strange sense of unreality. This stunning blonde—a terrorist. How absurd.

The inspector lowered himself carefully into the motorboat and headed for the shore. But when he tried to climb up onto the pier, he was nearly knocked into the water by the dozens of journalists who jostled to get near him. Three policemen hurried to push the journalists out of Pascal's way.

"Who are they?"

"What do they want?"

Dozens of microphones were thrust at Pascal. Several struck his face, and he stepped back. Another four policemen arrived at a run, their truncheons raised. The journalists pulled back a few paces, and Pascal produced the paper Deborah had given him.

"I have here a statement from the hijackers."

Instantly, there was total silence, broken only by the whir and click of cameras. Pascal began to read:

> During recent months, a historical crime has been perpetrated at Geneva. Persons calling themselves the representatives of nations sit in a conference hall, negotiating what they refer to as a peace treaty between the state of Israel, the Arab states, and the Palestinians. These persons have absolutely no right to engage in any such activity. There is no distinction between the Palestinians and the state of Israel. There is only one single land of Palestine, belonging to the Israeli-Palestinian people. Any solution based on any other viewpoint will perpetuate hatred and strife in the Middle East.

"Read it slowly!" interrupted several journalists. Pascal looked up. The cameras were snapping him from every conceivable angle, while the journalists' pens scribbled incessantly.

> We, the Ishmaelites, therefore present the following two demands. We demand that the Geneva Conference disperse, and not reconvene. Simultaneously with the conference's dispersal, its participants are to publish a joint communiqué.

Pascal broke off. This was what the girl was talking about. This and . . .

"What's the matter, Inspector?"

"What's wrong?"

Pascal shook himself out of his reverie. "Nothing, nothing at all." He looked down at the paper.

> The joint communiqué shall state that the conference recognizes only one single state to the west of the Jordan—the state of Palestine, whose citizens are Israelis and Palestinians.

Pascal paused one more, to permit the journalists to catch up.

> The second demand: the release by Israel of thirty-six freedom fighters, headed by Maruan Awad.

"What was that?"

"What was that name?"

Raising his voice, Pascal repeated, "Maruan Awad."

"How do you spell that?"

"These names . . ."

Pascal resumed his reading.

We give those concerned as much time as they need to fulfill our demands. We shall anchor here, facing the Palais des Nations, for as long as is necessary, in the name of Palestinian-Israeli justice. The Ishmaelites make their demands in the interests of peace. Although we have taken the precaution of arming ourselves, this is solely for protection. No one on board will be harmed or mistreated. Each hostage will, however, participate with us in a hunger strike to symbolize the suffering our peoples have withstood over the decades. This strike will continue until our demands are met.

Pascal raised his eyes to indicate the end of the communiqúe. He almost lost his balance as the journalists made a wild dash for the phones in the nearby cafes. Those who remained with him had seemingly gone insane: they yelled in his ear, shouted questions, tugged at his uniform.

"Alert the special unit!" Pascal said to the officer standing next to him. He gave the order unthinkingly, even though his mind had not yet actually absorbed all that had happened in the last hour.

As he walked to his car, he tried to string together the events he had just witnessed into some kind of logical sequence. Before climbing inside, Pascal turned once more toward the television cameras. He'd never received so much publicity before, and he had to confess that he rather liked it. He almost smiled, but then restrained himself. This was a time for an earnest, thoughtful, and somewhat anxious expression.

Only after he was in the car did Pascal allow his weariness to show. Slumping backward in his seat, he closed his eyes.

"Where to, Inspector?"

"The Mayor."

Forty-five minutes later the Swiss Foreign Minister had informed the ambassadors of both Israel and the United States of the terrorists' demands and Deborah's demand for Awad.

CHAPTER 14

THE COUNCIL CHAMBER at the Palais des Nations had once again turned into the arena for a political confrontation.

As soon as the chairman read out the bulletin reporting the hijacking, pandemonium broke loose. A few moments before, Arabs and Israelis had been conducting a serious, but polite, discussion on one item of a peace proposal; now, they were all on their feet, bellowing accusations and insults.

The signal for the stormy disagreement was given by the Jordanian representative, who received the floor. He spoke quietly, but his face was tense.

"Mr. Chairman, I must admit that I am not surprised by the developments. From the moment this conference opened, it was clear to us that the Israelis were doing their utmost to create obstacles. I am convinced that they came here with the sole purpose of undermining this effort to **(113)** bring peace to the Middle East. They hoped that we would help them achieve that goal. When they realized that that was not to be, they planned this disgraceful act."

The Israeli representative waved his hand excitedly and the chairman nodded tiredly toward him.

"I find it difficult to believe, Mr. Chairman, that the Jordanian representative believes the words he just uttered. Since the establishment of the state of Israel, its governments have made every possible effort to bring about peace." He looked in the direction of the Egyptian representative. "For the sake of that goal, my government agreed to withdraw from all of Sinai, despite the enormous oil reserves found there. For many years, we asked our neighbors to negotiate with us. We had great hopes for this conference, and we came here with a fierce desire to end the war in our region. Only a Machiavellian mind could believe that we came here desiring the failure of the conference and that we would endeavor to bring it about by means of the very terror which has victimized us all these years. I hereby declare, wholeheartedly, that the government of Israel knew nothing of the criminal kidnapping; it condemns it as it always condemns acts of terror."

"What about Lebanon?" shouted the Syrian representative from his seat, without bothering to ask for the floor. "What was that if not terror? You denounce terror by others, but you use it when it serves your interests."

"Our actions in Lebanon were taken in the interests of self-defense," replied the Israeli representative heatedly. "You yourselves occupied Lebanon and terrorized its population."

"That's a disgraceful lie!" cried the Syrian representative.

The Syrian delegation stood up in unison and began filing out of the chamber. "Gentlemen, gentlemen!" the chairman cried after them. The head of the Syrian delegation halted. "We will not sit with hyprocrites and liars!" he exclaimed, and headed for the exit.

The perplexed Jordanians looked at the Egyptians, who responded with questioning glances. The American deputy and the Russian delegates hurried out to pacify the angry parties, but they were too late. The Egyptians and Jordanians were already on their feet.

"Would you believe it?" said the head of the Israeli delegation to his deputy, who was seated on his right.

"How did *that* happen?"

The members of the Israeli delegation rose and they too began to leave the chamber. The enormous floor of the council chamber was now occupied by only three men, who stood helplessly looking at one another.

"We were so close to an agreement," whispered an American undersecretary to the United Nations.

"It was too good to be true," said the French ambassador.

The American shrugged his shoulders. "It couldn't have been that close, I suppose, or that good, if an incident like this was capable of setting off such a tempest." He began to walk out of the chamber, with the Frenchman and the Norwegian ambassador at his heels. The American halted and glanced up at the gigantic bas-relief. "Be just and have no fear." He shook his head. "What happens," he asked, "when everybody has his own particular justice?"

"That's when the trouble starts," said the Norwegian ambassador.

CHAPTER 15

UNITED STATES President Frank Kelly was satisfied with the memorandum just presented by Kenneth Garden, chairman of his reelection committee. The President was assured of the votes of 543 convention delegates, while 127 were promised to the opponent. He would be chosen on the first ballot with an overwhelming majority.

"Fine work," he said to Garden, whose face shone with pleasure at the compliment.

"You too, Ronnie," he praised Ronald Taylor, the Secretary of State. The President's tone was one of genuine affection.

In fact, more than anyone else, the Secretary of State had to be credited with Kelly's firm hold on the nomination. Five months earlier, it had looked like a lost cause. The Arab states had begun to take steps to impose an oil embargo, inflation was soaring, and the public's patience
was wearing thin. The prospect of the President failing to

gain his own party's nomination began to look very likely. His contender for the spot, Timothy Marsden, was coming up strong behind him, and it looked like many of his former supporters might choose the dark horse candidate.

It had been Taylor who insisted that the Geneva Conference would alter the picture dramatically. "It will give some hope of warding off the oil embargo, of course. But, what's more important, it will give the public something to help them forget rocketing prices. Peace in the making— Arabs and Jews together. The ups and downs of the negotiations. Who will pay any attention to inflation then? People will just remember that they have a President who can make peace when it seems impossible."

Garden was doubtful. He thought people were far more interested in the price of bread and vegetables than in prospects for peace. As it turned out, he was wrong. Taylor had the pulse of the American people.

The President walked over to pat Taylor on the shoulder. "What about another miracle?" he suggested.

"No problem. As long as you don't ask for plain simple things."

"I'd like peace. A comprehensive peace treaty before the elections."

Taylor smiled. "Yes. That *would* be pretty good."

"What are the prospects?"

"Who knows? We're talking about Jews and Arabs, remember. The hardest nuts to crack."

"See what you can do to coax them along. I'll see you tomorrow."

Taylor and Garden rose and were about to leave when Dick Radshaw, the President's secretary, hurried in and handed Kelly a note. The President's expression became a mixture of astonishment and horror.

"Tell them," said the President after a long pause.

Radshaw briefed the others quickly on the hijacking of the boat in Geneva and the enforced hunger strike. Taylor walked over to the bar and poured himself a whisky on the rocks. "Is there anything else?" he asked.

"Yes," said the President, brandishing the note in their faces. "Plenty. They just released a list of the hos-

tages' names. Susan Kraft is on that boat. He turned again
to Bradshaw. "How many hostages are there altogether?"

"Seventy-eight."

"Americans?"

"Sixty-three."

"Hell! Damn it!"

The room was silent for several moments.

"We haven't got any time," Garden muttered, remind-
ing everybody that the party convention would convene
in four days to select its candidate for president.

"Okay," said Kelly, regaining his composure. "Let's
examine the situation. Go on, Radshaw."

His secretary read the hijackers' demands. When he
concluded, the President began talking—almost to himself—in a thoughtful, anxious tone.

"This is nonsense. They can get any joint communiqué they want. In any case, it's not binding. The delegations can disperse and then reassemble when the whole
episode is concluded."

"That's not so easy, Mr. President," said Taylor. "I
know these customers. It will be very difficult to get them
back to Geneva. You remember how hard it was to get
them there in the first place."

"I don't give a nickel for that," said the President
impatiently. "That will be after the convention."

"But before the elections."

"True, true. But we'll worry about that in due time.
The main thing now is to finish this damn affair, and do it
fast, before the convention. Above all, without any bloodshed. Christ, all I need is to come to the convention with
the blood of a few dozen American citizens on my hands."

"I'm worried about the Israelis," Taylor said. "They
aren't eager to release any of their prisoners."

"We aren't going to ask them what they're eager to
do," said the President with venom in his voice. "We'll
tell them." He turned to Taylor. "You see to it. Use any
means."

"Wouldn't it be better if Silver deals with them?"

The two men looked at each other.

"Yes," said the President at last. "Yes. Very good."

Twenty-five minutes later, when Defense Secretary Silver strode into the Oval Office, he already knew about the hijacking. He was slightly surprised when President Kelly notified him that he had been chosen to handle the problem, but none of the advisers offered to expand on Kelly's decision.

"Silver, we don't want heroes," said the President after a brief greeting. "Just the release of the hostages. I don't care how you do it. But do it," he ordered.

He placed his hand on Silver's shoulder. "I'm relying on you. Believe me, there's far more involved than the safety of the hostages here. The manner in which this affair is settled will influence the results of the next election. My election."

Silver looked over at Taylor, who was sitting in an armchair to his left. Before the Secretary of State had a chance to respond to Silver's silent question, the President said quickly, "Taylor is occupied with other pressing matters. I need you, Marty."

When they were outside Kelly's office and had taken a few steps in silence together down the long corridor, Taylor suddenly let out a stifled laugh. "The old man's exaggerating, as usual. He'll grab the Presidency, even if this whole damn country goes up in smoke."

"Do you really believe that?" asked Silver.

Taylor grinned. "We'd better believe it. Otherwise, we'll all be out of work."

Silver nodded good-bye and climbed into the black limousine awaiting him. The situation was something he would just have to handle, as he had other affairs in the past. And when he had taken care of it, he would be Kelly's right-hand man again, maybe even closer to him than Taylor was. Sure, the President wanted him now because he was Jewish, but when he had solved the problem, and done his work just the way he always did, he would have proved to everyone—to himself most of all, perhaps—that his Jewishness didn't matter. Odd, wasn't it? The very process of his Americanization had been so easy for him, so clear-cut. He fit in here. He had changed

the clothes, dropped the accent, established the friend-
ships, just like he was to the manor born. And now, this
special assignment, just because he was a Jew. Well, maybe
there was some truth in that old suspicion he had har-
bored all his life—that he had developed his American
character out of convenience as well as conviction. Still, it
was his now—no one could take it away from him. Damn
it, he'd solve this mess. He'd show them. But if he couldn't?

"Home?" asked the chauffeur, who had been standing
quietly next to the car, ignoring the fact that Silver was
lost in thought.

"No," he responded quickly. "To the office."

His secretary followed him into his private office and
waited until he was seated. "General Dickenson wants to
see you. He says it's urgent. General Rogers called and
said . . ."

"Call the Israeli ambassador and tell him I want to see
him immediately."

"What about . . . ?"

"Never mind the generals," he shouted. "I want the
Israeli ambassador."

The secretary ran out. Silver picked up one of the
documents on his desk and began reading. But he could
not concentrate.

"Taylor is now occupied with other pressing matters,"
the President had said.

The President had also said that the fate of the Presidency hung in the balance. And if so, no other matters
could be more pressing. Certainly not four days prior to
the convention. The President would want the hijacking
dealt with in the best possible way. By the most suitable
person.

Him? Martin Silver?

He had very few illusions about himself. He knew
that he was good at his job, but he also knew that he was
the least suitable person to handle this matter. It required
diplomatic skills. He had none. He had never been a diplo-
mat, in his public or his private life. He was strong-
minded, resolute, opinionated even. He didn't know how
to compromise.

And, as long as he was summing up his failings, he should add "unable to communicate effectively" to the list. All his life he had felt uncomfortable at parties where he was expected to make small talk. He couldn't slip a political phrase or slogan into a conversation and make it sound convincing. He was good with facts, he could define things succinctly and accurately, but what good would that do him here? When you sit down at a bargaining table, when you're negotiating for human lives, you have to know how to compromise, something he had always equated with indecisiveness.

And then, too, he was never sure, deep within himself, how successfully the American government leader had buried the immigrant, the *yeshiva bucher* who had broken free of those huddled masses on Ellis Island.

Silver got up, walked slowly to the window, and looked out at Washington. No one could ever say that he had compromised with regard to the basic elements of his life. Certainly not about his country. God, how he loved this place! It had taken a while, but a deep and lasting love always needs time in which to nourish.

When he had first come, that first day, he nearly turned back. In Poland, his father had been a respected member of the Jewish community, a successful businessman who made sure that his family had the best of everything. In Brooklyn, the streets were filthy, the houses crowded, and the work like slave labor—if work could be found. And then there was the language, which he could not understand. When he tried to pronounce the few words he knew, he was ridiculed.

Martin was constantly troubled by the thought that he might have been wrong and Moshe Lieberman right. Perhaps Israel would have been the correct choice after all.

"Why?" his mother would ask. "Why don't you correspond with Moshe?"

"We have separate lives now." But he knew that was not the reason.

As he grew accustomed to his new life, he began to see the America beyond Brooklyn. The freedom, the openness, the security. Topics of conversation like the weather or the score of the last Dodger game were a breath of fresh air. In Poland, they had had to wonder when the next pogrom might occur, when their business might be closed down.

He went to night school to get a high school diploma and delivered for his parents' grocery store during the day. They were up at 4:30 in the morning to receive the merchandise, worked all day with one ten-minute break for lunch, and closed the shop after 11:00 P.M., an hour after Martin returned home from school.

Martin would arrive at school each night physically and mentally exhausted, but as soon as he took his seat in the classroom he would discover new mental strength. An education would rescue him from the life of a delivery boy, and so he worked and studied, worked and studied. Without compromise.

He could see it ahead of him now, the America he had dreamed of. He had discovered the world of chemistry, and the love of it propelled him through night school and on to college. He marveled to see how a fixed set of substances, in various combinations and amounts, could produce endless results. He was mesmerized by the creation of new materials from existing ones. He found here what he had always been searching for. Formulas in place of words. Facts in place of theories.

When he graduated first in his class, he considered the academic life. To teach others, to conduct experiments at his leisure, and to lead a quiet, secure life appealed to Martin. Instead, however, he chose to take a position as one of many researchers at the largest chemical company in the United States. The possibilities, he knew, were limitless.

Now he knew he had been right to emigrate to America and Moshe had been wrong. There was no need for a Jewish state. America was home to anyone who chose to live there. Jews, Arabs, Africans, Italians. And he knew he had been right in believing that the United States was, indeed, neither a Poland nor a Germany.

He was perfectly sincere in believing that being a

good American meant adopting the American way of life, without compromise or reservation. The synagogue, the Jewish and Zionist organizations, the Jewish festivals— all these ran counter to the American way of life.

When he decided to marry Joan, he told himself—with complete intellectual honesty—that he was not doing so merely because she was Protestant. "I love her!" he shouted at his father, when his family went into mourning for him. "Is it a crime to love a woman who is not Jewish?"

"No. It's no crime," his father said. "It's alienation. Who will accompany you to synagogue on Yom Kippur?"

"I don't want to go to synagogue on Yom Kippur."

"Who will light the Sabbath candles?"

"I don't light candles."

His father's bearded face was intense. "And who will say the prayer for the dead after you?" Martin was about to say he did not want anyone to say the Kaddish for him, but he knew that would be a lie; consequently, he said, "My son, of course."

His father shook his head glumly. "Martin, your son and your other children, they won't be Jews. They won't say Kaddish. At best, they'll pray for you—in church. But it is not the same. They will never know the meaning of the bond we share."

"They'll decide for themselves whether to be Jews or Protestants."

"You are ignorant, my son. You don't want to know," his father said sadly. "If their mother is Protestant, they'll be Protestants. Cold, genteel, reciting pledges not prayers. They'll have no choice in the matter."

Twenty-two years later, Silver was elected chairman of the board of the chemical corporation. He was only forty-seven. This was the culmination of his dreams. He saw himself as a fulfilled man who had achieved far more than he had ever hoped. Now he could relax. He had no ambitions left.

When President Kelly offered him the position of Secretary of Defense, he was surprised, and then disturbed. He was perfectly satisfied with his work. He had never nursed political ambitions. The offer upset the professional and mental balance which he had so carefully constructed.

The problem was that even refusal would not return the balance. He would forever ask himself if he had done the right thing, and the question itself would disturb his peace of mind.

After a lengthy struggle with his conscience, he concluded that once the balance had been upset he might as well accept the position. Especially since it involved a serious challenge.

His main concern was what politics meant and what it demanded of all those who embraced it. It was not a profession, really, but rather a way of life. A way of life that repelled Silver.

The President reassured him on this matter. He had chosen him for the role because of his scientific and administrative talents. He did not expect him to become involved in politics or diplomacy.

The President kept his promise. The only time he did not was when he had sent Silver to Israel as his representative to the official burial ceremony.

This was the second time.

Why?

The answer was obvious. He was Jewish. Both instances had to do with Israel.

He felt dizzy, returned to his desk, picked up the glass of water, and drank it.

"It is not for you to choose."

Who had uttered those words?

Moshe Lieberman. A few years ago.

But he is wrong. I am what I choose to be.

He started as the buzzer on his desk signaled him. He pressed the intercom button.

"The ambassador of Israel."

"Just a minute."

He took a handkerchief out of his jacket pocket and wiped the beads of perspiration from his forehead. Then he sat in his chair and took a deep breath.

He pressed down firmly on the intercom buzzer. "Show him in."

The man who walked into Silver's room was of average height and solid build. His gait was brisk, almost skittish. He wore gold-rimmed glasses which accentuated the fullness of his face.

Silver stood to greet him and extended his hand. "I am pleased to see you, Mr. Ambassador," he said in a joyless tone.

"Pleased to see you, Mr. Secretary," replied Arieh Doron.

Silver usually showed his guests to the corner of his office, where a couch and armchairs stood. But he wanted this meeting to be as formal as possible.

"Please take a seat," he said, pointing to a chair near his desk. He returned to his own chair, on the opposite side, and cleared his throat. He would not waste time on niceties. He would just deal with the issue at hand.

"Now, Mr. Doron," he said brusquely, "I have been charged with reporting to your government concerning the United States' view of the boat hijacking in Geneva. It is of supreme importance that the matter be concluded quickly and without any mishaps. To further this aim, the United States expects all concerned to respond to the hijackers' demands. And when I say that, Mr. Doron, I am quoting the President's precise words."

"I understand."

"This shouldn't really be too difficult for your government. We have reliable reports that the hijackers will be satisfied by the release of one single prisoner. In addition to the public broadcasting of their communiqués, of course, but that's a trifling matter."

"But there are thirty-six prisoners on the hijackers' list."

"One prisoner, Mr. Ambassador. His name is . . ." Silver fumbled in his pocket and produced a sheet of paper. "Yes, Maruan Awad. That's it. Maruan Awad."

"Awad? My government has already denied that he is in Israel. I don't believe that . . ."

The Israeli ambassador broke off as the Defense Secretary's hand hit the desk. Silver leaned forward, and he spoke in a rapid whisper.

"I suggest you stop playing games with me. We don't

have time. We know you are holding Awad, as well as four other terrorists you deny having ever seen. Make no mistake regarding the mood in the White House, Mr. Doron, and report this to your government."

"I will do so, of course. But if I may be permitted, I would like to make one comment."

"Go ahead."

"You are aware of my government's official position. We have always been of the opinion that giving in to terrorist blackmail invites further blackmail. I don't know what my government's position will be in this particular case, but. . . ."

"There is no official position!" Silver interrupted angrily. "Every case must be examined on its merit. If your government wishes to do so, it can determine its position with regard to hijackings in which the hostages are Jews. It is not empowered, and it is not entitled, to apply that position with regard to American citizens."

"Jews, sir?"

For several seconds, Silver's mouth hung open.

"You know what I meant, damn it. Israelis, of course."

CHAPTER 16

LIEBERMAN ARRIVED fifty minutes after the time set for the meeting. He made no apologies and gave no explanation.

This irritated the Prime Minister, but he said nothing. He still remembered—indeed, he would never forget—the one and only time he had demanded an explanation from Lieberman. The answer was curt: "You must believe that there's a reason. No explanation can be a substitute for trust," the head of the Mossad had reminded him.

Those who knew Lieberman relied on him completely. They *had* to trust him. But they did not have to like him, and few did. He never asked for friendship or affection; nor did he receive any. Many actually feared him. Even the Prime Minister felt uncomfortable when Lieberman entered his office. He had met the man dozens of times, he thought to himself. Dozens? Hundreds, if not thousands of times. And each time, there was the same sense of unease. **(127)**

Why should he be afraid of the man? After all, he was Lieberman's direct superior.

Or was he? Formally, of course, he was. Lieberman reported to him, unlike the head of military intelligence, who reported to the Defense Minister. He did have power over the man's decisions and could veto them if he so chose. But then there was the informal aspect of their relationship. However much he disliked it, he had to admit that Lieberman occasionally did whatever he wished. How many times, he asked himself, had he given his approval to operations which were not entirely to his liking?

He could rationalize these times away by saying that, well, he respected Lieberman's judgment. He had the experience and the expertise to go about his business competently. He was intelligent, honest, decisive—all this and more.

And there was something else. Of all the men surrounding the Prime Minister, Lieberman was the only one who judged matters purely on their own merits, the only one totally free of political considerations, or of anxiety about others' opinions. Lieberman was not concerned about popularity, party interests, elections. At times, the Prime Minister wished he would display just a little political realism, since every decision he made had a political impact of some kind. But this would go against the man's principles and his instincts.

There was another reason to trust Lieberman implicitly. He was the only man with anything to lose. The most the politicians could forfeit was their political career. This man always staked everything, including his own life.

"Are you in the picture?" the Prime Minister asked.

Lieberman nodded.

"Who are they?"

"A very small extremist group known as the Ishmaelites who support a bi-national state."

"Arab-Jewish?"

"Israeli-Palestinian."

"What's the difference?" growled the Foreign Minister impatiently.

"All the difference in the world, as far as they're concerned. It's the specifics of each they concentrate on. They make a complete distinction between Israeli and Jewish, and between Palestinian and Arab. The whole thing rests on the land of Israel belonging to those who were born and bred here."

"From which of those groups are the hijackers?" asked the Prime Minister.

"Both."

The Prime Minister ran his fingers through his thinning hair. "That makes matters even more complicated. Israelis among the hijackers, and all the hostages are foreign. What a combination!" He got out of his chair. "How much time do we have?"

"There is no doubt in my mind that the timing of the hijacking is not accidental. They are aiming at the Presidential convention, which takes place in three days."

The Foreign Minister removed his glasses and wiped his forehead with a handkerchief. "What choice do we have? Gentlemen, on this occasion, we aren't considering Israeli hostages. We are talking about foreigners. Americans!"

The room was silent. Lieberman was aware of the meaning behind the man's words, the tense atmosphere in the office. In effect, his colleagues had already made their decision.

The trouble was that Lieberman had no alternative at this moment. All he had was his gut feeling that under no circumstances must they capitulate to the terrorists' blackmail. They had not done so with Entebbe; they must not do so in this instance. Israel could not afford the luxury of capitulation, because its most effective weapon was its aura of invincibility. This aura had already been seriously damaged by the Yom Kippur War. Now it had to be restored.

Lieberman bore no grudge against his companions. He was aware of the difficulties no less than they. Of course the problems were enormous.

The United States and other countries would bring tremendous pressure to bear, and a rift with the United States could have disastrous effects.

"What do you propose?" Lieberman asked the Foreign Minister, mainly to gain time to think.

"We must give in to all their demands. Without delay. Before we enter into a confrontation with the United States."

"What do you say?" the Prime Minister asked Lieberman, who did not avert his gaze.

"I think we have to deal with the demands separately."

"Why?"

"I don't know," said Lieberman honestly. "That's why I need time."

The Prime Minister smiled, but Lieberman's reply angered the Foreign Minister even further. "The Americans want to know our position immediately. Not tomorrow, but right now. Doron sounded hysterical."

"There's no need for you to follow his example."

The Prime Minister's voice was icy, and the Foreign Minister sat down again. "Go on," he told Lieberman.

"We can take advantage of the demand for a joint communiqué and start negotiations. I don't see any difficulty in dragging it out for a while. No one will be very much harmed by fasting for a few days."

"What are you talking about?" shouted the Foreign Minister. "Do you think everyone is stupid?" He was on his feet again. "The Americans will draw up the joint communiqué and we and the Arabs will be told to sign it as it stands. The Arabs will probably sign without any delay to get the terrorist back. What happens then?"

"We will take the communiqué seriously."

The Foreign Minister shrugged helplessly and slumped back into his seat. There was a moment's silence, which was broken by the Prime Minister's deep voice. "And what then?"

Lieberman knew that he had won the first round. The Prime Minister was already inclined to agree to a strategy of gaining time.

"We might succeed in freeing the hostages."

This time, all glances were directed at the commander-in-chief of the Israeli Defense Forces.

"Prospects of success of a military operation are very slim," he said in his slow, quiet voice. "There are two reasons. First, the Swiss government will never permit it. My understanding is—" he glanced at the Foreign Minister—"my understanding is that we won't be able, nor will we desire, to treat Switzerland the way we treated Idi Amin."

"Definitely not!" the Foreign Minister concurred.

"Secondly, without the cooperation of the Swiss, our modes of operation would be severely restricted. Nowadays, the hijackers expect some kind of operation, so that there's considerable risk in any attempt. Many persons are liable to lose their lives. These people may say they're non-violent, but my report confirms that the boat is completely wired with plastique."

"Americans!" cried the Foreign Minister, waving his hand. "Let us not forget that most of them are Americans."

"American blood is no dearer or cheaper than Israeli blood," said the Prime Minister angrily. Then he stopped himself. "I'm sorry, that was unfair." The Israeli government had the right to endanger the lives of its own citizens, but it had no moral right to risk the lives of foreign nationals. "Well, actually," he added reflectively, "to tell the truth, I am inclined to agree with you. We don't have any choice. It seems that we are all in agreement. Accordingly, I propose that we now decide. . . ."

"We can't decide now."

Lieberman's voice was quiet, but his tone made the Prime Minister pause and turn around.

"Why not?"

"Because they want Maruan Awad. All the rest is of little interest to them, or at least to the woman."

"That merely makes the whole matter easier," said the Foreign Minister gleefully. "One terrorist! We'll let 'em have Awad."

"That's precisely what we can't let them have."

"Why?" the Foreign Minister demanded.

Lieberman did not reply. He just looked at the Prime Minister and then at the Defense Minister, who blurted out: "Oh God!"

"He's still alive, I hope," said the Prime Minister.

Lieberman nodded.

"Can you . . . er . . . do anything to . . . rectify his condition?"

"I don't know."

The Prime Minister glanced at the Foreign Minister. "You'd better get set for most detailed negotiations about the joint communiqué."

"It'll be a farce."

"As long as it drags on."

"The Americans won't be amused."

The Prime Minister turned to Lieberman. "You have a little time now. See what you can do about Awad."

Every inch of Awad's body was on fire. But the most terrible pain came from within. From his mind. His soul.

For two years, he managed to keep out of everyone's reach, thanks to his adherence to two strict rules: he never stayed too long in one place, and he was meticulous in selecting his close associates. He had abandoned one of those rules, and he had been caught. Deborah Rimon was an Israeli Jew. Only an utter fool could have deluded himself into believing that she was genuinely in love with him and that she really cared about the Palestinians.

It was this thought that tortured him the most, more than the parts of his body which had been wracked with pain for days from the techniques they had used on him. He had trusted that woman. He had trusted her, that Jewish whore, and she had betrayed him.

"How long has he been in this state?"

Lieberman stood over Awad, who was lying on the floor, his body twisted into an unnatural shape. He was holding his penis with both hands as he cried out in agony.

"Four or five days," said the warden.

"Has the doctor seen him?"

"Yes. He gave him some medication, which we administer every four hours."

"Foods?"

"Liquids. He can't take solid food."

"Will he recover?"

"The doctor claims he'll be all right in a day or two, provided we don't touch him."

"I see," Lieberman said.

Then he moved closer to Awad, until his shoes almost touched the prisoner's abdomen. Awad looked up at him in a supreme, yet futile, effort to hide the fear in his eyes.

Lieberman lifted his right foot and slowly, gently, moved it along Awad's body. First over the thick, muscular leg; then over the hip, the abdomen, the chest; and when he reached the hand, he suddenly thought, *This is the hand that cut off Gideon's limbs. And these are the eyes that stared at Gideon's face while he made each cut in his flesh, delivered each blow to his body.*

Lieberman removed his foot and placed it on the floor, taking a small step backward. "Do you remember the officer you killed on the Hermon?" he asked quietly.

Awad did not reply.

"Of course you remember," said Lieberman. "You amputated his hand. Cut off his legs. Severed his genitals. Of course you remember."

Awad continued to lie still.

"That officer had one great ambition," Lieberman continued, as though to himself. "He wanted peace. He thought you were human beings. He didn't know that you were vicious animals. But you and I know, don't we, Awad? You and I know the truth."

Awad's lips move slightly. "I . . . don't . . . remember . . . an officer. . . ."

The guard moved back in bewilderment as Lieberman's foot crashed into Awad's stomach. Awad emitted a terrible scream; his body contracted as though Lieberman had hit a spring hidden in his gut. Slowly, with heavy sighs, the body returned to its former shape.

The guard approached Lieberman and touched his arm. "The doctor said that . . ."

"I heard what the doctor said!" replied Lieberman, pulling back his arm. His eyes didn't budge from the prisoner.

"You don't even remember, Awad? You cut off a man's limbs and you don't even remember?"

Awad no longer made any effort to conceal the fear in his wide-open eyes.

"It was . . . a war . . . a long time ago. . . . I don't. . . ."

Lieberman's foot swung again, but this time it landed on Awad's face, and the guard expected to see the head dislocate from the shoulders. Blood streamed from Awad's mouth. And then his hands began to grope, as though in the dark, searching for support on the floor. He turned over on his stomach and tried to stand up. His first attempt resulted in his falling back on his face, but on the second attempt he managed to rise on all fours. He turned toward Lieberman and his eyes, which were blinded by blood, met Lieberman's steady, cold gaze. Then, with a supreme effort, he spat out a thick mixture of saliva and blood, some drops of which splashed onto Lieberman's leg.

The reaction was quick and accurate. The first kick landed again on Awad's face, but before he fell a second kick hit his chest and a third, his abdomen. Awad's body lay erect, but still, on the ground.

Lieberman took a handkerchief out of his pocket, stooped, and wiped the blood off his shoes. He then threw the handkerchief on Awad's body. "You should remember," he muttered to the silent body. "I'll make sure that you remember, like I do."

The guard bent over the prisoner's body and moved Awad's eyelid. "He's lost consciousness," he said. "I better call the doctor."

"Don't call anyone," ordered Lieberman.

"But he . . ."

"You heard what I said!"

"Yes, sir."

The guard rose to his feet and walked toward the door. Before he closed it, he turned and threw another glance at Awad. "If he does recover, it will take at least a few weeks."

Lieberman walked out of the cell. *As long as it takes more than four days*, he thought, I'm safe.

Lieberman left the isolated prison and had his driver take him to his small apartment in north Tel Aviv. His wife, Rivka, was sitting in front of the television set listening to the ten o'clock news when he walked in. With-out glancing at her husband, she asked in a toneless voice, "Do you want something to eat?"

"I'm not hungry."

The conversation ended there, as it did most even-ings. In the morning when they awakened, it was easier, somehow, to go about their ablutions and exchange a few words, but at night, the time that used to be theirs to share after Gideon was grown, they could not manage to speak to each other about anything. The rift had occurred when their son was killed, and both of them were aware of that. It wasn't as if they hadn't tried. God, had they tried in that first week. They wanted so desperately to comfort each other, and yet, it seemed their grief was too powerful to be shared. Each of them retreated into a somber corner, and within a month, there was an impenetrable wall between them. Gideon was gone, and so was their marriage.

Surely there had been something else that had bound them once. There must have been something other than their son which had maintained the link between them for twenty-eight years. Rivka spent hours trying to recall the time before she was pregnant, when Moshe was in the army and they struggled on his small salary. Surely they had laughed then, made love, and enjoyed the days they spent together. Perhaps, but now it was irrelevant. Over the years, they had undoubtedly shared numerous things which had nothing to do with Gideon. But when he was killed, nothing else seemed important. And Moshe himself had changed. He was harder now; there was a look in his eyes that made Rivka shiver. He seemed to see through her, searching beyond his own life to get back something he knew he could never recover. He craved vengeance. She recognized this, and she hated the craving for what it had done to him.

Lieberman walked through the living room to the bathroom. He opened the medicine cabinet and gulped down two sleeping pills. It had begun eight years ago with half a pill, which became a whole pill when Gideon was killed. Now, two pills did not always work.

"Are you coming to bed?" he called to her.

"I'll stay up a little longer."

A polite answer to a polite question. No more. Certainly there was no implied suggestion of sex between them. All that died on the Hermon with their son. They had tried it a few times, but one night Rivka had turned to him, sighing, and had said, "I'm sorry. I don't enjoy it any more." Then she had added, "I won't mind if you get it somewhere else."

He did not protest, nor did he look for it elsewhere. He had another need now, more visceral and vital than food or sex. His work became everything for him: home, wife, pleasure, suffering. Rivka was only a relic, an old reminder of a life he had once lived.

The more he tried to fall asleep, the less he succeeded. This night resembled scores of other nights which had preceded it. After half an hour, he conceded defeat. Turning on his bedside lamp, he picked up a cigarette and lit it. He stopped trying to subdue the thought which gave him no rest: since Awad could not be ready soon—he had made sure of that—some other alternative would be needed.

He picked up the green phone by his bedside. Almost instantaneously, he heard the voice of the duty officer at his headquarters. In a monotonous voice, Lieberman gave him a list of instructions, to be executed without delay.

CHAPTER 17

"MOM, WHAT IS IT? What's with Jimmy?" Eli touched his brother's forehead. "He's real hot." Eli's eyes were frightened.

"Yes, hon. He's got a high fever." Susan held Jimmy in her lap and comforted him. Eli wrapped himself in a blanket and huddled next to his mother, wondering what was going to happen next.

Deborah handed Nabil the binoculars and stretched. She was tired, terribly tired. An hour ago, she had shut her eyes for a while, but could not sleep. She'd decided that she was not cut out to spend a long time on a boat; the vessel's bobbing made her feel sick and weak.

She was peripherally aware of a child whimpering. Every bit of her body was strung tight, hypersensitive to the slightest sound. The child made it impossible for her to concentrate.

She strode out onto the deck. "What's the matter now?" she asked Susan. "Why can't you keep him quiet?" Susan shifted her body swiftly, as if to protect her child from any threat.

"He's uncomfortable and thirsty," she answered angrily. "It's literally physically painful for him to go without food for this length of time. I'm aware you have no concern for human needs, though, so I wouldn't expect you to understand."

"I don't intend to do him any harm. I'm truly sorry he's in pain."

"I see. Would you care to feel his forehead? He's running a very high fever," said Susan, testing.

Deborah stretched out a hand and placed it on the baby's head. He was burning up. She turned and pointed at Eli. "Is he yours too?" Susan nodded. "Where's your husband?"

"I'm a widow," Susan said without a pause.

Deborah bit her lip. What kind of person was she anyway? Surely she was not capable of putting a helpless infant's life in danger. "Don't worry," she said at last. "Everything is going to be all right. I'll be back in a minute."

She practically ran to the steering cabin and braced herself on the door frame. "Nabil, Yoram."

The two men joined her, keeping their eyes on the passengers as they shifted positions.

"We've got a very sick child here," Deborah whispered.

"Right," said Nabil. "So what do you suggest? Would you like to call the whole thing off?"

"What can we do?" asked Yoram hesitantly.

"We have no choice. We have to let the baby off, and his mother."

"I'm against it," said Nabil brusquely. "First, a sick kid is a good drawing card for us. And I'm concerned about the mother." He turned on Deborah fiercely. "You know how it is. She'll tell them what's happening here."

"How can that be of any use to them?"

"I don't know. But the fact is that in every case like this it has backfired. Every time. Haven't you learned a thing?"

Deborah glanced at the passengers and then at Yoram. His face was expressionless. Maybe Nabil was right; maybe it could be harmful. Still, she was not a machine, she had some feelings.

"Suppose the kid dies?" she pondered, wondering what could convince the men. "We'll lose the last shred of goodwill we may still have. That's Susan Kraft's child."

"All right," Nabil sneered. "Have it your way. We let the two of them go." Yoram hesitated, then nodded.

Deborah picked up the bullhorn and stepped over to the railing. "Hello Geneva, hello Geneva."

The reply came after a few seconds in a heavy French accent.

"We hear you."

"We have a sick baby on board. We're allowing him and his mother off the boat. Send a dinghy. The dinghy is to stop thirty meters from the boat. We will bring the mother and her baby to that point."

"The dinghy is on its way."

Deborah started for the passenger cabin.

The baby was still howling, as Susan made an attempt to hold him still and change his diapers.

"In a few minutes' time, they'll be coming to collect you and the child," said Deborah with a smile.

"What about my other son?"

"He's staying here!" Deborah snapped, her anger not so much directed at the mother as at herself for being obliged to make this decision.

Eli glanced at Susan and came over to stand next to her.

"I can't do that. I won't leave him." The words were neither a request nor a plea; they were a statement of fact. As she spoke, Susan put her free around the boy, cuddling him against her.

"I don't think the baby will survive if he stays here," Deborah protested softly. "His temperature is very high."

"I can't leave Eli," said Susan decisively.

Deborah sat down on the arm of the bench and bent forward, speaking in a whisper. "Look, I would gladly let the boy go, but it doesn't depend on me alone. I had enough difficulty getting you and the baby off. There's no hope that the others will consent to let your other son go. So—" she hesitated, and then added—"do me a favor, don't be difficult."

Susan stared at Deborah, trying to assess her intention. Was it conceivable? Was this woman really what she appeared? Could she actually combine a capacity for kidnapping and terrorism with feelings of tenderness?

Susan gazed at Eli, tears springing to her eyes despite her efforts to remain calm. "Do you understand what it's all about?" she asked tenderly.

The boy nodded solemnly.

"It's your decision, then," she said. "You know that Jimmy is very sick. But if you tell me to stay, I'll stay."

"You go. You have to. I'll be okay," Eli told her in a broken voice.

Hugging him to her and pressing her lips to his forehead, Susan let the tears come. She heard the wailing siren of an ambulance from far away on the shore.

"The dinghy's coming," Deborah said, taking Susan's arm. She gathered Jimmy close and followed Deborah to the forward deck. As they climbed down the rope ladder, Susan glanced back at Eli, standing silent and alone, trying not to seem scared as his mother was taken away from him, perhaps forever. She forced herself to look away.

Deborah returned to the passengers' cabin to make sure everything was in order. As she passed among the benches, she suddenly felt a hand seize her arm.

A man was leaning forward in his seat, half doubled over. "I wanted to tell you that you did a fine thing just now. Really fine. But I have a terrible stomach-ache, miss, and I know I have a high fever."

Deborah stared down at him. His face was twisted with self-pity. As though of its own accord, her right hand came up and landed a powerful blow on the man's chin. She put everything into that blow: her weariness, her passion, and her yearnings. But it brought her no release. She returned to her post in the steering cabin, and when she shut her eyes she felt big warm tears begin to run down her face and she had neither the strength nor the will to stop them.

Afterward, she felt relieved, as if she had gotten rid of some of the terror and hatred in her system. But then Nabil came in with Yoram moments later, and he started in with his criticism again.

"It was a mistake," he said, shaking his head. She looked up and stared at him blankly.

"He's right," Yoram chimed in. "We should have had the courage of our convictions."

"Courage," Deborah laughed mirthlessly. "You're one to talk. Tell me, how *did* you manage to survive the Hermon?"

His handsome face clouded, and he turned away.

CHAPTER 18

OLD ABRAM LEVENSTEIN walked slowly up to the brightly lit entrance of the imposing green house. He wasn't looking forward to this gathering. Usually nothing would tempt him to walk into a house full of strangers. Today of all days he wanted to be alone, to bear in private the shock and sorrow of the news about his son in Geneva. But the woman who had called to invite him to a meeting of the hostages' families had persuaded Levenstein that he should be better informed about the hijacking and that it was up to the hostages' relatives to "do something about it." So Levenstein had decided it was his duty to make the trip.

By ten past eight that evening, the front hall of John Morrison's house was filled to overflowing. In the center of the room, rows of chairs faced a rectangular table standing beneath an enormous painting of a sailing vessel; three additional chairs placed behind the table faced into the room.

When Abram Levenstein walked in, he failed to find a single vacant seat; embarrassed, he remained standing, leaning on his cane. An observant servant noticed the old man and hurried to an adjoining room to bring an armchair. Gratefully, Levenstein slumped into it.

He was seventy-three. At his time of life, he had not expected his peaceful routine to be disrupted by a drama of this nature. His wife had died three years previously. Ever since, his sole support in life came from his only son, his daughter-in-law, and their two children. He had seen them off two weeks ago on a lengthy tour of Europe. One day after getting a postcard they had sent from Geneva, he read the newspaper account of the boat hijacking. It never occurred to him that there could be any link between this incident and his own family, and he did not read the report very carefully. It was one of his neighbors who asked him later that evening if David Levenstein was not, by any chance, his son. A few hours later, he got Frances Morrison's phone call.

A handsome, well-dressed man with the air of a successful executive now arose from behind the table. The room fell silent. "Ladies and gentlemen," he addressed them, "my name is John Morrison. I want to thank you for coming." His deep voice was quiet and matter-of-fact, and everyone listened attentively. "I don't know how you feel at this moment. I feel that these unfortunate circumstances have made us all into one big family with one big concern."

Levenstein had to strain to hear, but he distinctly caught the word "family," and it bothered him. The people in this room—blacks, goyim—were not related to him. He had nothing against them, but neither did he feel anything for them. They were casual acquaintances, no more.

"There's no need to explain the purpose of this meeting," Morrison continued. "Several days have passed since our relatives, including my nephew, were taken captive, and they are in increasing peril with every passing hour. The Israeli government refuses to concede to the hijackers' demands, and I don't think that our government is doing as much as it should to get the hostages back."

Levenstein stood up and walked forward five rows. He wanted to be certain that he was hearing properly. What was the connection between the government and his family? What was this "increasing peril" the man had mentioned? Were things as bad as all that? Of course, he knew that the situation was grave, but to hear it like this. . . . Levenstein did not like the whole thing. He was used to keeping such matters to himself; at most, he would confide them to his Maker. But expressed in public, and with such pathos, it sounded rather, well, commercialized. Perhaps it was the atmosphere. The stifled sobs. Yes, in Poland such an atmosphere was the prelude to a pogrom. And even though Mr. Morrison did not say a single word about the Jews, Levenstein felt it coming.

Morrison's tone now became practical. "My friends, if we don't take action, no one else will do it for us. We are the people the hostages are relying on. We cannot—we dare not—rely on our government alone in this matter. We certainly can't rely on a foreign government."

A woman's sobbing voice broke the silence. "Those damn Israelis! They're playing with our children's lives!" The room erupted. Shouts mingled with one another, fists were brandished, faces contorted. Morrison banged the table loudly, trying to restore order.

There were a few moments of readjustment as people tried to control themselves. In the ensuing silence, everyone could hear the tearful mumbling of a middle-aged woman. "They'll never get out of there alive."

"We are not helpless," Morrison assured them, "if we act in unison. I myself have thought of some actions which may do some good. But first, I propose that we elect one of the group to be in charge and to act as our representative."

A middle-aged woman stood up. "I nominate John Morrison. He's better informed than any of us. Who's in favor of Mr. Morrison?" Everyone raised his hand. Morrison was about to speak, when Levenstein stood up and said hoarsely, "Wouldn't it be better to elect a larger body—three people, say?"

Levenstein was astounded at his own daring. He had never before addressed an assembly of strangers, but he was horrified by what was happening and he spoke as though driven by an inner force. He sat down again, overcome by the weariness of a man who had broken out of his characteristic role.

Morrison's voice was considerate. "What is your name, sir?"

"Levenstein," the old man replied hesitantly. "Abram Levenstein."

Morrison cleared his throat and pronounced the name, stressing every syllable. "A-bram Lev-en-stein." He paused. "Mr. Levenstein, I don't think we want top-heavy committees. Our sole concern is to save the hostages."

A loud bass voice rose from the back of the room. "We certainly don't want any Jew in on this affair!" Instantaneously, everyone in the room was on his feet, yelling.

"We care about the hostages just as much as you do!"

"What is this, segregation?"

"If they kill anybody, they'll kill the Jews first!"

"You people only care about Israel!"

"Please! Please!" cried Morrison. "We must avoid any controversy among ourselves. But—" and he turned to face the old man,—"Mr. Levenstein, I think you'll agree with me that under these particular circumstances, it would not be sensible for . . . er . . . well . . . Jews to take part in the action."

The old man's voice was weak and puzzled. "Jews? The Israelis say I'm an American. And you call me a Jew. I've been living in this country for forty years!"

"I have no doubt about that. But Mr. Levenstein, these circumstances are exceptional. Too many lives are at stake. And those lives depend, to a great degree, on the behavior of the Israeli government. Please believe me when I say that it's for your own good. I feel that when Israel is involved . . . well. . . ."

Levenstein did not hear the end of his sentence because of the din in his ears. With every remaining ounce of strength, he shouted, "I'm an American! My son, my daughter-in-law, and my two grandchildren are all on the boat!"

He fell back into his chair, completely spent. He sat there just a moment to recover, then picked up his cane and made for the door. Another guest rose to offer a hand, but Levenstein shook him off. He walked out, shutting the door hard behind him.

Once safely home, Levenstein lay in his bed, trying to forget the evening's unpleasantness. But he couldn't, and many hours passed before he slept.

CHAPTER 19

AT 7:33 A.M. LIEBERMAN SAT down at his desk and glanced through the files lying neatly on the brown desktop. What he read satisfied him that the duty officer had carried out his instructions efficiently.

The desk contained three sets of files, papers, and photographs. The first set contained a list of the hostages, with a few brief additional details such as marital status, age, and former names, if any. In the center were the names and photos of the hijackers. To the left, information about Geneva—every tree, every road, every building—and the precise position of the boat.

He began on the left with a detailed description of the Palais des Nations. He leafed through it absentmindedly and laid it aside. Then there was the airport, the mausoleum of the Duke of Brunswick, the flower clock near the lake, the *jet d'eau*, the Russian Orthodox church, the Einerfade Palace. All this was of no interest.

The picture of the boat was somewhat murky and blurred. But it sufficed to pinpoint the precise position of the vessel. In the background, white stone buildings—apartment blocks, apparently—showed up clearly; in the distance on both sides, snow-covered mountains.

There was nothing else of note in the photograph, but Lieberman continued gazing at it because it looked familiar. He leafed through the photographs he had studied earlier. *That's it: the* jet d'eau. The same buildings, the same snow-covered mountains. Placing the two photographs on top of one another, he opened up the middle drawer and took out a magnifying glass. From the right-hand drawer, he produced a ruler and a red pencil and began drawing straight lines on both pictures. When he finished, he again submitted both pictures to a close scrutiny through the magnifying glass. He smiled. There could be no doubt about it. The boat was anchored precisely at, or very close to, the spot where the fountain spurted up. The fountain was not functioning when the boat was photographed.

Lieberman was so immersed in what he was doing that he did not hear his secretary until she addressed him for a third time. He lifted his head.

"I'm sorry," she said.

"That's all right. What's the matter?"

"The Prime Minister. He wants you to come instantly."

"Okay. Get Porat."

Several minutes later Porat entered. Lieberman handed him the photographs. "The fountain?" Porat asked.

"Exactly. The *jet d'eau.* Find out what happened."

"Yes."

Porat left the room and Lieberman returned to his desk. He quickly leafed through the other documents. Pictures of the hijackers. Nabil Butrus. Deborah Rimon. Yoram Negbi.

His glance lingered on the last snapshot. Something stirred in his memory. He could have asked for additional information, but there was no time for that now.

Lieberman picked out several of the papers and photographs, slipped them into his attaché case, and walked out of the office. His car was waiting beside the exit, and he climbed in and sank into the back seat. On the way to Jerusalem, he would have forty-five minutes at his disposal, without interruption. He opened his briefcase and pulled out the list of hostages, reading the dull, routine information yet again. Sometimes one line or just a word could make the effort worthwhile.

He found nothing of any use in the list of hostages. Below the list there was the blurred photograph of Susan Kraft being released from the boat. The picture was attached to a report from the Israeli delegate to the UN bodies in Geneva. He wrote that he had attempted to perform the task with which Lieberman had charged him. Immediately after the woman's release, he had tried to meet her, so as to learn everything possible about what was happening on board the boat. After great difficulties, he managed to get near her, but she adamantly refused to talk. The envoy reported that she repeated over and over again, "I have another child on that boat."

From the report, Lieberman went back for another look at the photograph. Susan Kraft. American. Thirty-five years old. Executive, VP of RDP Broadcasting. Widowed. Mother of two children. Address: Manhattan, New York. Maiden name: Kingsley. Security check completed 1972. And then, inside brackets, in small letters: "See Eli Goren file."

Lieberman picked up the receiver of the car's telephone. Instantly, he heard his secretary's voice. "The Eli Goren file," he said.

Two minutes later, he heard his secretary's voice again. "It's here in front of me."

"Susan Kraft."

She leafed through the file.

"Yes. Chicago. Her name was Kingsley then."

"Get me the Prime Minister."

He heard a ring and then the voice of the secretary followed by the Prime Minister's familiar brisk tone.

"Where are you? We're waiting for you."

"I can't come. I propose that we meet this evening."

There was a brief silence.

"Is ten all right?"

"Excellent."

"Something new?"

"Maybe. Be seeing you."

Lieberman put down the receiver and spoke to the driver. "Do you know the Delek filling station near Herzlia?"

"Just before the lights?"

"Yes."

At the next intersection, the driver swung the car around and headed in the opposite direction.

There were two cars parked at the Delek filling station outside Herzlia. Lieberman's car drove past them and pulled up outside the office. From his seat, Lieberman could see the head of Eli Goren, bent over his desk. *He's going gray,* Lieberman thought to himself, touching his hair and smoothing it back.

He walked into the office. When Goren lifted his head, Lieberman could read the ambivalence in the man's face. Aside from his pleasure at seeing an old friend, there were the suspicious questions: *What's he doing here? What does he want?*

"You work too much," said Lieberman.

"So do you."

"I'm not working now."

"You're always working."

Goren stood up and grasped Lieberman's outstretched hand. They walked out of the office, savoring the warm sun.

"Don't you miss us?" Lieberman asked.

"Like I miss a hole in the head."

"You're really content? With this?" He waved at the fuel pumps.

"No. But I'm very contented with that thing." Goren smiled as he pointed at the cash register.

"How are the kids?"

"Terrific."

"Miriam?"

"Fine, fine."

"We need you."

There was a moment's silence. Finally, Goren asked, "How long is it since we last met?"

"Six years. Seven, maybe."

"Come with me. There's something I want to show you."

Lieberman got into the back seat of his car, and Goren followed.

"Where to?" the driver asked.

"I'll direct you," said Goren.

After a ten-minute drive, Goren told the driver to pull up. They were on the road which ran along the shore, but the sea could not be seen from where they were parked, the view blocked by an enormous picturesque house. It was light brown, with a red-tiled roof. The large tract of land around the house was enclosed by a green stone wall.

"Now what?" asked Lieberman.

"Do you know what this is?"

"A house."

"No, my house."

"Very nice," said Lieberman, genuinely respectful.

Goren laughed silently. "Much more than nice, Moshe. Construction was completed six months ago. It's a palace. Swimming pool at the back, greenhouse on the side over there."

"Elegant."

"In the basement, I have a billiard room, an exercise room, and a Ping-Pong table."

"I'm impressed."

"There's a color TV in every room. A quadro system. All the furniture is imported from Scandinavia."

"Yes . . ."

"This is something you don't give up, Moshe. Something with no risks involved."

"As I said, we need you."

"As you can see, I don't need you."

Goren lowered his eyes a little, to meet Lieberman's gaze. "I took part in three wars, while other men stayed home and made money. I went on seven missions abroad while other men continued making money. At first, there was at least the compensation of being a hero. Then they made me into a *shlemiel*, a square. What happened? Did I change? Did the jobs change?" He smiled. "The country's changed. Values have changed."

He broke off, breathing deeply. His voice was relaxed. "So I've also changed. And made a success of it. I've got all the money I need to live out my life in honor and comfort. I have time to spend with my family now. The only worry I have is looking left and right when I cross the street. Do you know how long it took me to get used to not having to look behind me as well?"

"I can imagine."

Goren laid a friendly hand on Lieberman's shoulder. "That's right. You still have to look behind you. Come and join me. We can work together."

Lieberman smiled. "Somebody has to take care of the state surrounding your garden."

"Somebody else."

"That's the trouble. There are so few who can. Fewer every day."

"Moshe, I am thirty-seven. How many more years do I have? I want to live them, and I want to live them well."

There was another silence. Cars drove past. Half to himself, half to Lieberman, Goren said, "Don't you understand? Don't you understand that nobody cares any more?"

"You don't really believe that."

"You're a lost cause."

The sun was hurting Lieberman's eyes, and he turned away from it.

"Without you, this thing has no chance."

"I'm not the only man who served with the naval commandos as well as the Secret Service."

Lieberman chuckled. He was not surprised that Goren connected his visit with the boat in Geneva. "You're the only one I can genuinely use here."

"Sorry. That's no problem of mine."

He was about to go into the house, when Lieberman grabbed his arm. "But this *is* a problem of yours."

Goren looked on curiously as Lieberman reached into

his jacket pocket and brought out a photograph, which he held out to Goren. Goren gazed at the picture and crinkled up his eyes. Then he threw an angry glance at Lieberman.

"It's a lousy picture," he whispered.

"She was on the boat," said Lieberman.

"She *was* on the boat?"

"Yes. She and her baby have been released."

A look of pain flashed across Goren's face, but he hurriedly replaced it with one of unconcern.

"In that case, everything's all right."

"Her older boy remained behind on the boat."

"She has another son?"

"About thirteen years old."

"That's a pity. But there's no change in my answer." Goren turned and began to walk away.

"His name is Eli," said Lieberman.

Goren halted. "Whose name?"

"The child's."

Goren's leap was so swift that Lieberman's driver, who never took his eyes off his superior, was late in observing it. He only grasped what was happening when Goren's hands were already gripping Lieberman's throat. The driver leapt from the car and knocked Goren to the ground.

"That's enough!"

The driver's hand froze. He stood up.

"Are you all right, sir?"

"You can go back to the car."

The driver glanced at Goren, who was picking himself up.

"But—"

"Go back to the car!"

Goren dusted himself off, as if in a daze.

"Why Eli?" he asked, as though nothing had happened.

"Don't know."

"Do you have a plan?"

"Glimmerings."

They began to walk, with Lieberman talking and

Goren listening. After Lieberman finished, Goren started in. Every now and then, Lieberman nodded his head in agreement.

"I like the look of it," said Lieberman finally.

"I'm crazy," said Goren sadly.

"Can you leave right away?"

Goren glanced at his watch. "Two hours."

"Come to the Sdeh Dov airfield. A special plane will be waiting."

Lieberman got into his car, which pulled away instantly. Goren remained standing, gazing after him. Then he looked at the photograph he was still holding. "You damn bastard," he whispered. "Damn foolish bastard."

Only after the car disappeared from sight did Goren move. Producing a bunch of keys, he opened the steel gate. A German shepherd ran up, leaping happily at his chest. Goren entered the house, with the dog at his heels. Just as he was about to hang up his coat, his wife, Miriam, appeared and kissed him lightly on the cheek.

"Why are you so late?"

"I was doing accounts."

"Who was that?"

He was surprised. "Who do you mean?"

"I saw you standing outside with somebody."

"Oh, Lieberman. Is there anything for your starving husband?"

He walked into the kitchen, evading her eyes.

"Moshe Lieberman?" Goren was silent. "What did he want?" she asked, her voice chilly.

Goren did not understand his own reaction. "I want something to eat!" he yelled in a rage.

Miriam's face remained impassive, and her voice was scarcely audible. "I want to know what he wanted, and what you told him. And I want to know right now."

A chubby six-year-old with a flushed face ran in, his large school satchel still on his shoulders. He flung the satchel down and proclaimed, "I could eat a whole cow."

Goren seized the opportunity for a diversion. Picking his son up, he planted a resounding kiss on his cheek. "Why are you so red in the face?"

"We had physical training."

They ate their lunch in silence. "I'm going out on my bike," said the boy when he had finished. Before anyone had time to reply, he was outside.

The moment she heard the front door bang, Miriam raised her eyes. "That was no ordinary promise you gave me and the children."

"I know."

"If you break that promise, we'll leave you."

He did not reply. She stood up. He heard her steps on the stairs, and then he heard the bedroom door close. He picked up a slice of bread, but his hand froze halfway to his mouth. Laying down the bread, he stood up and walked into the lounge, settling down in his favorite armchair.

From here, a glance through the great glass door showed a vast expanse of sea, more than the eye could scan. Together with the incessant roar of the waves and the whistling breeze, it all combined into a rich symphony of sight and sound. He could always sit here, think, and take it all in. He was comforted by the reassuring caress of waves, sky, and wind.

Of course, Miriam was right. His promise was the foundation for their marriage, the motivation for their survival as a family. He had given it to her after she presented her ultimatum: leave the service or we divorce. She told him that she was not prepared to live with a man who vanished for weeks and months—or, as occurred the last time, for a year and a half. Without his promise to leave the service and never rejoin, she would not remain with him, nor would she bear his children.

When he gave her all the assurances she asked for, she was uncertain whether or not to rejoice. It was so easy. Too easy. She suspected that he held some link with his prolonged sojourn in the United States. But she never dared ask, and in the course of time, she mellowed, although she never entirely forgot. Eli kept his promise. On several occasions, he even said that he was grateful to her for getting him to leave the service.

Goren rubbed his eyes, listening to the sounds of his home: his son Dror outside on his bicycle, three-year-old

Dalia turning over in her cot. And this house. And the station. And Miriam.

Hoisting himself out of his armchair, he went back into the kitchen. There was a smooth white board for messages on the wall. Goren picked up the black pencil attached to it. In large letters, he scrawled one word. Then he walked out.

In the bedroom, Miriam heard the car start. She raced down the stairs to the kitchen door. There, on the board, she saw the one word she had feared all these years.

"Sorry."

CHAPTER 20

MARTIN SILVER and Ronald Taylor met Israeli Ambassador Doron at the eastern entrance to the White House. The three men made their way quickly to the Oval Office, a herd of journalists following closely at their heels.

The President welcomed Doron with a warm smile and recited the ritual slogans about the United State's commitment to Israel's security and welfare. The moment the last photographer left the room, Kelly's smile vanished. He regarded Doron with a severe expression.

"Mr. Doron, let me come straight to the point. We want to know why your government is delaying its decision. American lives are in danger. Where does the Israeli government stand on this?"

"There is no decision yet."

"What do you mean, no decision?" said Taylor. "What are you people waiting for? Are you considering a military operation?"

(157)

"All I can say right now is that we still have time."

"What difference does that make? What do you need time for, anyway?"

"We need time to think," replied Doron quietly.

"About a military operation?" asked Silver.

Doron sounded apologetic as he answered, "I'm sorry. All I can say at this stage is that we're thinking."

The President got out of his chair and began pacing around the room. Suppose the situation did become dangerous. No one could guarantee that these unpredictable people would maintain their non-violent stance. There could be shooting, bloodshed, gigantic headlines. Reports were already pouring in about the demonstrations around the country. If this continued, Kelly knew what the outcome would be. His rival, Senator Timothy Marsden, would deliver an acceptance speech after winning the nomination for President.

He wheeled around in front of Doron. "That's out of the question, do you hear? I won't permit you people to risk American lives. I demand that you announce your acceptance of the hijackers' demands. I want that announcement within the next twenty-four hours!" His face was white as he swung around and marched out of the room.

Taylor took off his glasses and polished them on his handkerchief. Silver slowly hoisted himself out of his seat. He stood hovering over Doron. "It's about time you realized that Israel is not a United States protectorate," he said evenly. "It was perfectly all right to act like heroes at home, on your own turf, when you were dealing with the lives of your own people. You may need that kind of—" he stumbled over the word, "—of stimulation. You may even like it."

"We dislike it as much as you do," Doron answered. "But we have fewer options than you."

Silver brushed away the explanation. "Whatever the reason, you heard the President's ultimatum. This situation is different."

"It's the same as all the others," Doron rebutted. "Terrorists grab hostages. Period. If you give in, there'll be no end to it."

"So you *are* preparing some military action!" said Silver, his voice half-threatening, half-questioning.

"We are thinking."

"This is infuriating," said Silver.

Taylor rose from his seat. "We're going around in circles. Can we at least receive your assurance that you will do nothing without consulting us beforehand?"

Silver gave a short laugh. "Will you believe them if they do promise?"

Doron's voice was low, almost inaudible, but he stressed each word. "Coming from anyone else," said the Israeli ambassador, "I would take that as an anti-Semitic remark."

"Don't you criticize me!" shouted Silver. "We've seen your press statements. 'Frequent consultations with the United States.' What consultations? We talk and you don't listen. The only answer we get from you is that you're thinking. Listen," he said, lowering his voice, "I just need to understand one thing. Are you really prepared to disrupt your relationships with us on account of the release of some . . . Maruan Awad? Can you just explain to me why he is more important to you than we are?"

"I've already told you," replied Doron. "Maruan Awad is not in our custody."

"That's a plain lie."

Doron stood up. "I'm not prepared to continue the conversation if you intend to proceed in this manner." He began to walk toward the door, and nearly collided with the President.

"Where are you going?" Kelly demanded. "Have you reached some kind of agreement?"

"He denies that Awad is in Israeli hands," Taylor reported dryly.

The President glared at Doron. "You're playing hide-and-seek. Don't you think it's time to stop?" He turned to Taylor. "Did you give him the statement?"

Taylor thrust his hand into his jacket pocket and brought out a sheet of paper. He handed it to Doron, who sat down and began to read it through.

The heading was: Joint communiqué of the states participating in the Middle East peace conference.

1. The delegations of the states participating in the peace conference hereby proclaim that the conference is dispersed and will not be reconvened.

2. The Middle East peace conference hereby affirms that to the west of the river Jordan there is one single state—the state of Palestine—whose citizens are Israelis and Palestinians.

Taylor handed Doron a pen. "Be so good as to sign."

Doron did not budge. "I must first consult my government."

The President's face flushed. "Consult them? About what?"

"After all, it's purely a stall," Silver protested. "A signature taken under pressure isn't binding."

Doron stood up. "I'm sorry. I am not empowered to sign."

The President walked over to him. His voice was calm and emotionless. "I don't believe a word you're saying. I don't believe in your government's intentions. I warn you! If you do anything—anything at all!—the consequences will be extremely grave. I expect you to announce your consent today. That's final!"

Taylor came over and handed Doron the communiqué. "You'll need it for your—what did you call it?—consultations," he said with an ironic smile.

Doron allowed the sheet of paper to be pressed into his hand, and he hurried from the room.

The President looked at Taylor, then at Silver. "Well, what do you think?"

"I'm with you. He's bluffing."

The President walked slowly back to his desk and sat down. Then he said to Silver, "They're going to try and pull something. I want to know what it is. Martin, go pay a visit to your old friend in the Mossad."

The sandwich on the plane was tasteless. Silver wasn't sure if it was just his mood every time he got in a military aircraft, but somehow the fare seemed worse than on commercial jets. He tried to sleep, but couldn't clear his head sufficiently to let the tiredness take hold. Finally, he just sat, staring out into the billowing white clouds, wondering what in hell he was going to do when he landed in Israel.

A limousine was waiting for him at the military airport. As he settled into the back seat, he swore at himself under his breath. He had vowed, that day years ago, that he would never return to Israel. Once was enough. But the feeling flooded over him again: here you are, Martin, in the land of Zion. What did it mean to him now? No matter how often he asked the question, he couldn't fix on an answer. There were too many answers.

Lieberman looked older, harder to him. As the two men shook hands, Silver was acutely aware of their differences. *The death of his son shows in his face*, he thought.

"You look well, Moshe," he said automatically.

"You're a liar. I do not. Neither do you. I take it your President has been coming down on you pretty hard about our behavior."

Silver was determined to be cool. "I'd like to know what you're up to, Moshe."

Lieberman laughed. "What I'm up to? Well now, who do you think is running this government?"

"I'm not sure, really." Silver paused and then ventured, "Maybe you are."

"Hell no, Mordechai. I'm just an underground operator. The large plans take shape in other offices than this one."

"Listen, Moshe. All this is beside the point. The only thing that really concerns me—and which should concern you and your colleagues—is the safety of the hostages. This hunger strike business is very nice for the international press, but what happens if those terrorists get itchy?"

Lieberman shook his head and pushed away from his desk. "They aren't terrorists, they're children. There's nothing to worry about." He had a sudden, vivid image of Deborah Rimon's frail naked body lying on the bed next to Awad. "They have some vague idealized notion of a Utopian state, a melting pot where racial differences, religious beliefs don't matter. Where wealth is shared and there is no war." He paused. "I believe there were those not too long ago who imagined the United States that way."

Silver was silent. He could see that Lieberman's cynical exterior was no longer a mask, a protective disguise, but truly reflected the man within. "Well," he started on another tack, "I don't have to point out to you that you have made mistakes in the past. Bad ones. You were lucky with Entebbe, but then it was practically set up for you. This is harder. You've got to get eighty people out of a boat in the middle of Lake Geneva, and do it soon."

"You sound like such a rabbi, Mordechai," Lieberman said, smiling. "Our moral responsibilities to eighty people, etc., etc. Well, I am convinced you're worried about only one person on board that boat, the son of a well-known television reporter who will blast you in the media as soon as she gets back on American soil. And when she does that, your President Kelly is President no longer. She will see to it that your ineptness and ours is spread about liberally over the public airwaves. So, that's your problem. To be frank, we have other considerations."

Silver grew indignant. How *dare* the man scoff at his motives? "You question my reasons. Well then, Moshe, I must point out that you cannot escape the same criticism. Two of your hijackers are Jews from prominent families. You would have wiped them out by now if they were all Arabs. And that's the plain truth."

"You think their Jewishness matters to me? It doesn't. I made my peace with that a long time ago. When I'm in this office, the world is divided between allies and enemies, whether they are Jews or non-Jews. But you, Mordechai," Lieberman stressed the name, "you have some serious thinking to do on that score. Look, I can tell you matters are well in hand. That's all I can say."

Silver felt utterly defeated. "What news am I to take back to my country?"

"I cannot speak for my government, but for what it's worth," he said as Silver was about to protest, "you can tell your President and your people that they are looking for an easy way out, and there is none. You capitulate to hijackers, and you write your own ticket to disaster. I don't care if that communiqué is a fake, nor should you. The hijackers won't be much appeased by it either, but it's a stalling tactic. The only way now is to trust us, something that is difficult for your country to do. But, Mordechai, you are my friend. Can you trust me?"

On the plane back to Washington, Silver remembered Lieberman's question. His last thought before he fell asleep was, *No, Moshe. I cannot trust you. I cannot even understand you.*

CHAPTER 21

THE FIRST THING Goren did after his plane landed in Geneva was to buy a local paper. He had little difficulty in finding what he was looking for. The headline was printed in twenty-point type. *"The Reporter's Inside Story: The Woman Who Came Back From Hell."* Beneath it was a photograph of Susan Kraft climbing into the ambulance, her son clutched in her arms.

The story made the most of her celebrity status: the little reporter, fresh from the University of Chicago, who scooped the biggest interviews of the decade; the brave woman who made it through her husband's tragic death from cancer only three years earlier to become one of the foremost TV personalities on the news. Goren read the information greedily. It was not until he was interrupted by a hard shove in the back that he realized he was standing right in the middle of the passenger lounge, (164) blocking the way. He moved aside and went over to the

Pan Am office. There was no one around, thankfully. Leaning on the reception desk, he continued his reading.

There was something unreal about all this, he thought, reading a daily paper for intimate details of a woman with whom he had been so intimately acquainted.

He continued his reading till he found what he was looking for. "Immediately after her baby was hospitalized, Mrs. Kraft was taken to her suite in the Bristol Hotel, where she is staying as the guest of the city."

Goren folded up the paper and put it into his coat pocket. Walking out, he entered the first waiting cab.

"Where to?" asked the driver.

"The Bristol Hotel."

Goren was surprised to find how short the distance was from the airport to the city. Ten minutes after entering the cab, he paid the driver and entered the lobby of the luxury hotel. After a few steps, he halted, his eyes swiftly scanning the scene—the low square coffee tables to the right, surrounded by heavy brown and red armchairs; a tangled vine growing out of a large round pot; four automatic elevators; the enormous crystal chandeliers; the small bar on the left, flanked by a serving trolley loaded with cakes and drinks; a wall-to-wall flowered carpet; jewelry and clothing boutiques, a bookstall, a pharmacy, a Hertz office and an Avis office; the cashier's counter; the reception desk, staffed by a pleasant young woman who was expert at making negative replies seem almost positive.

"I'm sorry, sir, but we have nothing available, and we're heavily booked for the next three weeks."

"What do you suggest I do?"

"That's a tough one. It's the conference, you see. And now the hijacking too." She looked at him, expecting him to thank her and leave. But he stood stolidly before her, waiting expectantly. "I'll see what I can do." She shrugged.

She walked into a back room. Goren turned around to survey the people who were milling about the lobby. Most of them were journalists exchanging information.

"I found something."

Goren spun around and encountered the young woman's smile. She handed him a note. "The Du Midi Hotel. Small but very pleasant."

"Far from here?"

"Two streets away. Just a few minutes' walk if you don't have much luggage."

Out of the corner of his eye he saw two men perform the subtle ballet he himself had learned in the undercover services. One, seated diagonally across from the reception desk, lowered his *Figaro* slightly and made eye contact with the other, who approached the magazine rack as if searching for something to read. Faintly, Goren heard the words, "Replacement in 1127."

Goren walked toward the revolving exit door, shrugging slightly. He decided to wait outside for a few moments to lull the suspicions of the desk clerk. Then he walked back inside and headed for the elevators.

The lighting on the eleventh floor corridor was dim, and he could scarcely make out the sign which indicated that Rooms 1101–1130 were to the right and 1131–1161 to the left. Turning right, he halted outside a door bearing a bronze number plate with the figures 1127.

Susan clutched the telephone receiver in both hands, unable to believe the course of the conversation with her producer. She recited the words monotonously, her mind consumed with other thoughts. "The doctors say that Jimmy is going to be all right. . . . They aren't sure yet . . . a few days. I've already told you . . . yes . . . yes . . ."

Finally she could no longer restrain herself, and she blurted out, "You can forget that, Jerry. I have another child on that boat. I don't know when I'll see him again. And now you want to put me through the pain of a television interview? Well, you can take your ratings and . . ."

There was silence on the other end. "Hello! Hello!" she shouted into the phone.

"I'm here." She heard the producer's voice crackling on the overseas line. "You have no right to act like an overwrought housewife, Susan. You're a public figure. You've got to share what you've been through with the rest of America."

She took a breath. "You're a cold fish, Jerry. Christ, I feel for your family."

"I am sure that you'll reconsider. You're a trooper, Sue." He clicked off.

Then she heard the knock on the door.

"Who's there?" Susan's voice was edgy and impatient.

"I have a message for you, Madame." Goren swallowed. "From the manager of the hotel."

The door opened slightly and Eli Goren's eyes met those of Susan Kraft. She did not know who he was.

"What message?" she asked impatiently.

Goren stepped forward, pushing back the door gently but firmly.

"What is this?" she cried, but instantly she clapped her hand to her mouth as she recognized him. Stepping back into the room, she slumped down on the pale-blue couch. Goren walked in after her, closing the door behind him and drawing the chain across.

"Hello," he said.

She sat and stared at him in disbelief. Her eyes expressed something which Goren couldn't define. Hatred? Fear?

"You're the last person I wanted to see here," she whispered. "I know what it means when you show up."

He began to approach her. "You're wrong. I . . ."

"No!"

He halted.

"No!" she repeated. "Don't lie to me again. Fourteen months of lies were quite enough!"

Years ago, the time they spent together had seemed a lifetime. It was as though he had never lived without her. Did all that last no more than fourteen months?

It was planned as an easy mission. After two consecutive forays into Arab countries, Goren was chosen to spend a few months in the United States, a comfortable place to work. He was sent to Illinois, where he registered at the University of Chicago. His job was to penetrate the ranks of the Arab and Palestinian students, who were very active on campus.

One late afternoon in January, he dashed into the sociology building to escape the raging snowstorm outside. He brushed the thick snow from his boots in the corridor and entered the lecture hall. The class had already started, and he sank into the first vacant seat he saw—on the right, in the second to last row.

Pulling out a notebook and pen, he asked the girl sitting beside him, "What's he covered so far?"

"Tell you later!" she said impatiently.

He glanced at her. She was slim, almost skinny. Her auburn hair was pulled back. She was bent forward, her eyes on the lecturer, while her right hand scribbled rapidly in her notebook. Every now and then, her free hand would push back the small silver spectacles perched on her pert, freckled nose.

She stook up the moment the lecturer finished. Only then did she look at him. "Excuse me," she said, indicating his legs, which were blocking the way.

"You promised . . ."

"I promised?"

"Definitely. You promised to tell me what I missed."

"Did I?" She glanced distractedly at her watch. "I have to get home. I'm expecting an urgent phone call. I'm sorry."

"I'll come with you."

"You could ask anybody else."

"But I want to get it from you. You promised."

Her impatience erupted. "Look, if you're handing me a line, you're wasting your time. Since I promised, you can come along with me, but if you have anything else in mind—well, you're really wasting your time."

"I have plenty of time."

She lived four blocks from the campus. When they reached her apartment, both of them were thoroughly covered with snow. She looked at him and at the water dripping from his clothes, and a flush of anger covered her pale features.

"What have I done now?" asked Goren.

"This whole thing looks like some cheap movie. What am I supposed to do? Offer you some dry clothes? It's ludicrous!"

Eli made no reply. Instead, he flung out his arms helplessly, shaking drops all over her.

"Oh, all right," she growled, and went into the next room.

This was certainly no run-of-the-mill student's apartment. The furnishing was of a slightly better quality, though it certainly was not flashy. Everything in the apartment was functional, chosen with modest good taste. The parents had evidently made great efforts to provide their daughter with every comfort.

She came back, wearing jeans and an oversized sweater, and thrust a bundle of clothes at him. "Go in there," she commanded, indicating the other room.

Her bedroom was white. Everything there was white: the wide bed, the closet, the lamp shades. Only the wall-to-wall carpeting was beige. Not bad for a student.

The pants she gave him hung down a little over his shoes, but the shirt fit well.

When he walked back into the other room, she was sitting on the couch, glancing through a notebook. "Are these your boyfriend's?" he asked, indicating the clothes he was wearing.

Without replying to his question, she held out the notebook. "Here are my notes. You can copy them."

Taking the notebook, he leafed through it and then tossed it back at her. "I'm not interested," he said.

"So why are you bugging me?"

"I'm interested in you."

"Oh, fine. You can leave now."

He stood stolidly in front of her. "No coffee?"

"Listen," she said, exasperated. "Let's just admit you made a mistake and we'll say good-bye like friends. Okay?"

"My clothes are still wet."

"You can take the ones you're wearing. Bring them back whenever you get the chance. Better still, give them to me at the next lecture."

"I'm really excellent company." He gave her a boyish smile. "All my friends say so."

She sighed deeply and stood up. "How can I phrase

this graciously? I have a lot to do and not a great deal of time in which to do it. Get the message?"

The telephone rang and she went to answer it.

"Oh, it's you. Yes . . . I've been wanting to speak to you. Look," she covered the receiver with her hand and turned to Eli. "Do you mind? This is personal." He shrugged and went into the kitchen.

"All right, Phil," she said into the phone. "I'm not one to put any faith in rumors, but Samantha tells me you slept together when she went to the city last weekend. I'm just going to be blunt about it and ask you outright. Is she telling the truth?"

When Susan heard the response, she coughed slightly and cleared her throat. "Yeah. Well, I asked for it. Enough. No explanations," she said tensely as he tried to cut her off. "I'm going to need some time. Lots of it." She placed the receiver in the cradle.

Eli put his head down on the kitchen table and shut his eyes for just a second. He could hear her voice getting angry, then softening. Finally, it faded away. When he opened his eyes again, he looked at his watch. 2:00 A.M. He had a terrible pain in his back when he stood up.

It was only when he noticed the notebook lying on the table next to him that he remembered where he was, and the girl with the freckles. Stretching and testing his cramped muscles, he felt his backbone creak. He walked through the dark living room to the bedroom and slowly pushed the door open.

She seemed different without her glasses and with her hair spread over the pillow. It partly covered her face and gave her a vulnerable look he hadn't seen before. She appeared smaller and more fragile in the great expanse of the wide bed.

Silently, Eli undressed, dropping his clothes on the floor. Wearing only his shorts, he carefully lifted the blanket on the vacant side of the bed; he noticed only a slight squeak of bedsprings as he put his weight on the mattress. A wonderful sense of mischief swept over his body, which still ached from hours bent over on a kitchen table. Turning his back to her motionless form, he fell asleep as soon as he closed his eyes.

When he awoke, the room was flooded with sunlight. He rubbed his eyes and looked over his shoulder at Susan. She was wide awake, staring at him as if he were an apparition. She couldn't believe her eyes.

He smiled apologetically. "That table was not very comfortable. I could have been permanently deformed."

She said nothing, did nothing. She just continued to stare.

"Angry?" he asked.

She didn't respond, so he turned over on his side to face her, propping his head on his left hand. His expression was grave as he lifted his right hand hesitantly to stroke her cheek.

She closed her eyes and felt the tears coming. God, what a time for this to happen. All her hopes for her and Phil . . . and now this guy just invites himself into bed. She didn't want to see what was happening. Slowly, she slipped down toward him and lay flat, pressing herself against him. His body was warm, accepting. In a fever of need and wanting, she let him take her. She flung her arms around him and held on for dear life, kissing him, sucking at his mouth, giving herself over to the feeling. Afterward, she lay breathing heavily as he held her.

"You may wonder what came over me," she said at last.

Goren was silent. His attention was focused on the small freckled face. He was actually astonished that she hadn't thrown him on the floor and kicked him out. Just a few moments earlier, this wild woman had been all over him.

"Well, what are you waiting for?" she asked. "Now you tell me I'm the one you've been searching for all your life. That you've been pursuing your goal like some dark star across the Chicago campus for months."

"I'm just happy to be here. Why don't you shut up?"

"I'm afraid I must spoil the idyll. I have a fiancé."

"I guess I know that already. It was thanks to him that I fell asleep on the kitchen table."

For the first time, then, he heard her laugh, a sudden eruption of almost happy sound which surprised him no less than her earlier sexual outburst. She turned to him and hugged him.

Goren heard no further mention of her fiancé. He did not ask, and she offered no explanations. And he never came to claim his wet clothes. Within a week, he packed his scanty belongings, paid what he owed to his landlord, and moved in with Susan Kingsley.

He was twenty-four, she was twenty-two, and every experience became precious: studying together, going for walks in the snow, their small squabbles, their tempestuous peacemaking. Above all, warming each other's cold feet during the icy winter nights.

Susan, therefore, was profoundly upset when she came in one evening in March and Goren wasn't home. He was not back by midnight, nor by two o'clock. She made no calls to find out his possible whereabouts, not wanting friends to assume that something was wrong between them. Once she thought of calling the police, but she did not look forward to hearing them say, "Just go to sleep, lady. He's probably out tying one on with the boys." Eventually, sick from worry and anger, telling herself over and over that they were individuals with lives of their own and that she had no right to be jealous, she sank into a fitful, restless doze.

It was after five in the morning when a slight noise awakened her. She heard the front door open and close and did not budge. He would be hanging up his coat. A few moments later, Goren entered the bedroom on tiptoe and began to undress. When he finished, he noticed that her eyes were open. He walked to the bed, sat down beside her, and stroked her cheek, her eyes, her hair.

"Miss me?" he asked.

"I was cold." She shifted away from his hand.

He slipped in beside her and took her resistant body in his arms. "My poor darling. Better now?" He ran his tongue along her lower lip.

"Where were you?" she demanded, pulling back.

His body began to move against hers. "Later, sweetheart, I'll tell you later."

She was repelled by him in that moment. How could he say nothing and then expect her to respond to him sexually. She did not smell liquor on his breath, and she knew he just wasn't the type for a one-night stand, so what the hell was going on?

"Listen, Eli, I'm sorry, but this isn't going to get very far. I'm too exhausted, okay? Try me again in the morning."

With that, she turned over and lay staring at the ceiling until dawn.

He was still asleep when she made breakfast. Placing the steaming cup of coffee and the warm toast on the table, she picked up the morning paper. Viet Cong forces advancing. President Johnson hospitalized for a checkup. Two Arabs murdered in Chicago. Mayor Daley warns of situation in the slums.

She put the paper down, sipped the coffee, and bit into a slice of toast. She hadn't yet prepared her paper on the population structure of Britain. Well, there was always the weekend. Ever since Eli came into her life, everything seemed to get postponed to the weekend. And then from the weekend to the middle of the next week. And so on. Well, so what? Anyway, her mind wasn't on Great Britain right now.

Suddenly, as she stared at the headline, the words became clear, and she snatched up the paper. "Two Arabs murdered last night at their downtown home," ran the report. "The two Palestinians were well known to the police, apparently members of the Al Fatah terrorist organization. The motive for the murder remains unknown, but the police are considering the possibility that it may have been committed by Israeli agents." The report was flanked by a large picture showing two bodies, one sprawled on a bed, the other halfway from the bed to the floor, as though the man had been caught while trying to escape. The corpse's contorted face was clearly visible; what caught Susan's attention were the eyes—their expression of utter terror.

She laid the paper aside. How atrocious! Why did the
Israelis do it? And then, she sensed a tremor running
through her body. "Israeli agents." Her mind went crazy
with an impossible fantasy. "Israeli agents!" She shook
her head vehemently. "That's ridiculus. Just because he
got home late?"

But that dull fear did not leave her. "It can't be! It can't
be!" she told herself. Then she opened the hall closet and
rummaged around, swinging hangers away. She felt terribly guilty and yet something compelled her to keep searching. And then, in his left coat pocket, she found a package
wrapped in thick brown paper.

Mesmerized, she gazed at the package. "I musn't. . . .
If I don't touch it, nothing will happen. I mustn't touch it.
For my own sake. For both our sakes." But she knew that
it was too late. Now, she had to know. And when she
stretched out her hand, she was not at all surprised to feel
the cold metal of a pistol butt.

She suddenly realized how little she knew about him.
He had told her that he was born in Israel and lived there
all his life, but that he had decided to emigrate three years
previously. "It's tough living there," he said, without
elaborating.

Stealing into the bedroom, she opened the closet
quietly and picked out the clothes she was going to wear,
laying them on the armchair. She took off her robe and her
nightgown.

He woke up, looked at her, and grinned broadly. "What
a wonderful sight to wake up to."

She put on her panties.

"No. Come here," he pleaded.

She put on her bra.

"What's the matter?" he asked.

"I'm in a hurry."

"That's not the reason."

She sat down on the bed beside him. "Why did you
leave Israel?"

"I've already told you."

"Tell me again. And this time tell me the truth."

His voice hardened. "I've never asked you what you do when you take an occasional weekend in New York, why you go there, and why you never invite me to come along with you."

She nodded. "I've often wondered why you don't ask. Now I understand."

"What the hell are you talking about?"

"You don't ask questions so that you don't have to answer any."

He lifted himself up, placing his arm around her waist and trying to draw her toward him.

Tearing herself away, she ran out of the room and came back, clutching the paper. She flung it on the bed with the photo of the dead Arabs facing him. Eli's expression did not change. "What's the meaning of this dramatic scene? What is all this?"

"Don't lie to me," she pleaded. "Please."

He said nothing. She pulled on her blouse and then her skirt. After combing her hair, she sat down beside him once more on the bed. "I don't know anything about your wars, and I don't want to know," she said. "I don't know who's right and who's wrong." Gently, she stroked his face. "I just know one thing. Every time I look at you, every time I kiss you, every time you are inside me, I'll always see those two bodies . . . and all the other bodies I don't know anything about."

Her lips touched his forehead. He shut his eyes. When he reopened them, she had left the room. He heard the outside door slam.

Susan was not sure what to expect when she came home that evening. She preferred not to see him, but with all her being she wanted him to be there. All day long, she had been turning things over in her mind, her conflicting thoughts and feelings tormenting her unmercifully. He was a spy. No, a murderer! But for him it was a war. Did that make any difference? Not as far as she was concerned. She could not live with it. But for God's sake, if she couldn't live with Eli, could she live without him? Wasn't she being too hasty?

It was with this thought that she walked into the bedroom. Eli was nowhere to be seen. She opened the closet where he hung his clothes. It was empty.

As he stood close enough to touch Susan once more, Goren knew that he had made a mistake. He should have stayed home. This thing was not for him. Not the meeting with Susan nor the business on which he had come.

"Why did you give your son my name?"

"His name isn't Eh-lee, it's Ee-lie."

"The same thing."

"What difference does it make now?" Her face was expressionless. "If you're concerned, he was born a year and a half after my marriage."

"The papers say he's thirteen."

"Really? Well, take it from one who knows. You should never believe what you read in the papers." Suddenly, her tone changed. "Why, after so many years?"

Goren gave her a cynical smile. "I wanted the autograph of the famous Susan Kraft."

"Why did you come here?" She sounded frightened.

"I need your help."

"What?"

"Everything you can tell me about the boat. About the hijackers. Anything at all."

Susan leapt for the phone and began to dial. In a split second, Goren grabbed her wrist. He slammed his other hand onto the phone cradle.

"What the hell are you doing?"

"Phoning the police. I won't let you do it." She put the receiver down. "I told you. Back in Chicago. Your wars are of no interest to me. I want my son, and I want him alive!"

"Whether or not this war is of any interest to you, you're right in the middle of it."

She approached the phone again, and Goren seized her hand. "Don't be stupid. It's the only chance."

"What do you mean?"

Could he tell her? Could he avoid telling her?

"Do you know what the hijackers want?"

She nodded. "Of course. I was briefed by the Inspector of Police here, after I was released. He wanted information too. And I didn't give it to him."

"Above all else, the hijackers want one of their men who's imprisoned in Israel. His name is Maruan Awad."

"Then for God's sake, let him go!"

"That's the whole thing. We can't."

"Why?" Her voice shook. He sounded so authoritative. How was she going to get Eli back?

"I can't say more than that. You've got to believe me."

"You're lying—the way you did in Chicago."

"You must believe me," said Goren quietly. "They can't get what they want. Do you understand what that means?"

She looked at him, dazed. "You mean they'll let everyone starve? These . . . pacifists?"

"Do you have any doubts about that?"

"Definitely. That woman, you know, she doesn't look as though she's capable of watching anyone die of slow starvation. Of killing."

Eli gazed into her eyes. "Do I look as though I'm capable of killing?"

He saw that she was beginning to understand. "It would make matters very simple if the people who are capable of killing showed it. The reason why they don't look any different from other people is that in most cases they aren't different. They are people like you, like your friends. It's just that they live under different circumstances."

She covered her face with her hands. "Oh God. I don't know. I have to tell the police. Somebody has to do something."

"If you do that, and an action is taken, they'll forget the meaning of the word 'non-violent.' The lake is a potential powder keg. Is that what you want?"

"I don't know anymore. But somebody has got to do something."

"Precisely."

"What if it fails?" she asked.

"Chances will still be better than they are at present."

She looked at him for a long time, and then she sat down on the couch, her hands still, her back straight, her face tense. As he had seen her so many times over the years on television. The compleat interviewer. The reporter who dug in and held on for dear life until she got the story. Now she was on the other side. She began to answer his questions as her memory served her. When he finished making his notes, he mumbled, "The problem is going to be keeping them from getting to the detonator."

Susan was silent. Goren closed his notebook and put it in his pocket.

"Okay," he said. "I guess that's that."

She did not move. He began to walk toward the door. He stopped when he heard her voice. "Did they send you because of me?"

"Yes."

"Would you have come if I weren't here?"

"No."

She stood up and approached him slowly. When her body touched his, he embraced her and she leaned her head on his chest.

CHAPTER 22

AMBASSADOR DORON was completely disoriented when the phone rang. The room was pitch black, and his mind was a total blank covered with a thick haze of sleep. He could not remember where he was, why he was here, or even the day or the time. The only thing he knew with any certainty was that he could easily sleep another thirty hours.

"Hello," he said hoarsely.

"I'm sorry to disturb you, sir, but I have Rabbi Horowitz on the line, and he says it's urgent. . . ."

"All right."

The President. Taylor. Silver. The boat in Geneva. Things began to sort themselves out. Doron sat up and held the receiver between his chin and chest while he lit a cigarette.

"Arieh . . ."

Doron felt goosebumps form on his flesh. Every time he heard the voice of the chairman of the Jewish Presidents' Conference, with his Yiddish accent, his repetitious, clipped phrases, and his sing-song ingratiating intonation, it annoyed him anew. The man was an old-world Uriah Heep.

"I'm glad to be talking with you once more, Arieh."

"So am I."

"Times are difficult, Arieh. We had a meeting today. All the presidents. They were all there. I have to notify you. It's very important. Very important."

"Yes?"

"Not over the phone, Arieh. Not over the phone. When can you see me? I know you're a busy man, but it's important."

"Where are you, Rabbi?"

"Where do you think? In Washington, of course."

"You can come straight over, if you're not busy."

"I'm never busy when Jewish concerns are involved."

By the time Rabbi Horowitz arrived, Doron felt quite refreshed. The weariness and depression he had experienced after his talks at the White House had vanished, and he even felt more welcoming toward the old rabbi. He stretched out his arms to greet Horowitz as the latter hastened to embrace him. Doron poured two whiskies.

"You don't change, Arieh. You just don't change."

"It's the climate of the Holy Land, a good place to live."

Rabbi Horowitz laughed. "I agree, Arieh. You are fortunate people. Truly fortunate people. . . ."

"You're welcome to come and join us."

Rabbi Horowitz laid down his glass. "There's nothing I want more, and you know it. But someone has to look after the affairs of the Jewish people here."

Doron smiled. "No question about that. In my country, we only have three million Jews, and you have six million. We're no more than your subordinates. You are the true leader of the Jewish people."

Once again, Rabbi Horowitz burst out laughing. "You're laughing at me, Arieh," he said, but Doron knew that the man was flattered.

He was short and thin, with a pale, wrinkled face; he had lost most of his hair long ago. He enjoyed little regard in the Jewish academic world, nor did he have any ambitions in that direction. Most of his energy was channeled into Jewish communal politics. He was one of the scores of politicians who made a career and a living from dealing with Jewish problems.

He had reached the head of his field. Starting as the leader of a small community in Cleveland, he had achieved international prominence. His counsel was sought, not in Jerusalem alone, but also in the State Department and even in the White House. At first, he felt quite overawed in such surroundings, but in time he began to comprehend what enormous power had fallen to him—although he never completely grasped why.

But of course, Rabbi Horowitz was not a man to articulate his doubts in public. If the President of the United States believed that the Jews commanded secret powers, who was Rabbi Horowitz to disagree with him?

At the same time, he was well aware that if the illusion of Jewish power was to be maintained, it must never be put to the test.

And this was precisely what seemed about to happen because of that accursed boat in Lake Geneva!

"Times are difficult," he repeated, opening his briefcase and producing a bundle of newspapers. Everything the rabbi wanted Doron to read was marked in red ink.

"Israel must respond to the hijackers' demands." "No dealing in American blood!" "The United States must exert pressure on Israel." The headlines spoke for themselves. Doron put the papers back on the table.

"It'll pass," he said.

"It'll pass if everything ends well."

"We all hope it will."

"You don't understand," said the rabbi. "It isn't Israel. It's the Jews. My sense of smell never deceives me. And I smell anti-Semitism, Arieh. I smell anti-Semitism."

Doron smiled ironically. "What are you afraid of? The worse thing that can happen is that you'll be obliged to come and live in Israel."

"This is no time for jokes. I'm speaking in earnest."

Doron looked pensive. "Rabbi, some say the state of
Israel was founded by people who aspired to restore ancient traditions. Others say the state was founded on
ideals. You and I know both views are mistaken. Israel
was founded on *fear*. It was founded by people fleeing
from persecution and massacre, who wanted, finally, after
centuries of mistreatment, to take control of their own
fate and that of their children. In short, Rabbi Horowitz,
the instinct of self-preservation is what created the state
of Israel."

"So that's old history."

"But I'm talking about the future. Do you know what
can induce American Jews to come to Israel? Discrimina-
tion. Persecution. Bombs."

"Is that what you wish for us, Arieh?"

Doron smiled. "No, of course not." But the rabbi did
not seem convinced by his denial.

"Tell me, if all of us Jews come to live in Israel, who
will you go to for money? Who will look after your interests in Washington?"

Doron smiled again. "That's what I've always liked
about you, Rabbi Horowitz. Invariably, your first concern
is for other people. But in this case, your concern is superfluous. If all the Jews were to come to Israel, we wouldn't
need all that. If you brought yourselves, your talents, your
money—who would need American money? Who would
need political support? Just imagine what would happen
if we had another five or six million Jews living in Israel."

Rabbi Horowitz shrugged. Their conversation was
drawing further away from the topic he had come to
discuss. "We can argue about that all night. The point is
that the Jews are not immigrating to Israel. The point is
that you need help in Washington and you need us to
get that help." He paused briefly to permit himself a couple
of deep breaths. "On this matter, we are on the side of the
U.S. government, Arieh. We won't give you our support.
We won't give you our support."

"That would be a very tragic development, Rabbi.
Every American administration has tried to sow divisions
between the Jews and Israel. They failed—and therein lies

our strength. The moment there's any crack—any crack at all—in the wall of Jewish unity, we're finished. All of us!"

Rabbi Horowitz rose to his feet. "In that case, don't let it happen, Arieh. We support the administration's demand that you respond to the hijackers' conditions. So for God's sake, Arieh, don't play any foolish games!"

A western breeze whipped up the lake. The waves were not large, but they were powerful enough to keep the boat rocking from side to side. Several of the hostages were sick; every now and then, someone would lurch to the side of the deck and attempt to throw up. But on empty stomachs, there was no possibility of relief. Many on board were in severely weakened conditions—the worst part of a long fast is always the first days, when the body protests the lack of nourishment and peristalsis persists even in the absence of food. Some had fevers, some were dizzy. All were terrified.

Eli sat huddled in a blanket, staring out the cabin window and wishing he were back with Jimmy and his mother in his own backyard at home. A young man wearing a blue windbreaker and jeans strolled over and said hello in a thick German accent.

"You look like you're doing pretty well here, but you will let me know if you need some help, yes? My name is Jan."

"I'm Eli."

The German boy sat down on the bench, pulled a deck of cards from his jeans pocket, and asked Eli if he wanted to play. Eli nodded, and Jan started to deal. Suddenly, there was a shout from the other side of the boat.

"You know what you all look like?" the voice was yelling. "Like a bunch of sheep waiting to be slaughtered."

Eli and Jan went around to see who was making the commotion. It was Bill Peterson, the American who had tried to get off the boat earlier, the one Deborah had slapped. From various sections on the deck, there were stirrings and mutterings as people worried how the hijackers would react. Several heads turned toward Nabil, who strode rapidly to the man and landed a powerful blow on his shoulder. Peterson slumped down on the bench. "That dirty Arab," he rasped.

Deborah, who had seen the incident, walked across the deck nervously. This man was evidently a violent type and would have to be watched closely. She went over to Jan and the boy.

"How are you two doing?" she asked casually, watching Peterson anxiously.

"Okay," said Eli. He wet his lips. "Miss," he asked quietly, "do you have any way of knowing how much longer this is going to last?"

"I don't know exactly," she answered. "But it won't be long."

"I'll make damn sure it doesn't last long!" Bill Peterson was on her before she had a chance to catch her breath. He flung himself at her, reaching for the gun in her belt. Without a second thought, Deborah jumped back. Her hand flew to her waist and jerked out the automatic. She did not take her finger off the trigger until she had emptied the whole magazine.

The incident took no more than a few seconds. Peterson lay at Deborah's feet with blood pouring from his face and chest. She stared at the body in disbelief. Jan pressed Eli's head to his shoulder to conceal the sight from him. His own eyes were full of horror.

Several of the hostages screamed, others jumped to their feet trying to see what had happened. There were hysterical cries from all corners of the boat.

Nabil stood at the end of the gangway, his feet planted firmly and his submachine gun raised. "Everybody—sit down!" he ordered. "Anybody who moves will be shot!" Within seconds, it was quiet again, except for some excited whispers and sobs.

Slowly, Deborah walked to the steering cabin and slumped down on the wooden seat. Her mind was a vacuum. She could see nothing but the bullet-riddled body with the blood gushing up from the wounds. Her mind was still unable to connect the gun in her hand with that corpse. In the space of a few seconds, she had changed completely. She had become a murderer.

*   *   *

Goren lay beside Susan Kraft, aware of the slight pressure of her leg on his. As close as they had been for the past hours, there was no joy between them. Nothing but a sense of profound sadness, of futility, of an absence of choice. She took his hand, stroking his fingers and then his palm. Her hand froze when it touched the cold metal of the ring he wore on his left hand.

"I have two children," he said.

She studied him a moment. "I'm trying to imagine how it would have been if things had gone differently years ago," she said at last.

He smiled, "That's hard. We'd probably be divorced, with the same two kids. Three, maybe."

She slapped him lightly on the chest. "Don't be a cynic."

"Okay. Don't you be a romantic. It doesn't help us, it's just painful."

She snuggled against him until she found a comfortable position, with her head in the crook of his shoulder.

"You never told me how you got into this."

"Into what?"

"You know."

"I suppose it was an accident. I got my discharge from the army, and I had nothing particular I wanted to do."

"So you went to the employment agency, and they sent you to the intelligence service."

He laughed. "No. Not exactly."

"Then how, dammit?"

"It doesn't matter."

"Well, then, why?"

"You wouldn't understand."

"Give me a chance."

He sighed. "To understand, you'd have to see thirty-two children's bodies fished out of the water. It's a horrifying sight. The commander of the navy said that if we'd had better intelligence, it wouldn't have happened. I heard him say it."

"Is that true?" she asked.

The phone rang and startled them both. "Yes, this is

Mrs. Kraft," she said into the receiver. She turned slightly to him. "It's the pediatric ward."

"Oh, that's grand. When can he be discharged? . . . Fine, I'll pick him up then." She put the phone down and sighed contentedly. "Jimmy's doing much better. Probably better than us," she added softly.

Goren stretched out to the night table on his side of the bed and looked at his watch. He switched on the radio and turned the dial until he got a newscast.

"A burst of fire was heard from the boat a few moments ago," the voice droned. "So far, no explanation has been given for the shooting. But immediately afterward, the hijackers requested a doctor to come aboard. They also asked for an ambulance to stand by. It seems, then, that there may be injuries."

Goren was immediately on his feet and dressing. Susan sat gripping the sheet, her expressionless eyes fixed on the opposite wall. "They're killing them . . . they're going to kill Eli. . . ."

Goren grabbed her by the shoulders and shook her. "Don't say that. There are always lousy rumors in a hijacking. I'm convinced nothing happened."

If Susan heard him, she gave no indication. She began to sob. Goren tried to comfort her, pressing her against him until her sobbing died down. He let go of her then, lifted the phone receiver, and dialed.

"What happened?" he asked.

He listened for about a minute and then hung up. He took Susan's face in both his hands. "There's only one casualty. An adult."

Slowly, she lay back on the pillow and closed her eyes. Goren gazed at her, feeling an old longing fill him and spill over. He pulled up the sheet and covered her body carefully, but she did not respond as he knelt beside her and kissed her twice, on each of her tightly closed eyes.

CHAPTER 23

THE STREET IN FRONT of the Israeli Embassy in Washington erupted into angry shouts, which Ambassador Doron could hear clearly even through his office windows. He could read the slogans on the huge banners held by the picketers below. "No American blood for Jewish wars!" "Release the terrorists!" "Jews, you shall not kill!" "I want my boy back!"

"Jews," said Doron softly. "Not Israelis. Jews."

"I told you it was directed against us, Arieh," said Rabbi Horowitz, who was hunched in the armchair in the corner of the room. "Do you see that now?"

Rabbi Horowitz was about to go on when suddenly a missile came flying through the window. He threw himself flat on the floor. There was an asymmetrical hole in the windowpane, and a heavy stone rested on the blue carpet.

"Get away from the window!" the rabbi shouted at Doron. But Doron did not budge.

A dozen policemen were scuffling with the demonstrators. All around them, the television cameras hummed while the press reporters stood a short distance away, jotting down their impressions or interviewing the demonstrators.

"It isn't hard to imagine how that'll look tonight, with Cronkite's voice in the background," said Doron.

Abram Levenstein saw the anti-Jewish demonstrators on the news that night. He had seen worse as a young man, and he had never been particularly impressed by people who contended that it was different in America. As far as Levenstein was concerned, a goy was a goy everywhere, and his attitude toward Jews had nothing to do with his character or way of life. It was merely a question of opportunity.

Actually, he couldn't have cared less. To him, events in the United States were marginal and trivial. At this time, the focal point of Levenstein's existence was a boat in the center of a lake, thousands of miles away. It was impossible for Levenstein to go there, but he could be near his family—in spirit, at least—through his Maker. The synagogue was the only place where Levenstein felt truly at home. Everyone there spoke his language; they thought, rejoiced, prayed, and feared just like him. No matter that it was just a dirty little room where the air bore an overpowering stench of mildew. Or that it contained no more than a dozen men, each one an island unto himself. In this room, and with these men, Levenstein felt safe.

As he started to remove his hat to place the yarmulke on his head, he heard footsteps behind him and turned to see Clarence Boynes coming up the steps from the basement. Thin and stooped, with a wild array of pure white hair springing up from his charcoal-colored forehead, Boynes had been the shabbes goy at this synagogue as long as Levenstein had worshipped there. He was more than a janitor to those who frequented the temple; he was a kind and careful man who, it was often remarked, would have been a diligent scholar of the Torah had he not been born black.

"G'day, Mr. Levenstein," Boynes said softly, wiping his face with the back of his hand. "I been reading 'bout your family, and I'm awful sorry."

Levenstein extended a delicate, liver-spotted hand. "Thank you for your concern, my friend. I can't think of much else to do but to come here and ask the Lord for His interference."

"That's just the thing. You know He never lets His people down. Leastwise, I'm counting on that—always have. You go on in now."

He opened the door and steadied Levenstein's arm as he walked inside. *Poor old man*, thought Boynes. *Those people is all he got 'ceptin' for God, of course.*

Tears started from Levenstein's eyes when a man with a white beard opened the Holy Ark to reveal the two Scrolls of the Law whose red velvet covering was stained and whose gilt crowns had long since lost their glitter. All that Levenstein could see was that these were the Books of the Law, the Holy of Holies, and the sight of them was enough to banish the terrible thoughts which had haunted him these past few days.

"My God," he whispered. "Please, please . . ." He watched the slow progress of the old man who bore the Torah among the benches. The members of the congregation pressed toward the aisle; one by one they took the velvet covering between their fingers and raised it to their lips, kissing it fervently. Levenstein was sitting in the last row near the doorway. He was the last to do his obeisance, but his fervor was the greatest. Heart and soul, as he pressed his lips to the velvet, he was at one with the long round scroll.

Consequently, he did not hear the scuffle outside, or the sound of Clarence's first cry. But then the door to the synagogue was flung open.

"Dirty Yids," screamed a man with hate-filled eyes. He was brandishing a pickax and had a revolver tucked into his belt.

"You stay out of there," Clarence was yelling, but

another looter, a huge, muscular man, flung him aside. As
he crashed his fist into Clarence's ribs and hurled a small
rectangular object, the janitor reached out for Abram Levenstein. He could almost touch him.

But the explosion came too quickly; afterward, neither of them heard anything else. When the police arrived,
among the corpses they brought out were the shattered
bodies of two old men, one white and one black, who had
been tossed together on top of the charred remnants of a
Torah scroll.

Defense Secretary Martin Silver had come in from the
airport only two hours earlier. The reports of the demonstrations disturbed him, but he was not really surprised.
There was always some scapegoat in a time of crisis. Jews
or blacks, Iranians or Chicanos—it just depended on the
particular crisis.

The buzzer startled him. "The Israeli ambassador is
here, sir."

"Show him in."

He shook Doron's hand firmly. "I regret what's been
happening. It's terrible. Of course, I've given strict orders
to step up your security."

"Thank you, Mr. Secretary," Doron replied.

"At the same time," Silver went on, "you musn't be too
shocked. In a hostage situation, particularly when family
members are involved, people can behave in strange ways."

"The demonstrations in Los Angeles, Cleveland, and a
dozen other cities were not staged by relatives of the
hostages," the ambassador remarked coolly.

"No, no," Silver hurriedly conceded, anxious to let the
subject drop. "Well, Mr. Ambassador?"

From his jacket pocket, Doron brought out a sheet of
paper and handed it to Silver. The Defense Secretary's
expression showed his rising anger as he read through the
memo. When he finished, he thrust the paper down on his
desk.

"You are making a mockery of us. You agree to nothing which the United States has already approved."

"That's the text I received from my government."
Doron shrugged.

Silver took another look at the sheet of paper. "Concerning paragraph 1: you object to it being expressly stated that the conference is not to be reconvened. In paragraph 2, you object to mention of the word 'Palestine.' Then you object to reference to a state composed of Jews and Arabs. . . ." Silver raised his eyes. "There would have to be a special Geneva conference to negotiate the text of this document!" Stalking around to the far side of his desk, he tore the sheet of paper to shreds and threw them in the wastebasket.

"Of course, we all understand what you're trying to do. You know perfectly well that the joint communiqué is meaningless. This whole game can mean only one thing: that you aren't prepared to hand over Awad."

"It's not a matter . . ."

Silver raised his hand. "Let me finish," he demanded. "I'm not going to make trouble about this as long as I'm sure you have some reasonable plan. Do you?"

There was silence.

"Because if you don't—" Silver's voice rose, "—you are deliberately passing a sentence of death on dozens of innocent people!"

Doron had to admit that Silver's anger was justified. At this moment, his indignation was directed not at the Secretary of Defense but at his own government. *What was going on over there? Why didn't they give any indication of their plans?*

"There is no government more sensitive to human life than the government of Israel," he said diplomatically.

"You're entitled to think so," Silver snapped, "just as I'm entitled to disagree with you. Several of your operations failed to prove that. They proved only that your good luck far exceeded your responsibility and concern for the welfare of the hostages. I'm not prepared to put my trust in your luck!"

He rose and Doron did likewise. "Mr. Doron," said the Defense Secretary, "you heard what the President said. We expect a clear statement from you within the next few hours."

On the way home, Silver gave some thought to his visit with Lieberman. Strange. . . . Had circumstances been otherwise, he and his old friend might today have each other's positions, each other's homes and lives. But as the car drove down the main street of Georgetown toward his house, he came abruptly back to the present.

"What's this?"

Dozens of people were standing at his front gate. The driver stopped. "I don't know, sir. Looks like a demonstration. Shall I turn back?"

But it was too late. Several of the demonstrators had recognized the official limousine and were running toward it.

"Drive on!" Silver ordered. The driver eased the car forward to the entrance, but he was forced to halt before he could turn. The vehicle was suddenly surrounded.

The car windows were closed, and Silver could see nothing but the signs the demonstrators thrust at him: "We want our children!" "Israel—release the terrorists!" "Middle Eastern Terrorism—Never Again!" Silver's eyes focused on one sign which bore a personal note: "Jew Silver—are you with US or with Israel?"

Silver was outraged. How dare these people accuse him of being biased? He had worked long and hard to become an American, and he had publicly proved his loyalty. Now he was seeing how much good it had done him. Others would still assume that he was in some way different, lacking in something. No, not lacking. That he possessed the one thing they themselves lacked, the thing they feared and hated because it was an unknown. His Jewishness.

The police were able to push the crowds back to allow the car to squeeze past, and his driver stopped suddenly at the side entrance to his house so that he could jump out.

Silver entered his house and sank into an armchair. His daughter, Barbara, entered the room and put a cup of hot tea on the table near him. She had been watching the scene outside from the window and knew just how her father would react. She smiled weakly and sat on the rug, placing her head in his lap. He stroked her brown hair. Usually she resented it, complaining that he treated her like a baby although she was about to graduate from college. But this time she said nothing. Several seconds later, she placed her hand on his.

"They have no right to treat you like that."

"No."

"You may have been born Jewish, but that doesn't exactly count anymore, does it Dad? . . . I mean, you're not *real* Jewish."

He looked at her, his lower lip dropped, his eyes were wide open. What could he say? *Any child born of a Jewish mother.* . . . How did one answer such a question? "I'm American," he finally said.

"I know . . . but . . . I mean. . . . Do you *feel* Jewish?"

He became a little irritated.

"I told you that I'm an American and that's how I feel."

But Barbara persevered. "Do you have special feelings for Israel? Or is it like any other country?"

He put down his tea. "I have no special feelings for Israel. Does that answer your questions?"

She rose on her knees and turned toward him. "Does that answer *your* questions?" she asked. "And where does that leave me? What am I? Jewish? Not Jewish? What do you think, Dad?"

He stroked her face. "I think you are a young, beautiful, and intelligent woman."

She pulled her face away. "That's no answer."

His face was flushed. "It is the only answer I can give you. Other than that, you are what you choose to be."

"You chose. It didn't work."

Her words pierced right through him. *It is not for you to choose.* He heard his father's voice ringing in his ears. And Moshe's.

"It did work," he cried. "A handful of hooligans doesn't change that."

She stood and looked at a point over his head. "Maybe you should let somebody else handle this affair? Maybe . . ."

He jumped to his feet and, before he realized what he was doing, he slapped her face. For the first time in his life he had struck his daughter.

In that brief moment, he thought, *She is not my daughter and I am not her father. She is a non-Jewish woman looking at a Jewish man who just struck her.* But all that lasted no longer than a fraction of a second. The hateful look in Barbara's eyes softened and the thought disappeared from Silver's mind. He stretched out his arms and brought her head to his chest. "I am sorry, baby," he said, "so sorry."

When she left the room, Silver sat down and hid his face in his hands. What did it mean? That he had failed? He'd believed he could blend in. Was it all an illusion?

Silver raised his head. Nonsense. It was the confusion of the day.

As soon as this damned affair was over, life would return to normal. He could not be wrong after having been right for so many years. Impossible!

CHAPTER 24

"THE PRIME MINISTER is expecting you."

Lieberman nodded at the secretary and went in without knocking. The man seated across the room scowled at him.

"Have you heard about the killing?" the Prime Minister demanded.

"One man."

"What do you mean, one? One is the beginning. They're executing the hostages!"

"I don't think so. If that was their intention, they would have let us know. Otherwise, it would serve no purpose."

"How do you explain it, then?"

"They're jumpy, just as we are."

The Prime Minister looked at his watch. "I have a meeting now with Yedidia Rimon and General Negbi."

"What for?"

The Prime Minister closed his eyes in weariness. "Because they are the terrorists' parents." He pressed a buzzer on his desk. "Ask them to come in."

Yedidia Rimon and General Negbi entered and were greeted warmly by the Prime Minister. Lieberman remained seated in the far corner of the room.

The Israeli leader knew them both very well, Rimon in his public capacity, Negbi in his military one. He had often discussed matters of state with both men and at times had consulted one or the other on highly confidential matters. One could not find two more loyal and devoted Israelis.

He cleared his throat. "I've asked you to come because I felt it was my obligation to inform you where things stand just now. We are engaged in constant consultations with the United States. I want to assure you that we intend to resolve this incident in a peaceful way. We will make . . ."

"What if you fail?"

The Prime Minister didn't like General Negbi's tone of voice. It sounded more like a challenge than a question.

"In such a case we would have to review our position."

"Do you contemplate a military rescue operation?"

How much can I trust them now? the Prime Minister asked himself, and immediately answered, *Not at all. They are not impartial bystanders. They are parents.*

"No military operation is being discussed at this stage," he said, glancing at Lieberman, whose face remained expressionless.

"Why not?" said General Negbi. "What are you waiting for?"

"We want to avoid casualties. Among the hostages as well as the kidnappers."

"Why?" said the General heatedly. "They are terrorists and they deserve no such consideration."

Yedidia Rimon shifted his position in the chair. "Why did they become terrorists?" he said quietly. "This is the question we should ask ourselves, General Negbi. Maybe it is our fault. Maybe they are trying to do now what we neglected to do all these years. Maybe our children are tellings us, General, something we should listen to."

"I have no doubt, Mr. Rimon, that you have some soul-searching to do," Negbi retorted. "Your speeches and writings about the poor Palestinians . . . well. I hope you are satisfied now."

"I have never advocated a Palestinian state, and definitely not a Palestinian-Jewish state. On the other hand, your militancy . . ."

"Rimon! Negbi!" the Prime Minister protested. "I am sure there will be plenty of time for soul-searching after this incident is over. For all of us."

He got up slowly, looking very tired and tense. He walked to the other side of his desk, closer to his visitors. "I think I can understand your pain and frustration. But it is crucial that we maintain our calm now. We will report to you when there are new developments. Is there anything else I can do for you?"

General Negbi shook his head. Rimon paused, then asked, "Do you remember her?"

"I . . ."

"Deborah, I mean."

"Yes."

"She is my last child," the old man murmured, trying to overcome the tears in his voice. "Please remember."

"I will," the Prime Minister said. "I will."

Rimon walked out. The General was about to follow him, but suddenly he turned and went to the far corner of the room. Lieberman stood up.

"On the Hermon," said the General, "I wish it had been my son instead of yours." And he quickly left the room.

The buzzer sounded. The Prime Minister pressed the button, and his secretary's voice came through. "The ministers and the commander-in-chief are here."

"Tell them to come in."

The Foreign Minister started talking the minute he was through the door, without waiting for the other leaders to sit down. "The situation in America is deteriorating. Demonstrations everywhere! Temples bombed!"

"Calm yourself," said the Prime Minister.

"We must conclude this whole affair at once. We must sign the communiqué and release Awad."

"That's out of the question," said Lieberman.

"What alternative do we have?" asked the Defense Minister.

The Prime Minister turned to the head of the Mossad. "Go ahead."

Lieberman opened his briefcase and brought out three documents, which he laid on the desk in front of him.

"Obviously," he began, "the alternative is to rescue the hostages."

He spoke for eight minutes. When he concluded, the Defense Minister shifted uneasily in his seat. "The difficulty is that they expect something. They're not overlooking anything, not even the most bizarre plan."

"We needn't make a decision at this moment," said the Prime Minister. "Obviously, we cannot implement this plan—or any other plan—without American backing." He turned to Lieberman. "You do understand that, don't you?"

Lieberman did not respond.

"Without American backing, our position will be intolerable if we fail. I can't take responsibility for a botched rescue attempt."

"We can try," said the Defense Minister. "If there's one thing the President needs at this moment, it's some dramatic success."

The Foreign Minister grinned. "And if there's one thing he doesn't need, it's some dramatic setback. Apparently he is not, as their expression goes, a shoo-in. I wouldn't dare propose such a plan to them."

"Doron will take care of it," said the Prime Minister. "I think that's all for now, gentlemen. Moshe, will you wait just a minute?"

"I hope you understand," he continued when the others had filed out.

"I don't like the idea of letting the Americans in on our plan," said Lieberman. "That's risky."

"We can't do it without them. It's as simple as that "

Sitting in his car on the way to Tel Aviv, the Prime Minister's words kept running through his mind. "Our situation will be intolerable if we fail." In other words, the American backing was not the critical issue. The critical issue was avoiding failure.

Lieberman asked the driver to wait when they pulled up at his front door. He packed a small suitcase and hurried back to the car.

"To the airport," he directed. But then he changed his mind. "No, first drive to the prison."

Maruan Awad saw nothing unusual in the fact that the cockroach standing motionless on the ceiling was now his only friend in the entire world.

Anyone whose existence is totally confined within four walls must find some creature to whom to address his thoughts and reflections, and to be the object of his affection and concern. All these are life's most basic components; forfeiting any one of them means taking the risk of losing one's humanity.

There could have been no better listener than the cockroach. He already knew everything there was to know about Deborah. He had heard the most detailed descriptions of her body, her responsiveness, her treachery. But suddenly, Awad broke off, aware that someone else was listening.

"Awad!" Lieberman came in and laid a bundle of clothing on the bed. "Get dressed!"

A wave of joy swept over him, followed by a more powerful wave of fear. "Where are you taking me?"

"Get dressed!"

Silently, moving his battered body slowly and carefully, he put on his unpressed blue suit.

"Let's go," said Lieberman, nodding to the warden who stood in the doorway.

Awad began to walk through the doorway. Suddenly he halted and glanced back, up at the ceiling. Nothing. His eyes swept the cell, his agitation apparent. Suddenly, he flung himself to the ground and looked under the bed. His lips broke into a smile. There he was, standing motionless in a corner. Awad's eyes moistened. "Good-bye, dear friend," he mumbled.

The warden walked up to Awad, grabbed him by the collar, and hauled him to the car waiting outside. "To the hut," Lieberman order the driver.

After a ten-minute drive along the Tel Aviv-Jerusalem road, the driver turned right on a dirt track leading into an orange grove. For the next quarter of an hour, the car jumped and lurched, sending up clouds of dust. Finally, it approached a small green-painted hut, almost entirely concealed by the fruit trees.

Only Lieberman and his closest confidants knew of the existence of "the hut." The structure had no official function, and it did not appear in any inventory. Lieberman had bought it several years previously and maintained it with the sole purpose of ensuring that there be one place over which he had total control.

He got out of the car and knocked on the door of the hut. Instantly, a light appeared in the window.

"Who's there?"

"Moshe."

The door opened. Lieberman beckoned to the driver, who got out of the car, hauling Awad after him.

"I've brought you a guest," said Lieberman to the man at the door. "No one knows he's here. It must remain so."

"I understand."

Lieberman and his driver walked back to the car. "To the airport," Lieberman ordered.

Now they couldn't release him, even if they wanted to. If the Prime Minister got any hysterical ideas about dealing, he'd be thwarted before he could make a real error. Pulling a small notebook from his jacket pocket, Lieberman reached over for the car telephone. "Give me 418028," he said into the receiver.

After a couple of rings, he heard the sleepy voice of the state radio's correspondent for military and defense affairs.

"Lieberman here."

"I am listening."

"I've got something for you—just as long as you stick to the rules."

"Go ahead. I'm writing."

"Tomorrow, at 2:00 A.M., no earlier, start broadcasting the news that the government has released Awad and that he is on his way to Geneva. I repeat: tomorrow. 2:00 A.M."

"That kills the story. Who listens to the radio at 2:00 A.M.?"

"Whoever needs to listen." Lieberman slammed down the receiver. On the horizon, he could see the top of the Ben Gurion Airport's control tower.

CHAPTER 25

"YOU SEE WHAT I mean, Mr. Doron?"

Arieh Doron approached President Kelly, who was standing at the window gazing out at the milling crowd.

"Make no mistake, Mr. Ambassador," the President said in a confidential tone, "I want to be President for a second term. But the way things have been going these past few days, my prospects are plummeting to zero. I hope you bring news of favorable developments."

Doron glanced around the room. Silver's face was impassive; Taylor was rummaging through his attaché case.

"We have a plan. We believe it can work."

"Yes? Go on. . . ."

"A rescue plan."

Silver sprang to his feet, but a wave of the President's hand stemmed his protest. "Let him speak," said the President.

Doron outlined Lieberman's plan. When he finished, he sat down in the vacant chair beside Silver and waited.

Stunned into silence, the President simply stared at Doron. He made an effort to keep his tone matter-of-fact. "Have you weighed the risks?"

"That has been done. And I would not have been authorized to discuss this if the chances of success weren't considered good."

"How good?" demanded the President. "Fifty percent? Sixty? Seventy-five?"

"Something on that order."

The President approached Doron. "I'll be more generous. Ninety percent. No. Ninety-five. Does that satisfy you?"

Doron nodded. But now, the President could no longer control his voice. "Well, it doesn't satisfy me!" he shouted. "Do you know what will happen to me if your scheme backfires?"

Doron did not reply.

"Dozens of people will be killed," said Silver.

The President wheeled about to face him. "You can add one American President to the casualty list. But who cares? Israel doesn't give a damn what happens to me."

He turned again to face Doron, his voice low and tense. "For the past four years, you people haven't had a better friend than me here in Washington. Believe me, yours isn't the most popular cause around here. Still, I've never taken any steps which I thought might harm you, directly or indirectly.

"No, you received everything you asked for. Money? More than double the whole foreign aid allocation. Everybody was yelling, inflation, New York, oil—but you got what you wanted.

"Arms? You've never been equipped the way you are today. Political backing? Taylor, how many times have you told me that you're superfluous and that I'd better transfer your powers to the Israeli Foreign Minister?"

Taylor nodded his head. The President went on angrily, "What did I get in return? Gratitude? Praise? Nothing but gripes and complaints. Whenever anybody here talked about a Palestinian settlement, your newspapers started yelling as if we were about to drop an atom bomb on you. Your press always makes me look like a cheap crook."

Doron started to object, but the President silenced him with a wave of his arm. "I don't care about that. I said to myself: Listen, a small state, surrounded by enemies—you have to show some understanding. It's legitimate for them to be suspicious, even petty. Whatever they demand, whatever they receive, their situation is unenviable. Isn't that what I always told you, Ron?"

"Yes, sir."

"And now, I ask you, Mr. Doron. Will you grant me something in return? You people aren't fools. You've noticed how Marsden is gaining on me. Is that what you want? Do you believe that you'll be better off with Marsden in the White House? If you'd listened to him in the debates on the Middle East, I don't think you'd be too pleased."

"Of course we appreciate everything you've done for us," said Doron hoarsely.

"Oh, really?" retorted the President. "I begin to doubt it when you bring me a plan which will seal it up for Marsden at the convention tomorrow night. Tell me, does it make any political sense to hold on to a few damned terrorists and lose a friendly President?"

Kelly's plea embarrassed Doron. Here was a President of the U.S., a world leader, practically beside himself with fear of losing an election.

Not that his claims were entirely accurate. Doron had taken part in the endless arguments with the President over every dollar Israel requested, over every missile, every combat plane. Each time, Israel had been required to give something in exchange—some moderate political declaration, some assurance to cut down on future requests, some guarantee to stay in line, some concession to Egypt or Syria.

But he had to concede that there was considerable truth in the President's words. No nation could be expected to give without demanding something in return. That

was the political game. And while the United States demanded a price, it gave generously—whereas other states
demanded much, and gave nothing.

But what could he say? If it were up to him, he would
hand Awad and his companions over to the hijackers
forthwith. Doron was far from certain, however, that
everything was being reported to him. He had no idea
what the hell was brewing in Jerusalem.

"Mr. President, I promise to explain your exact feelings to my government. But I have to know whether your
opposition to the plan is final."

"Nothing could be more final!" thundered Kelly.

He turned to leave the room, beckoning to Silver.
"Come into my private office," he said.

When he had closed the door, the President threw off
his jacket and loosened his tie, "Whiskey?"

The President handed Silver a drink and sat down
facing him with his own glass in hand.

"How long have we known each other?" asked Kelly
thoughtfully.

"Ten years. Twelve, maybe."

"That's a long time."

"It can be."

"It's been a long time," repeated Kelly.

Silver smiled nervously. "You sound like a man who's
about to tell his mistress they're through."

The President did not find the remark amusing. "What
I'm about to ask of you isn't easy for me. I can only hope
that you understand the situation I'm in. I want to begin
by telling you that throughout many years of working
together, I've never had the slightest grounds for complaint
against you. I've always trusted you both as a loyal ad-
viser and a friend." The President took a long gulp from
his glass.

"However—" said Silver ironically.

"No 'howevers.' I made a mistake. I shouldn't have
assigned you the handling of this affair. Now they're
screaming for your head, and I am obliged to give it to 'em."

Silver nodded. He'd read the signs in the media. Nothing really unfavorable was said about him; there were

only hints and slurs. Was there the slightest conflict of interest? Was there just one chance in a hundred that the Israeli government was encouraged by the fact that the United States government had entrusted this hijacking affair to a Jew? Could one dismiss the possibility that the Defense Secretary's decisions were dictated by his origins?

"It goes without saying," added the President, "that this has nothing to do with your duties as Secretary of Defense. I don't have to tell you that I'm going to ask you to stay in your job for another four years." He grimaced. "If I'm reelected," he added in a low voice.

Silver put his empty glass down. "Do you want a letter?"

Kelly banged his hand on the small table beside him. "Damn it, Martin, I didn't invent this game. But the outcome changes daily. Tomorrow it could change again. So don't put on this offended act. In my place you wouldn't act any differently, and you know it!"

"I'm really trying to think what I'd do if I were in your situation, Mr. President. But I just can't. For the first time in my life, I understand that people like me simply cannot put themselves in the situation of people. . . ," he paused, considering his phrasing, ". . . of your background. Do you want a letter?"

"Don't be ridiculous. On your way out, issue a statement to the journalists."

After his brief encounter with the press, in which he said only a couple of carefully chosen words, Silver ordered his driver to take him back to his office. But then he changed his mind. He lacked the energy to pretend that nothing had happened.

His wife did not look at all surprised when he arrived home early. "I heard on the radio," she explained as she helped him off with his jacket.

He walked into his study and sat in his favorite armchair. She brought him a drink and sat on the arm of the chair beside him.

He grinned strangely. "This time, it's not demonstrations. It's not hooligans. It's the President of the United States."

"It's not fair," she said.

"Why not? After all, I'm a Jew, dealing with a Jewish issue."

She searched for the right words which would make her meaning clear without upsetting him. "With someone else there would be a conflict. But not with you. I know you well, darling. I know you wouldn't adopt some position concerning Israel just because you're Jewish."

He looked at her, and suddenly let out a tremendous burst of laughter. She was expressing her faith in him, paying him a compliment. How absurd.

She looked offended, and he hastened to pacify her. "I know you mean well, Joan, but it sounded so awful."

"What?"

"To the same extent, you could have said that I'm capable of reaching some decision concerning my family while overlooking the fact that it's my family. Is that moral? Is that virtuous? Would it be right of me to refrain from taking advantage of my position to help the Jews, when I myself am a Jew?"

"You were appointed to your position as an American, not as a Jew!" she said firmly.

He nodded, and then added softly, as if talking to himself, "I was appointed as myself, Martin Silver. I'm an American, yes. And I am a Jew." His own words stung him. He remembered his long conversations with Moshe. If he was right now, he had been wrong all his life. And if he had made such a fundamental error for so many years, what did his choices amount to? His alienation toward his people, his flag-waving patriotism, his Christian wife. He couldn't lie now, just when he was summoning up the courage to face himself. Yes, his children. His father had spoken the truth: they were Protestants. His home was a gentile home. He was an alien here, the only member of his family who did not belong to the exclusive club.

Suddenly, he found no good reason for not returning to his office.

CHAPTER 26

THE PRIME MINISTER picked up the phone on the first ring.

"Yes, yes," he said eagerly.

He listened to Doron's soft, monotonous drone. "I see," he said, and put down the receiver. Pressing the buzzer, he picked up the intercom. "Give me Lieberman."

The Foreign Minister and the Defense Minister looked at him impatiently.

"The Americans are against it," the Prime Minister told them.

"What did I tell you?" sighed the Foreign Minister.

The Prime Minister's aide entered. "Lieberman is out," he said.

"What do you mean 'out'?" the Prime Minister shouted. "He always leaves word where he can be found."

"His secretary says she doesn't know."

"Nonsense. Let me talk to her!" He grabbed the phone.

"Hello, this is the Prime Minister."

"Yes, sir."

"Where is Lieberman?"

There was a short silence. "I don't know, sir."

The Prime Minister lowered his voice. "Listen," he said gently. "This is a national emergency. Do you understand?"

There was another brief pause. "I'm sorry, sir. I can't say."

The Prime Minister was incredulous. "You can't say? Do you understand who you're talking to?"

"I'm sorry, sir. I have express orders not to tell anyone."

"I'm not just anyone!"

The woman's voice remained calm. "I am forbidden to tell even you, sir."

The Prime Minister struggled to control himself.

"What's your name? Or is that another secret?"

"Zipporah, sir."

"Listen, Zipporah. This is a matter of life and death."

"I understand, sir."

"Well?"

"I'm sorry, sir. But Mr. Lieberman ordered me not to say a word, even if I was told that it's a national emergency."

The Prime Minister's expression was that of a man who has just learned that he is not what he thinks he is. "Zipporah, I'll give orders to have you arrested if you don't tell me instantly."

The woman's voice remained completely cool. "I'm sorry, sir. Truly. But when I receive an order, I don't disobey it."

Furiously, the Prime Minister flung down the receiver. After a few seconds, a thin smile crept across his lips. "The lucky bastard," he mumbled. "Why can't I find a secretary like that?" Then he turned back to the others.

"Lieberman has vanished. The earth has simply swallowed him up."

"He must be up to something," said the Defense Minister.

"That's what's worrying me," the Prime Minister agreed. "But I can't believe he'd try anything. I expressly told him not to act before we'd heard from the Americans."

"What do you intend to do?" asked the Foreign Minister. "Just sit here and wait?"

"What do you propose?"

"I think we should announce that we are willing to release Awad without delay."

Of course, the Prime Minister thought. *A brilliant suggestion.* Logically, Awad's immediate release was vital. Sick or well, in one piece or several—that made no difference anymore. It had to be done, for the sake of the United States. Didn't it always come to that? No matter how events unfolded, he always ended up having to do something for the United States, to ensure continued aid and backing.

He called his aide again and asked him to get the chief warden of the security prison on the phone. When the man picked up, the Prime Minister ordered him to get Awad ready for immediate release.

The head warden sounded confused. "I can't do that, sir."

"What did you say?"

"He isn't here. Mr. Lieberman came during the night and took him away."

"Where to?"

"I have no idea."

"He didn't tell you?"

"He didn't tell anyone."

The Prime Minister banged down the receiver. "What's going on here? Who's running this confounded state anyway?"

"What's with Awad?" asked the Defense Minister cautiously.

"He's vanished with Lieberman. He transferred him somewhere else."

"So what's the problem?" asked the Foreign Minister. "How many prisons are there in the country?"

The Prime Minister shook his head. "That's a waste of time. If Lieberman wants to conceal Awad, we won't find him."

"He doesn't have this kind of power!" shouted the Foreign Minister. "He's got to be told to stop this insanity immediately!"

"I'm quite willing to tell him so," replied the Prime Minister. "But where the hell is he?"

Lieberman gave Marcel Danun a warm handshake. "Everything ready?"

"Everything you asked for."

As I expected, Lieberman thought. Marcel, head of European operations during the past two years, rarely said no. But what pleased Lieberman particularly was that even when he couldn't perform, he never excused himself. It was as though he were saying: You have to assume that I did my very best. If you don't assume so— well, that's your problem.

They were seated in Danun's room at the Ambassador Hotel, near the wide window looking out at one of the many canals which crisscrossed Amsterdam.

"I've rented a Cessna Stationer six," said Danun.

"What's its landing path?"

"Sixty meters."

"Good. The pilot?"

"He's okay."

"Do you know him?"

"He's done two jobs for me. Very expensive, but he's worth it."

Lieberman took the proffered cigarette. He lit it, and gulped down the smoke. His head spun. "What about Halid Ismail?"

Danun pulled a photograph from his pocket. "He's young," Lieberman muttered, examining the picture carefully as though intent on learning not only the look of the face and body but also the innermost secrets of the man's soul.

Having memorized his subject, he ripped the picture into tiny pieces, went into the bathroom, and flushed them down the toilet. Then he returned to the room, took off his shirt and pants, and clambered into bed wearing only his shorts. This was a well-established routine between the two men. Danun placed his feet on a chair and glanced out the window at the people sitting along the banks of the canal watching the boats glide past.

Lieberman woke an hour and a half later. Danun was in the same position. The sun was setting and its crimson rays poured through the window, highlighting Danun's swarthy face. As usual, his lips were set in a half-smile, giving him the tranquil demeanor of a man without a care in the world.

Stepping out of bed, Lieberman stretched his arms and yawned deeply.

"Feel better?" Danun asked.

"Fine. Thanks for standing guard."

He went into the bathroom and showered, then put on his suit and overcoat. "Let's go," he said.

A twenty-five minute drive brought them to the Israeli Embassy in Amsterdam. The ambassador was alone there, waiting for them near the entrance. He led Lieberman and Danun to his private office, then left. He had already put through the call to the Prime Minister.

Lieberman picked up the receiver which was lying on the desk. "Hello," he said into the phone.

"What are you doing in Amsterdam?" The Prime Minister was trying to sound calm, but Lieberman heard the edge in his voice.

"There was no time for arguments," Lieberman explained. "Please, trust me."

The Prime Minister glanced at the Foreign and Defense ministers, seated opposite him across the desk. He knew that they would be of no assistance now. It would have to be his own decision.

"May God have mercy upon us," he whispered into the receiver. Before replacing it, he added, "Good luck."

Lieberman put the phone down slowly. He rose, and Danun followed him. The ambassador showed them out. "Shalom," he said as they turned away. It was the first word he had uttered since their arrival.

Lieberman and Danun got into their rented car and headed for the Street of Love.

Two men watched Halid Ismail and his tall blonde companion as they strolled down the dimly lit street.

"Dammit," Danun hissed. "What will we do with the woman?"

"We'll have to continue," said Lieberman.

Halid and the prostitute entered a hotel. She led the young man through several corridors and into a dark room with peeling walls. It was the first time Halid had ever dared such an adventure, and he was ready to faint with excitement.

The woman locked the door. Unable to restrain himself any longer, Halid pulled her to him and began to shower kisses on her bosom, her neck, her ears. He kept trying to press his lips to hers, but she turned her head away. Finally, she managed to slip out of his grasp.

"Just a minute, kid," she snapped, zipping up her skirt.

"What's the matter?" Halid asked plaintively.

"Let's see your money first."

Halid reached into his jacket pocket and pulled out a handful of bills. "Is that all right?"

"You're a sweetie," she said, rapidly counting the bills and then stuffing them into her purse. "Now, I'm all yours."

Moments later, Halid had sunk into a deep sleep. The woman grinned. She felt as though she had stolen the money. This cute kid finished before he had even begun. She hoped he would become a regular client. She liked quickies.

The question was: should she stay all night or should she go back to her own apartment? True, he had paid for the whole night, but judging from his thunderous snores, he wasn't about to wake up and make additional demands. On the other hand, she might do well to be around when he did awaken the next morning. It might be possible to arrange a further rendezvous.

She turned over on her side and was beginning to feel drowsy when she suddenly heard a dull thud in the neighboring room. Her body stiffened. She could just make out the sound of footsteps. She shook Halid's arm, and he groaned. She shook him again, harder this time. But by the time his eyes were open, the two men were already in the room.

"Wait! Please!" the woman screamed as she sat up,

staring at the gun barrel. "I don't know this man. I'm just . . ." Her face still wore the same surprised expression when her lifeless body tumbled backward.

Halid made a desperate effort to burrow under the blankets. Lieberman stepped over and yanked the bedclothes off him. "Get dressed!" he commanded.

"What do you want?" Halid asked, terrified.

"Are you Halid Ismail?"

"Yes."

"You were in Paris in March? March the twenty-first?"

Halid hesitated. "What do you want?" he asked again.

"You are to come with us," Lieberman said. "You have nothing to be afraid of—if you will do as you are told."

"Why? Why me?"

Lieberman took two steps forward. "Because you have parents and four brothers and a sister in Nabatiyeh. If you are concerned about them, you will not ask any more questions. Let's go!"

Cautiously, Halid crept out of the bed, not taking his eyes off the two men, expecting their pistols to go off at any moment.

"Hurry up!" Danun urged.

Halid stared at the woman. Her eyes were open, her head hung slackly. The sheet covering her body was soaked with blood.

CHAPTER 27

THE RAIN FELL incessantly, doing little to soothe Deborah's overwrought nerves.

She was seated on the upper deck, one hand resting carelessly on the detonator handle, the other holding a cigarette. She glanced at the approaching dinghy: Yoram was holding the tiller, struggling to keep the teetering water containers from overturning.

Nabil walked over to the rail. Seizing the rope that Yoram flung up from the dinghy, he lashed it to a bar attached to the rail.

When Yoram had climbed onto the deck, Deborah permitted herself to remove her from the detonator handle. Idly, she asked herself what she would do if anything were to happen to Yoram. Would she really set off the explosive charges? She did not know. One thing she did know: if she were to set off the charges, it would not be an act of courage. She could do it only out of fear—that monotonous, dead feeling she had had ever since she had pulled the trigger.

She left the steering cabin and stood in the doorway, scanning the passengers. Bizarre. Their panic had vanished. Having grown accustomed to their situation, they were docile and obedient. Those who were feeling light-headed from the fast lay still, resting calmly. Some of the women were doing their laundry. Two groups of men were playing cards. A bunch of children were playing hide-and-seek. Every now and then, someone would glance at Deborah and nod a greeting. Some even smiled at her. In some strange way, she had become one of them. Sharing the same fate, trapped in the same place; whatever happened to them would happen to her, too.

Deborah was having trouble remembering the face of the man she had killed. Yesterday, the incident had seemed like a tragedy she would never be able to live with. Today, she knew that she was capable of killing again, if that were the only way she could get Awad back.

Yoram came over and sat beside her, exhausted by the effort of hauling the heavy water cans up onto the boat. Several yards from them Nabil stood facing the passengers, his submachine gun at the ready.

"It's quiet," said Yoram offhandedly. "I wonder what they're planning."

There was no response.

The passengers began to form up into four lines, with volunteers ladling out the water. There was no pushing or shouting. Everything was well-organized: the lines, the volunteers, the acceptance of a simple glass of water. They had all fallen into the rhythm of their survival routine.

"They must be planning something," said Yoram.

"You keep repeating yourself," Deborah snapped. She pointed at the passengers. "Do they look as though they're capable of doing anything?"

"I don't mean them. I mean Israel."

"Nonsense," said Deborah. "One light push and the boat is blown sky-high. They know that."

Yoram smiled grimly. "One of the first things I learned in the army was never to think in terms of logic or likelihood. Those are luxuries which only the strong or numerous can afford."

"So what do you propose?"

"Let's change our plans. Do something to catch them off-guard."

"We're not changing any plans!" Nabil bent toward his colleagues so that his gun was pointing directly at them as well as at the passengers in range.

Yoram blinked. "Don't you trust us?" he asked in disbelief.

"Why do you want to make new arrangements?"

"I told you. As a precaution."

"Just that? Have the two of you been planning things without me?"

Yoram turned to Deborah. "Would you believe it? He doesn't trust us!"

Deborah made no reply. She turned her back on both men, folded her arms, and just sat there, looking out over the dull water.

The rain continued to sweep the streets of Washington. Inside the car, Ambassador Doron could hear the swishing of the windshield wipers. Pennsylvania Avenue. K Street. The tall buildings. Government offices of imposing appearance. Quality. Quantity. Enormous power. The Americans had to be right. But the Israelis? It was presumptuous to try to be right when you had no more than three million citizens, when your balance of payments was in chronic deficit, and when you didn't have one oil well in the country.

The car halted. Doron jumped out and ran into the embassy, where his secretary was awaiting him. He took off his dripping overcoat.

"Did you get the Prime Minister?"

"I decided to wait. The President is giving a press conference."

They went up to the second floor, to the ambassador's private office. The television set in the corner was already on. The White House spokesman announced, "Ladies and gentlemen, the President of the United States."

The cameras shifted to the left, following the President's rapid stride as he hurried to the small dais and its battery of microphones. Kelly looked around, smiled, pulled two sheets of paper from his jacket pocket, put on an earnest expression, and began reading.

"Ladies and gentlemen of the press, for the past four days we all have been concerned with the boat hijacked in Lake Geneva. The city from which we expected tidings of peace has become the scene of a most shameful criminal act. From the very first moment, it was the view of the United States government that, in the absence of any alternative, and out of profound concern for the welfare of the hostages, the hijackers' demands would have to be met. It is my duty and privilege to stress that this view does not, in my opinion, contradict in any way the United States' fundamental and vigorous views concerning international terrorism. We still believe that acts of violence must be resisted by all means available. At the same time, ladies and gentlemen—" President Kelly raised his eyes, "we don't believe that the campaign against terrorism will be served by the deaths of the hostages on the boat."

The President turned a page. "Accordingly, we have spared no efforts to bring this affair to a satisfactory conclusion. We have approached all the governments concerned. I should point out that the Arab governments responded without delay, and they immediately signed the joint communiqué demanded by the hijackers."

The President cleared his throat and looked up again at the crowd, his expression grave. "It grieves me deeply that I cannot say the same about the Israeli government."

There was a silence. Doron and the secretary glanced at one another.

"All our requests have been rejected," the President went on. "Israel has refused to sign the joint communiqué. Israel has refused to release the prisoners held in her custody." The President raised his voice. "They *are* in Israeli custody. All of them. We are convinced of that."

There was a stir among the journalists. The President waited till silence was restored.

"Ladies and gentlemen of the press. In view of all this, I have arrived at the conclusion that the Unites States government can wait no longer for the Israeli cabinet to reach the decisions required by circumstances. Consequently, I have decided to notify the Israeli ambassador in Washington—the notification will reach him shortly—that, until further notice, he is no longer persona grata in the United States."

Several journalists made for the exits. The rest remained in their seats, waving their hands. The President folded the sheets of paper and turned to leave.

"Mr. President!" a woman's voice called out. "Does that mean a severance of diplomatic relations with Israel?"

"Not at this stage. It simply means that the presence of the ambassador is not appreciated at this time."

Dozens of questions rang out simultaneously, but the President had already left the podium. "Thank you," said the White House spokesman, and then he too departed. The telecast switched to a commentator, and Doron turned off the set.

The secretary picked up the red phone.

"Do you know what pains me more than anything else?" asked Doron pensively as she was dialing.

"What?"

"Did you see who was standing behind the President?"

"I didn't notice," she said.

"Rabbi Horowitz."

Wearily, Doron hoisted himself out of his seat. Taking the red phone, he repeated the main points of the President's statement. Then, after listening to the response, he replied, "All right," and put down the receiver.

"What did he say?"

"Nothing."

"What do you mean—'nothing'?"

"The Prime Minister says that Kelly's actions are of no importance now. All we can do is wait."

CHAPTER 28

"THAT WAS MAGNIFICENT," Jean Dromier announced aloud as he finished off the steak in tomato sauce. "I should cook for myself more often."

He wiped his mouth carefully on the linen napkin and stood, admiring the nice table he had set. The dishes could wait until later, he decided. As he was on his way into the living room for his pipe, the telephone rang. He considered not answering. Perhaps a quiet evening in front of the television, another glass of wine, an early bedtime. . . . He stared at the phone. People did not call so often these days. He lifted the receiver on the sixth ring.

"Mr. Dromier, this is National Electrique. We got the part you ordered. I knew you were anxious about it, so I took the liberty of calling you at home."

"Excellent. I'll be there first thing in the morning." said Dromier happily. Finally, he could go back to work.

"Three o'clock."

"In the afternoon?"

"In the morning. It's the only time we can deliver it."

Dromier was about to protest, but then he considered the advantages. Things would be going by the time the directors of the Geneva Water Corporation were even out of bed. They would see what sort of man they employed. The *jet d'eau* working overnight! Now that was service. "I'll be there," he told the voice on the other end of the phone. He hung up and began the hunt for his pipe. What a stroke of luck!

David Porat replaced the reciever of the pay phone and went back to his small hotel room to watch the clock.

The Cessna Stationer six naval plane winged its way toward Geneva. Moshe Lieberman was at the back, with Halid Ismail sitting beside him. Two seats to Halid's left sat Marcel Danun, his right hand gripping the pistol that rested on his knee.

The tiny plane tossed from side to side, scarcely able to contend with the powerful wind. Every now and then, it would suddenly plunge into a steep dive as it hit an air pocket. The raindrops falling on the plane's fuselage made an insistent, monotonous patter.

Lieberman felt uneasy, as he always did when confronted with something over which he had no control. Any mishap could cause a plane to stall and crash, and there would be nothing one could do about it. It was ten times worse in the Cessna, on a night like this.

Lieberman tried to distract himself by turning his thoughts to other matters. Gideon. The Prime Minister. Awad. But it was futile. The slightest lurch of the plane, the most distant flash of lightning, the merest rumble of thunder were sufficient to jerk his thoughts back to his present situation.

As for Marcel, the weather reminded him of his family and those infrequent evenings when the wind whistled outside and they would turn up the heater in their Tel Aviv home with everyone on the carpet—he and his wife and the three children. Laughing, shouting, tumbling all over one another. Happy. In another year or two, such evenings would be his to enjoy every night. Lieberman had promised him a staff job, and he would be perfectly content to sit at a desk and analyze other men's reports of danger and action.

Halid Ismail's mind was also occupied with thoughts of his family, especially his little sister, now a young woman. What if she ended up like that whore? His thoughts were interrupted when he noticed that Danun's fingers had lessened their grip on the pistol. An idea crossed his mind. Could he do it? Again he saw his sister, his stern, wrathful father, his younger brothers. Could he do it? What would happen to them? *But then,* he thought, *whatever would happen could not be prevented.* If the Israelis had marked them, they were probably doomed anyway.

Halid watched Danun's fingers, then his face. When he saw Danun's eyes close, he made his leap.

It happened so fast that Lieberman did not immediately grasp what was going on. By the time he understood the situation, Halid was lying on top of Danun. Lieberman jumped to his feet, grabbing Halid by the shoulder and pulling with all his might. And then he froze as a shot rang out.

Lieberman hoped it was Danun. He still needed Halid. The other man's part in the mission was over. He could manage on his own. But not without Halid.

Slowly, Halid began to move, drawing himself up gradually. The blood was still spurting from the gaping red hole in Danun's belly. Lieberman glared at the Arab, wishing he could kill him with his bare hands. *Not now,* he told himself. *Not yet.* Instead, he grabbed the young man by the arm and shoved him violently into his seat.

"What happened?" the pilot called out anxiously. "I thought I heard a shot."

"Everything's all right now," Lieberman responded. Then he leaned toward Halid and slapped his face with all his might. "Don't try that again."

Lieberman looked down at Danun, who stared back with hollow eyes. His hand still gripped the pistol.

"How do you feel?"

"How do I look?"

The blood gushed from the open wound. "Where's the first-aid kit?" Lieberman called up front.

The pilot handed back a box, and Lieberman fished around for anything that might help. Perfunctorily, he bandaged Marcel's wound, but it was of little use. The moment he finished the bandage was soaked through.

The man was in need of immediate medical attention. Lieberman stared at Halid, who was sitting calmly with a smug expression on his face. He clearly knew what was at stake. And so did Danun.

Lieberman stood, steadying himself against the plane's side. He stared at the wound in Danun's belly and tried to make himself think or feel. Suddenly, the man lying in front of him changed. It was Gideon. His son, Gideon. *Well then, Moshe Lieberman, make your decision on that basis. Your only son. If the plane does not land immediately, he dies. Can you still tell yourself that it's regrettable but casualties have to be expected, that they're part of the whole thing, that the success of the operation is more important than the life of one man?*

Lieberman leaned over. Gently, he took the gun from Danun. With his other hand, he touched the wounded man's head.

"What do I do?" asked the pilot.

"Go on as arranged," said Lieberman.

"Christ, this is terrible," President Kelly muttered. "Why do I have to make decisions like this?"

Ronald Taylor, who was standing motionless in the middle of the room, made no response.

"Is there no other way?" the President asked for the third time.

"We're not getting anywhere with them."

"Are you convinced that they really intend to take action?"

"No doubt about it."

The President grimaced. "Damned obstinate fools. Why can't they listen to reason, just for once?" He looked at Taylor. "Exactly what do you propose?"

"There are two options. One is to warn the hijackers, and—"

"Under no circumstances!"

Taylor fell silent. He gazed at the President, who was flushed with anger. "How dare you suggest such a thing?"

"I said it was an option."

"That's no option, damn it! Cooperating with the hijackers? And let the whole world know it?"

"There's a second option. Preventing the plane from landing."

"How?"

"Boats on the river."

"Who will know anything about it?"

"That can be arranged with the local authorities."

"It mustn't come from us. It mustn't lead back to us."

"Things have a way of getting to the press, Mr. President."

"That doesn't bother me, just as long as we can deny having anything to do with it, and just as long as no one can throw our denial back in our faces."

"That can be arranged."

"All right, then."

Susan Kraft walked up and down the length of the hotel room, trying to avoid Goren's eyes. "I don't know," she mumbled. "I should have gone straight to the police inspector and told him the whole thing."

She came close and let her body lean on his. "I'm so afraid."

"Everything's going to be all right."

"Will there be shooting?"

"Not necessarily."

"But you can't promise me."

"I can only promise to do everything—anything—to prevent it."

"Will you be taking part?" She raised her eyes.

He smiled. "Now you're looking for something new to worry about."

"You are!"

Goren kissed her lightly on the forehead, stroking her hair. "I've got to go now. Will you wait here for me?"

She shook her head. "I'm going to the hospital. I've got to pick up Jimmy." She kissed him, and he took her face between his hands. His eyes told her everything.

"Don't go. Please."

But he was already out the door.

He took the elevator down, walked across the hotel's crowded lobby, and swept through the revolving door. Glancing left and right, he hurried to the gray car parked near the entrance. He got in and the car sped away.

Eight minutes later the driver braked and stopped. Goren got out, taking a briefcase from the back seat. It was quite dark. Only the dim light of the street lamps illuminated the clock. The hands showed the time as 1:25. The dial was fashioned from pale red flowers, the hours were marked by pink roses and the minutes by light blue flowers, and the whole clock was framed in yellow flowers surrounded by a bed of dark red ones. Not a single petal out of place.

Beneath the clock and the lake stood a picturesque tourist restaurant, which was always packed on warm days. Dozens of diners would sit at the tables, enjoying the scent of the flowers and the view of the lake as they sipped on aperitif. The place was deserted now, the rain pelting down on the tables and the metal chairs piled on top of them.

Oblivious to the rain, Goren laid his briefcase on one of the tables and looked around. No one there. Opening the case, he pulled out a diving mask and put it on the table. He stripped down to his wetsuit and then took a pair of flippers and a small pistol from the case. Making sure that the gun was loaded, he pulled on a belt fitted with a holster, into which he slipped the pistol.

Goren walked over to the railing which bordered the lake. The hijacked boat lay no more than thirty yards away.

There were only a few dim lights on the vessel, and Goren could see only a few silhouettes. Every now and then, a head would appear at one of the portholes. Goren would have given a great deal to know whether it was a hostage or one of the hijackers he was seeing. His only real piece of luck so far had been to happen upon this isolated spot on the lake. The attention of those on the boat was focused on the other side, where hundreds of curious onlookers had stationed themselves. Even at this hour, Goren could see activity across the water.

Bending, he ran his hand over the wet grass and squatted down, preparing for an hour's wait.

CHAPTER 29

MARTIN SILVER glanced at his watch. 9:15. What the hell was he doing at the office at this hour? He had already read through all the letters and documents on his desk. He had already made a note of everything he would have to look into the next day. Nothing to do now but finish the dregs of the Johnny Walker bottle. Why didn't he go home where there was more?

The answer was simple: the office was the only place where he could be completely alone. He was uncomfortable in his study at home with his wife and children only a few feet away. Their very presence—even if they were asleep—would have intruded on his privacy.

And he had to be alone now. He could not simply dismiss the day's events as part of the risks of a political career. He had come to the crossroads he had avoided for so long; now he had to decide either to go straight on or to strike out in a new direction.

A knock at the door shook him from his reverie. He took the empty bottle and glass off the desk and placed them on the floor. "Come in," he called hoarsely.

The secretary on night duty walked in holding a sheet of paper. "You *did* ask to see all reports about the boat," she said apologetically.

"Right. Thank you."

He put on his reading glasses, but the words swam in front of his eyes. He had to hold the desk with both hands to steady himself before he could make out the text clearly. Even so, on first scanning the page, he could not get the meaning of the words. He began to read a second time, slowly, making a supreme effort to overcome the fogginess which clouded his brain. Only on the fourth reading did he understand it.

He put his glasses down on the desk and rubbed the bridge of his nose. Then he got up and walked to the bathroom adjoining his office, supporting himself against the furniture and walls as he went. He was going to have to make a decision now, regardless of how he felt. He turned on the cold tap, bent over, and let the water run over his head and neck.

You owe me nothing, Moshe Lieberman had said. Was that so? He must owe something to somebody.

He returned to his desk and picked up the phone. "Give me Ambassador Doron," he croaked in a half-whisper. He knew now that there was no turning back.

Doron was disappointed to hear Silver's voice. The Secretary of Defense had no further influence in this matter and therefore would not be a source of news. But as he listened, Doron realized that he was wrong. *Why is he doing this, for God's sake?* Doron pondered as he absorbed the information.

When Silver ended his monologue, Doron responded, "I appreciate what. . . ." But the line had already gone dead.

Minutes later, Doron was at his desk holding the red phone. When the Prime Minister picked up, he said, "The police inspector in Geneva intends to prevent the plane from coming down."

"What?" the Prime Minister gasped.

"At the bidding of the Americans," Doron explained tersely.

"I understand. Thanks."

Instantly, the Prime Minister summoned his secretary. "Notify the Mossad immediately. Doron says something is going on to halt the plans. They've got to get hold of Lieberman and their man in Geneva."

The secretary nodded and left the room. What in God's name could Lieberman be doing at this moment? He stood near the door and startled the secretary, who had nearly run into the room with his report.

"Sorry, sir," he said, recovering quickly. "But I've just found out that Goren is their man in Geneva. They can't get hold of him. Or Lieberman," he added, anticipating the next question.

The Prime Minister looked at his watch. 4:58. "Never mind," he said wearily. "It's too late anyway." Then he shook himself and banged his fist on the nearest chair. "News!" he ordered, and the secretary crossed the room to switch on the radio. They heard a time signal, then the voice of the broadcaster, who was having trouble suppressing his agitation.

"Our military correspondent quotes a reliable source as reporting that the Israeli government has decided to release Maruan Awad, who has been in custody for an unspecified length of time. Our correspondent learned that Awad has already left Israeli territory and is now being flown to Geneva. It has been established further that Awad is to be handed over to the hijackers by Halid Ismail, who was involved with the Ishmaelite group."

The Prime Minister stared.

"Do you think he really intends to release Awad?" the secretary asked.

"Don't be a fool," responded the Prime Minister.

Deborah could not believe that she had heard correctly. "What did they say? What did they say?"

"They're releasing Awad," said Nabil, smiling.

Deborah flung herself at him, alternately laughing

and crying. She had been almost certain she would never see Awad again.

"What's happening?"

Deborah ran to Yoram, who had come from the other side of the vessel. She hugged him too, telling him of the radio report. Yoram's worried expression remained unchanged. "Did they say anything about the joint communiqué?" he asked.

Deborah shrugged. The communiqué had never really been as important to her, and Yoram knew it.

"So what are you getting all excited about?" Yoram went on. "Listen here, Deborah. I didn't get into this whole thing just to free your lover. I came here to advance the cause of the Palestinian-Israeli state." He looked at Nabil. Stepping backward, he raised his submachine gun slightly. "If that wasn't your intention as well, I want to know now."

"We're in agreement," said Nabil hastily.

"We won't leave till we get the communiqué," said Deborah. "But this is something. They're ready to meet our demands."

"It might be a trick."

"He's being brought by Halid. That's what the broadcast said. What trick can there be?" Deborah walked up to Yoram. "Don't you see? They've given in."

Yoram's face was a cold mask. He stared at Deborah. "Given in what? We came here to disrupt the conference, to get a statement that would advance our cause. And all you can think about is Awad. No, Deborah. It's you who have given in."

She felt her cheeks grow hot. "Since when did you become such a big champion of the cause? If it wasn't for me you would have given up long ago."

"But I didn't. And you are. Now."

Suddenly, she saw the image of Peterson lying dead on the deck, and she felt a desperate need for a comforting gesture, a warm word. "Please, Yoram, don't talk to me like that. I have committed my life to the cause. You know that better than anybody else."

He kept looking at her, but his expression remained

cool. "No, I don't," he said quietly. "Not any more. But you can prove me wrong."

"How?"

"Don't accept Awad until the rest of our demands are met."

They looked at each other for long seconds. Finally, it was Deborah who lowered her eyes. "I can't," she whispered, and Yoram felt a terrible ache in his chest.

"Very well, then," he said. "But I am not leaving this boat till I achieve my objective."

"We've arrived," the pilot said quietly.

Lieberman glanced at his watch. 2:40. Too early.

"Make a few turns."

He leaned over and peered out the window. He couldn't see a thing—just a slight reflection off the lake below. "Can you see the boat?" he asked.

"Over there." The pilot pointed.

Lieberman strained his eyes. He could not make out the boat, but he guessed that the dim lights he saw marked its position.

"We'd better go down a little."

Lieberman left the window and kneeled beside Marcel Danun. The man's swarthy face was pale; perspiration was running down his neck and onto his shirt, which was soaked with a mixture of sweat and blood. Lieberman had changed the bandages three times, but they still failed to halt the stream of blood. An unpleasant odor began to pervade the little plane.

"How do you feel?"

Danun tried to open his eyes, but he was too weak. He mumbled something which Lieberman could not hear. He placed his ear near the wounded man's lips. "I'm going to die," he heard.

"Don't kid yourself," said Lieberman, trying to make his tone jocular. "In another half hour you'll be in the hospital."

A sardonic laugh sounded from the rear seat. "Bullshit," said Halid. "You're lying. He's going to die."

In a flash, Lieberman's powerful fingers were around Halid's throat, tightening their grip as the man struggled to breathe. Lieberman needed every ounce of restraint to overcome the temptation to shut the Arab's mouth once and for all. He loosened his grip.

"Mr. Lieberman?" The pilot was pointing down at the lake.

"What's that?"

"That's our whole mission—scrapped."

"What the hell do you mean?"

"Boats. They're blocking our landing path."

"Ridiculous. You can land."

"I can, but it'll be a long way from the boat."

"Out of the question."

"There's no other way."

Now he knew. Even the best and most meticulously prepared plan couldn't help hitting some snag. He glanced at his watch.

"Make another turn," he said quietly.

Eli Goren sprang up, his heart pounding madly as he realized he had dozed off. Horrified, he looked at his watch. 2:50. All right, nothing to worry about.

He saw at once that one of the tables had been moved, causing the chairs to tumble off it, and it was the noise that had awakened him. He glanced around nervously, then spotted a man weaving through the tables in the direction of the lake, swaying from side to side. He staggered past the tree where Goren was crouching and nearly brushed against him as he proceeded on his drunken stroll.

Goren had no choice: he would have to take the risk of revealing himself. More important that he got the man out of the way. He had only ten minutes. He was about to grab the man's arm, but in that instant the drunk saw him and fled in terror.

Goren peered into the sky. The drone of an engine. It wasn't far off. He glanced out at the boat, which was exactly in the same spot it had been in before he had fallen asleep. He looked along the shore, and jerked upright. Three boats were casting off from the pier. They were pointed directly at the hijacked vessel. *Maybe it's just a patrol,* Goren thought, trying to control his growing apprehension. *Maybe they were bringing out more water cans.* Anything, just as long as it wasn't what he feared.

He continued to watch the motorboats' progress. One of them halted about fifty yards to the north of the hijacked vessel. A second one approached, and the pilot of the first vessel climbed aboard; the unmanned boat remained motionless.

A third boat was stationed thirty yards further north. Its pilot also disembarked and, with the others, sped back to the shore in the first boat.

On Lake Geneva, facing the Palais des Nations, there were now three silent silhouettes: the hijacked pleasure boat flanked by two unmanned motorboats, whose forward lights were left on.

Goren felt tears of anger fill his eyes. Everything was going down the drain. This was madness! Who botched the operation?

He pulled himself together and gathered his strength. Perhaps *he* could do something. But what? Any movement might disclose his presence. And if that were to happen, he would be unable to help the rescue team when it arrived.

But if he didn't act, the team wouldn't be able to arrive.

Goren plunged into the water and swam as if his life depended on it.

CHAPTER 30

DEBORAH APPROACHED JAN and Eli with a warm smile on her face. "They're releasing Maruan Awad," she told them. "It will be over very soon, I promise."

"Deborah!" Nabil ran across the deck and grabbed her by the shoulder. "Look!"

Through the light drizzle she saw the lights of two motorboats which had been stationed nearby on the shore. They were moving toward the pleasure boat.

She grabbed the bullhorn. "Hello Geneva, hello Geneva. What's going on here?" she shouted.

There was no answer from the shore. Deborah took Yoram's binoculars. Numerous policemen were gathering on the shore—more of them than usual. There was something odd about their behavior and the way they were watching the boat. As though they were expecting some-

(234) thing to happen.

Somebody is trying to prevent Awad's release, Deborah thought in a fury. She put the bullhorn to her lips once again. "We demand that you remove those boats instantly. Instantly."

She saw scurrying on the shore. Then Yoram yanked at her shirt.

"Look!"

She turned in the direction he was pointing. They saw a man pull himself out of the water and clamber aboard the nearest of the two boats. He started the engine and headed for the other unmanned vessel.

Deborah looked up. She could see the lights of a small plane. The plane carrying Maruan Awad. On the water, the first motorboat now rapidly approached the second boat.

Deborah closed her eyes, praying that the man on the boat intended to clear the way for the plane and that he would make it—whoever he was.

"Prepare to land!" Lieberman told the pilot.

The pilot shook his head vigorously. "Sorry, I won't do it. It's suicide."

Lieberman put his hand in his jacket pocket and brought out his gun. "I won't hesitate to use it," he said.

"We'll all die," said the pilot.

"Yes," said Lieberman.

The pilot looked at him, realizing that he meant it.

He pressed down on the bar to his right, and the plane descended.

"Just so there's no misunderstanding," said Lieberman. "Twenty or thirty yards from the boat. No further."

"Don't listen to him," shouted Halid, moving forward toward the pilot. "He's crazy!"

Lieberman pointed his gun at Halid and stared at the Arab wordlessly. Slowly, Halid sidled back into his seat, taking a firm grip on the one in front.

The small plane rapidly approached the water, and the motionless motorboats. The pilot felt the sweat pouring down his hand, but he did not dare remove it from the metal bar.

Lieberman glanced at Marcel Danun. As far as he could see, the man had lost consciousness. If he was lucky.

The pilot looked down at the water, which was rushing up to meet them at a terrifying speed. Suddenly, one of the lights began to move. Lieberman and the pilot stared at it, mesmerized. The plane was rapidly approaching the boats. Four hundred feet, three hundred feet, two hundred feet. And now the second boat was also beginning to move, drawn along by the first. A few seconds later, the plane's undercarriage touched the water.

Goren screamed, ducking out of the way to dodge the wing. He was almost swept overboard by the wake. When he had recovered, he steered the two motorboats toward the shore. The trip seemed endless. The plane rocked on the water, dangerously close. When Goren had moored the two boats, he plunged back into the water. Slowly and quietly, doing his best not to attract attention, he began to swim toward the hijacked boat.

It was silent on the water. The only sound was the monotonous drone of the plane's engine. Everyone waited to see who would make the first move.

"You're on," Lieberman said curtly to Halid Ismail, whose face was still pressed against the back of the next seat. He was muttering a prayer to himself in Arabic, intoning the chant in a high, nasal voice.

Slowly the Arab raised his eyes, and Lieberman handed him a bullhorn. "You address yourself to Deborah Rimon. If you are asked any questions, you will answer shortly and to the point. Understood?"

Halid didn't respond. Lieberman grasped his hand firmly. "Make no mistake about what's going to happen to you if you try anything funny. And to your family." At the mention of his family, Lieberman saw fierce hatred spring into Halid's eyes. That was just fine with him. It meant that the Arab got the message.

Lieberman let go of Halid's hand. "Okay. Now."

Halid directed the bullhorn out the window and held it close to his mouth.

"Deborah Rimon," he shouted.

There was no response.

"Louder!" Lieberman commanded.

"Deborah Rimon!" Halid shouted once more.

"Deborah here."

"This is Halid Ismail."

Nabil snatched the loudspeaker out of Deborah's hand.

"Identify yourself. Where were you born?"

"Hebron."

"Where did you grow up?"

"Nabatiyeh."

"What mark do I have on my body?"

"A scar on your belly."

Deborah nodded and took the horn from Nabil.

"Welcome, Halid. Let me talk to Maruan."

Halid glanced at Lieberman, whose features remained expressionless.

"They'll only allow him to talk to you after you free the hostages."

"Out of the question!" Yoram said to Deborah. "You promised!"

"We must get Awad out! This may be our last chance!"

"I'm staying here," Yoram declared.

"I propose that Deborah and I go and receive Awad," said Nabil. "As soon as he's handed over, we'll come back to the boat."

"They won't hand him over."

"They won't endanger the hostages."

Deborah lifted the bullhorn.

"Nabil and I will get into a dinghy and come to fetch Awad. Yoram will remain on the boat. The moment we have custody of Awad, Yoram will release the hostages."

Lieberman nodded. "Agreed," Halid shouted.

From every side, all eyes were fixed on the boat. Even on the shore, where thousands had congregated, there was total silence.

Deborah placed her foot on the top rung of the rope ladder. Eli Goren, who was holding on to the bottom, hastily dived underneath the boat.

Deborah clambered into the rowboat next to the ladder, and Nabil followed. He picked up the oars and began rowing toward the plane. Neither of them saw Eli Goren grab the bottom of the rope ladder as soon as the boat moved off.

Nabil rowed, his back toward the plane. Deborah sat facing the plane, tightening her grasp on the submachine gun as the rowboat advanced.

"That's close enough," she said.

Nabil stopped rowing.

The rowboat was now halfway between the pleasure boat and the plane. Deborah picked up the bullhorn. "We're waiting," she shouted.

Her heart pounded wildly. How would he look? How would it be between them?

The plane's engine revved, and it taxied toward the rowboat. Fourteen yards . . . twelve yards . . . ten. . . .

Porat looked nervously at his watch. "What's the problem?"

"Another two turns and it's in," replied Jean Dromier. His forehead was covered with perspiration and he was breathing heavily. Hoisting himself up, he gave another twist to the heavy screwdriver. One more turn and the *jet d'eau* would start functioning again.

Taking a deep breath, he grasped the screwdriver and bore down.

With a mighty roar, the *jet d'eau* erupted in Lake Geneva, its powerful turbines sending up a jet of 110 gallons a second, at over 100 miles an hour, with a driving force of 7 tons.

The roaring jet stunned everyone on the boat, and it was unclear who fired the first shot. Nabil was the first to fall into the water, with two ugly red stains on his chest.

Deborah could not think. She only sensed that her submachine gun was blasting off. It continued firing even after the first bullet hit her in the belly. It only stopped when the second bullet struck her face, between her lip and her right cheek. The lower part of her body remained jammed in the boat, while her face sank into the water, surrounded by a halo of blonde hair which rippled around her like sheaves of ripe wheat.

"Get to the boat—fast!" Lieberman shouted to the pilot.

Out of the corner of his eye, he saw Halid trying to jump into the water. He was halfway out of the plane when the bullet hit his neck. Lieberman caught a glimpse of Goren scrambling up the rope ladder. Within seconds, Goren was on the deck, going for Yoram, who was racing toward the steering cabin.

The detonator, was all Goren could think of as he commanded his legs to propel him after the hijacker. He remembered Susan's description of the device. Raising his gun, he fired, but he was afraid of hitting the hostages and he missed his target. Yoram halted, glancing back, an expression of terror on his face. This moment was worse than any before—worse than the slide off the roof in training, worse than firing his first shot, worse even than facing his father's disapproval when he was transferred. He seized the first hostage within range. It was a young boy, who had been crouching in terror by the boat's side. Yoram jerked the child's arm and pulled him close, shielding himself from his pursuer with the small body.

Pointing his gun at the boy's head, Yoram slowly paced backward toward the steering cabin. Goren felt his guts turn over. Two paces, three, five. Another two or three steps, and Yoram's hand would be touching the detonator.

The two Israelis glared at each other. Yoram's thoughts were confused, panicked. *Could he shoot?* He was trembling. *The Hermon. The Syrians storming the door. Amos getting it in the guts. Gideon. . . .*

It sounded as though a single shot was fired. But after the two bodies tumbled onto the deck, it was clear what had happened. Yoram's throat was torn open. The child's head was blown apart.

The passengers stared at Goren in horror, uncertain whether to fear him or to trust him. He was still holding the gun. His complexion was pale; he looked nearly transparent.

Slowly, he approached the two corpses. Suddenly, a young man blocked his path. "Keep away from him," Jan growled.

"Who is the boy?" Goren asked in a terrified whisper. He had to know.

"Eli. Eli Kraft."

Everything began to revolve at a dizzying speed. Instinctively, Goren grabbed for the nearest seat. His eyes closed.

"You murdered him," he heard Jan mumble.

He felt a hand on his shoulder. He looked up at Lieberman. "Did you get him?"

"He's dead," Goren whispered. But he was not answering Lieberman's question.

"It's all over. You are free," the head of the Mossad told the assembled passengers. There were cries of joy from all sides as the people took in the news, embracing each other, crying and laughing at once. The German youth knelt by the small body on the deck. Lieberman crouched down beside him.

"I'm sorry," he said gently, but the young man did not respond. Lieberman straightened. The air was cool on his skin, and he shivered. He was soaked through. Everyone there was in the same condition because the *jet d'eau* was now sending up a continual stream of water. Lieberman looked around for the captain.

"Is there no way of turning that damn thing off?"

CHAPTER 31

MARTIN SILVER could read the President's mood the moment he entered the Oval Office. Kelly was seated at his writing desk, his head resting on his right hand; his angry gaze was fixed on the carpet.

Kenneth Garden, chairman of the President's reelection committee, was conversing in a whisper with Ronald Taylor. Dick Radshaw, the President's secretary, was pretending to read some documents he had brought in. Silver sat down beside him.

The President looked up. "Gentlemen," he said, "we have to accept the situation. The Israelis have made us look like a bunch of fools. It was all well and good that they liberated the hostages. Thank God, their operation was a brilliant success. But precisely for that reason, we come out looking stupid, and that's the way we're going to look at the convention tonight."

Garden was skeptical. "Even so," he said, "I don't see how that gives Marsden much of an advantage. He emphatically supported giving in to the hijackers. He certainly is in no position to criticize us while praising Israel."

"I agree," said Radshaw. "If the rescue operation destroys anyone, it's Marsden."

"Marsden wasn't in the White House," Taylor said pensively. "He can claim that he would have acted differently had he known the facts. He can claim anything. He didn't have to be right. And all he has to do now is convince the delegates that the President was wrong."

"That's what worries me," Kelly agreed. "We went on record saying that the operation had to be prevented."

"I don't see how that makes us culpable," Taylor protested.

"What do you mean?"

"We went on record, all right. And we know we actually tried to foil the operation. Aside from a few Israelis who also know, no one else does. We're still in the clear."

"What are you talking about?" the President snapped. "I went on television to announce that the Israeli ambassador was persona non grata." He paused and then added, "As you proposed."

Taylor felt no embarrassment or rancor—such was politics, after all. Now that the Israeli operation had been completed successfully, it was his proposal. "Mr. President, that does not worry me in the least. I believe that the outcome of the hijacking can be exploited to our advantage."

"How?"

Taylor explained his plan. When he finished, Kelly looked calmer; he even smiled.

"Okay," he said, "go to it."

The President got up, indicating that the meeting was over. The others were about to leave when Silver spoke up.

"There is something you ought to know, Mr. President," said the Secretary of Defense in a hoarse voice.

"What is it?" the President asked impatiently.

Silver cleared his throat. He wanted everything he

said to sound out clearly and distinctly. "I informed the Israelis about our plan to station boats on the lake."

An astonished silence fell upon the room. Taylor was the first to pull himself together. "I suggest, Mr. President, that we did not hear what the Secretary of Defense just told us."

Yes, thought Kelly. *That's it. No further complications.* He nodded.

"No," said Silver. The word reverberated in the room.

The President walked over to him. "Marty, you feel all right?" Silver nodded. The President went back to his chair and sat down. "What do you hope to achieve by this?" he asked wearily.

"I don't know," silver responded. "Maybe, something I lost a long time ago."

Garden fidgeted nervously. "Look, why don't we just skip it for now. If you still feel the same, we can discuss it after the convention."

Silver turned toward him. "Do you understand what I said? I, Martin Silver, United States Secretary of Defense, delivered defense information to another state." He spun around and faced the President. "I want you to dismiss me. Today."

"You're out of your mind!" Kelly exploded. "Today, on the eve of the convention, you want me to make it known that a Defense Secretary whom *I* appointed has revealed secret information? Why don't you simply ask me to walk over to the window and jump?"

"Be reasonable," Taylor said harshly. "If you think this will make you into a hero, you're mistaken. The public is not going to cheer you for helping to make the operation a success. The Israelis get the credit for that. But you, you'll be branded as a traitor. It'll destroy you . . . and your family."

Taylor could see that he had hit his mark. For the first time since his revelation, Silver seemed uncertain. He hadn't thought about the children.

"Look, the best solution for everybody concerned is to continue acting normally," Taylor went on. "The President will be reelected, there'll be new appointments, and nobody will give it a second thought. And if the President isn't reelected—" rapidly he interjected "which I don't imagine for a moment"— it will be even more natural for you to bow out of the public eye." He let his words sink in. "What do you say?"

Silver looked at Taylor, then at the President, Garden, and Radshaw. He got up and walked out of the room.

Arieh Doron found himself unable to savor this moment to the fullest. Somehow he couldn't help feeling that it was a Pyrrhic victory.

This time he was not summoned to Taylor's office; instead, the Secretary of State had come to see him. He smiled broadly as he walked through the door, and his handshake was hearty and firm.

"My deepest congratulations on your brilliant operation," said Taylor, beaming. "You should be proud."

Doron was not feeling particularly diplomatic at this moment. "That isn't what you thought five hours ago."

"My dear friend," Taylor said, maintaining his composure, "I don't think that it will be in our two countries' interests to hold a grudge. When will you people learn that you can't expect the whole world to adopt your methods?"

"Mr. Secretary, have you anything else to discuss with me?"

Taylor took off his glasses. "Yes, I certainly do. I propose that when we leave this room, we have an agreed-upon version of the events preceding the rescue operation."

"Of course," said Doron. "There is only one true version. And we both know what it is."

"Well, Mr. Doron," said Taylor, "let's see just what we *do* know. Is it the truth that you were prepared to endanger the lives of some eighty hostages for the sake of one Arab terrorist? You wouldn't admit it. So what is the truth, Mr. Doron? That the state of Israel, whose very existence depends largely on the United States, misled and deceived her benefactor? No. You'd say that Israel has done the United States a great favor, that Israel has done the dirty work the United States did not choose to do."

He took a deep breath. "No, Mr. Doron. You took the initiative, you carried out the operation, you succeeded. Those are the facts; I don't deny them. But that's only one side of the truth. The other side lies behind the facts. The circumstances. The chances taken. Whether or not the operation was necessary. Let's be frank with each other, Mr. Doron. That operation should never have been launched. It was lunacy."

"What are you driving at?" Doron asked.

Taylor came around the side of the desk and faced Doron. "The party's convention is opening tonight. Nobody there is going to listen to explanations. They all want snappy slogans that people can remember easily. That's why we need an agreed-upon version."

"A share of the credit," said Doron softly.

"Precisely," said Taylor. "We need it, and you need it."

"We do?"

"Definitely. The question of who will be the next President of the United States is as important to you people as it is to every American citizen." He took his next step cautiously. "If your story comes out, you're likely to be handing the nomination to Marsden on a silver platter. Is that what you want?"

Doron stood up and began to pace the room, thinking. "I'm not sure now that we prefer Kelly to Marsden," he said carefully. "It isn't just this affair. Several of our aid requests have been turned down lately. I still remember what a cold reception we got when we asked for the additional five hundred million. Perhaps we would have better luck with Marsden."

Taylor relaxed; he had reached familiar ground. Bargaining was his specialty. It gave him an electric thrill to be able to play this game as well as he did. He had come halfway. The other half would be much easier.

"I can assure you that the President will review the requests again," he said. And then he added, "In the most favorable light. He can't promise anything about the

Harding missiles, but you can consider the planes and the financial aid as settled."

"The President may not see things in such a 'favorable light' after he's reelected, Mr. Taylor. And then, he may not be reelected."

"It will be seen to before the elections."

"Can I have that in writing?"

"I'll send it to you the moment I return to my office." Taylor rose with a large smile on his face. "I'm glad we understand each other," he said as he shook hands with Doron.

"Till the next crisis."

"Let us hope that's not for a long time," said Taylor with a smile.

"If I am still here." There was a small smile on the ambassador's face.

Taylor pretended to remember one more item which would interest Doron. "Oh, yes. I've had a statement drawn up saying that the whole persona non grata thing was a mutually agreed-upon smoke screen."

After Taylor's departure Doron stood wrapped in thought. Then he stepped over to the television and pulled the knob. Instantly, the room was filled with the din of the delegates' hand-clapping as they cheered the President of the United States. Every now and then, the camera would focus on Kelly, his face perspiring but beaming with joy as he raised his arms high.

"At least he's not making the victory sign," Doron muttered to himself.

The applause thundered on, the delegates ignoring the chairman's appeals for silence so that the President could begin his address. They loved him; no doubt about it.

His secretary walked in. "Your car is waiting."

Doron nodded and left the room without turning off the set. He slid into the back seat of the long black limousine, brushing off the drops of rain which clung to his coat. "Please turn on the radio," he asked the driver.

Instantly, he heard the President's voice boom out. "Once again," he was saying, "we have demonstrated the unreserved friendship prevailing between the United

States and Israel. To all those who have ever criticized our support for this brave country I say never, never has the United States channeled its resources to a worthier cause. This small nation, fighting heroically for its existence, deserves the thanks, and the assistance, of the American people. And I assure you, it will get both!"

Once again, there was applause, whistling, and cheering. Doron could hear thousands of voices chanting, "Kelly for President!" "Long live Israel!"

"Switch off the radio, if you would," Doron told the driver. He leaned his head back and rested it against the upholstery. *What kind of country is this anyway?*

Doron refused to answer the question, even to himself.

CHAPTER 32

THE PLANE CARRYING Moshe Lieberman back to Israel taxied onto a side runway, where there were no journalists, cameras, or microphones. Just an ambulance and Lieberman's chief aide, David Porat.

"The Prime Minister requests that you contact him at once," Porat told him as they stood together in the chilly dawn.

Lieberman did not move. In a few seconds, two men brought a stretcher out of the plane. Marcel Danun's body was covered with a white sheet.

A third man, bearing a thick leather briefcase, followed the stretcher out.

"Dr. Zussman?"

The doctor stopped next to Lieberman.

"What was the cause of death?"

"Who are you, sir?"

"His commander."

The doctor glanced at Porat, who nodded his confirmation. "Loss of blood. A pity. If only it had been possible. . . ."

"Thanks," muttered Lieberman and hurried away toward the terminal.

"The whole country is going crazy," he heard Porat say directly behind him. "The Prime Minister, the Defense and Foreign ministers—they're all suddenly national heroes."

Lieberman got into the back of the car and Porat climbed in beside the driver. "To the Prime Minister's office," Porat directed.

"No," said Lieberman curtly. "To the hut."

A cold rain fell, the raindrops mixed with snowflakes. When they reached the orange grove, the dirt track was flooded, and the car nearly got stuck in the thick mud.

As they halted outside the hut, the curtain in the front window was jerked aside. Instantly, the door opened and Lieberman entered.

"How is he?" he asked.

"Quiet," said the guard.

Pulling out a key, the guard unlocked a heavy padlock on the massive iron door. Lieberman shoved the door open and entered. He was trying to get his eyes accustomed to the darkness when a yell froze his blood.

"Look out!" Porat shouted.

It was too late. Maruan Awad's hands were already at Lieberman's throat as he shouted, "I'll kill you, you dirty Jewish whore! I'll kill you!"

Porat grabbed Awad by the shoulders and pulled him away from Lieberman. The Arab continued to struggle till a blow from the guard sent him sprawling. Instantly, he calmed down, and his eyes widened in astonishment. "Why don't you let me kill her. That bitch—Rimon—she turned me in. Don't you understand?"

Lieberman looked at Porat, who shrugged. "He's out of his mind."

Lieberman turned back to Awad. "Get up." Awad's face lost its hate-filled expression. Suddenly he was child-like, fearful.

"Do you want to interrogate me again? Please, no. I've told everything. Ask Porat—he knows. Haven't I told everything?"

"Get up!" Lieberman commanded again. In a cold voice, he added, "There will be no further interrogation." Instantly, Awad scrambled to the side of the hut, but Lieberman grabbed him by the arm and shoved him out the door. Awad walked carefully, as though he had not been on his feet for days. He turned and looked helplessly at Lieberman.

The head of the Mossad nodded to him to walk on. "Wait here," he told Porat and the guard.

The two men went ahead through the light snow, Awad in front, Lieberman two paces behind him. Suddenly Awad stopped and wheeled around.

"I have to know. You have to tell me."

"What is it?"

"Did she betray me? Did she work for you?"

Lieberman looked into a pair of anxious, terrified black eyes. Once again, he could see Gideon on the Hermon. "Yes," he answered.

Awad's eyes were empty again. He started to walk ahead. Within moments, the two of them disappeared between the orange trees, vanishing from the view of Porat and the guard. Forty seconds later, the men heard two shots. Lieberman returned alone.

CHAPTER 33

ELI GOREN STOPPED at the reception desk of the Hotel Du Midi and set his valise on the floor. "Bill, please."

"You're leaving, sir?"

"Yes."

"I hope you enjoyed your stay."

"Yes."

The receptionist hastily finished up his bill and Goren pulled out a wad of notes and paid without checking it.

He walked outside. The street was deserted. It was cold, and the rain was still falling. Even so, he walked the several blocks to the Bristol.

He saw her as soon as he entered the lobby, surrounded by a crowd of journalists. Two men preceded her, clearing a path.

"Do you have anything to say about the death of your son?"

"Do you know who killed your son?"

"What's your view of the rescue operation?"

Susan's face was white and rigid. She was clutching Jimmy in her arms. One of her escorts shouted, "Leave Mrs. Kraft alone. She's already told you she has no comment."

The journalists kept at her as she crossed the lobby and went through the revolving doors. She was five yards from the cab when she noticed Goren.

Both of them stopped short, not knowing what to say. Then, not taking her eyes off him, she stepped forward and whispered, "I know you think there was no alternative. But there was. It all came down to the life of one Arab terrorist against my son's." She came closer and said in a voice he could scarcely hear, "Your son's."

He looked at her in horror. "But you said . . ."

Susan didn't answer. She climbed inside the cab and slammed the door after her.

Several journalists walked up to Goren.

"Are you a friend of Mrs. Kraft?"

He picked up his suitcase and started running. He only stopped when his strength gave out. Gasping for air, he sat on a wet bench on the curb. He was drenched through.

Gradually, Goren got his breath back. He stood and hailed an approaching cab. The cab stopped, and he climbed inside.

"To the airport," he said.

The voice of Edith Piaf came over the cab radio, strong and poignant. "*Je ne regrette rien. . . ,*" she sang. Goren shut his eyes. An announcer interrupted the verse. It was the six o'clock newscast.

"By an overwhelming majority, Frank Kelly was chosen as his party's candidate for reelection as President of the United States. Opinion polls predict an easy victory for Kelly in November elections. And now, our correspondent in Jerusalem. . . ."

Goren stiffened.

". . . An Israeli government spokesman today announced that the Israeli government never had any intention of releasing Maruan Awad, for the simple reason that

Awad has never been in Israeli custody. The spokesman added that the Israeli government will be grateful for any information likely to lead to the capture of the dangerous Arab terrorist. It is believed . . ."

The driver switched to another station. Dance music.

Goren was the last to board the plane. Two minutes later, the plane began to taxi for takeoff.

Goren could make out the dome of the Palais des Nations, the floral clock, the opera house, the lake. The *jet d'eau.*

In a few hours he would be back in Israel. And what then? Right now he was much too tired to think, or to care.

When he arrived home, Silver hurried to the closet in his study. He had not slept one hour in the last forty-eight, but it didn't seem to matter. He was elated, feverish, euphoric. He fumbled about on the shelves, pulled things out of drawers, and strewed them all over the floor. He only noticed his wife when she bent over beside him. She was holding a Scotch bottle and a glass. "Here's what you're looking for," she said, and he couldn't decide whether her tone was one of contempt or pity or both.

He ignored her and continued the search. Finally, at the bottom of the last drawer, he found what he was looking for: a small bundle wrapped in blue velvet. He picked it up, feeling the texture of the fabric in his hand, gazing at the package as though hypnotized by it. He could hear his father's voice distinctly as he urged him to take it.

"I don't need this, Dad."

"Don't be stubborn. Put it away somewhere. It's just a small bundle."

Silver stood up with the package under his arm and was at the front door when his wife confronted him. "Where are you going?"

He left the house without answering, without looking back. Where to go? And then he recalled the small, ancient building he always saw from his car window, with the large Star of David over the door. He started out in that direction, walking briskly. When he arrived, his forehead was covered with sweat. He stopped outside the building, looking up at the Star of David. Then he stepped firmly toward the entrance. Before crossing the threshold he opened the velvet bundle and removed a small, rounded, concave piece of material. He glanced at the Hebrew words embroidered on it in gold thread and then read them aloud. He raised his hand slowly and placed his *yarmulke* on his head.

Now he could enter the synagogue.